ELECTRIC
BREAKFAST

PAUL MELOY

MONTAG

First Montag Press E-Book and Paperback Original Edition March 2022

Montag Press ISBN: 978-1-957010-05-2
Design © 2022 Amit Dey

Montag Press Team:

Cover: Ben Baldwin
Edit: Brandon Nolta

A Montag Press Book
www.montagpress.com
Montag Press
777 Morton Street, Unit B
San Francisco CA 94129 USA

Montag Press, the burning book with the hatchet cover, the skewed word mark and the portrayal of the long-suffering fireman mascot are trademarks of Montag Press.

Printed & Digitally Originated in the United States of America
10 9 8 7 6 5 4 3 2 1

DEDICATION

For Emily

TABLE OF CONTENTS

Introduction vii

All Mouth 1

Remember Prosymnus 19

Reclamation Yard 46

Joe is a Barber 91

Dirty Black Summer 96

Electric Breakfast 116

Dogs with their Eyes Shut. 129

Driver Error 197

Carrion Cowboy 212

Night Closures 216

Villanova 250

Acknowledgements 274

Author Info 275

INTRODUCTION

by
Tim Lebbon

P aul Meloy is good at a lot of things. I know, because over the years I've known him (and it must be going on twenty years now), I've been lucky enough to become his friend. And now that you're lucky enough to have this splendid new book in your hands—and you're in for a treat—I'd like to tell you about just a few of these things. So here goes (and in no particular order):

Swearing—like a trooper, like my grandmother used to say. Some people swear a lot and it becomes background. You know what I mean, the words they use lose meaning, their language becomes busy and littered with ineffective expletives like a wall smothered with badly sketched landscape. When Meloy swears, you know it means something. His swearing stamps meaning onto every sentence, like one small, perfect, impactful work of art on that otherwise bare wall. He's a perfectionist of profanity, bestowing cutting obscenities like a true, twisted wordsmith. And you will remember.

Soup—yes, he makes a mean sweet potato and butternut squash soup. Who'd have thought it? And how should *I* know? Well, here's what happened...

For the past few years, myself and an assorted bunch of other writers have hired a cottage once or twice a year for a writing retreat. Now, I know what you're instantly going to think. *Yeah, okay Tim, a 'writers' retreat, eh? Drinking weekend, more like.* And you're partly right. But they've also become very productive weekends for everyone involved. We'll work hard during the day, retreating to our own work space (bedroom, dining room, conservatory, coal bunker), and writing through the day. There are various interludes for tea and biscuits, and a break for lunch of course, but usually we'll work on into the evening. Then it's time for one or two of us to cook dinner, and we'll have a drink and chat late into the night.

Paul's been to 3 or 4 of these weekends now, but I think it was West Wales where he first cooked his soup. We had 3 little cottages there. Paul had the smallest cottage to himself, and one afternoon the smell of cooking lured me in. There he was, glass of port in one hand and a spoon in the other while he carefully stirred a pan on the cooker. I noticed how particular he was, how careful and patient, and when I asked when the soup would be ready he said, 'Oh, a couple of hours'. We ate it with crusty bread and it was divine.

I've tried making the soup myself many times since. It's nice, perfectly edible, and even my kids like it, but I don't ... quite ... get there. Maybe I'm too hasty, or maybe I'm just not Meloy.

And this gets me, quite tangentially, onto one other thing that Paul is very good at. Writing, of course. I mean, this isn't a book of recipes.

I know for a fact that he puts as much care, patience, attention and love into his writing as he does into cooking that amazing soup. I've seen him doing it. During one of these writing weekends we went on, I wrote an 8,000 word story, and that included one day when the hangover was quite nasty. That's a huge output for one weekend.

Paul's output for these weekend has, I think, topped a couple of thousand words once or twice. And there you see the care he takes over his writing. For while I'll chuck a few chopped vegetables, an onion, and some stock into a pan, boil it up, whisk it and call it soup, Paul pays attention to what he's doing from the ground up. The finest ingredients treated in the right way. The correct processes involved, including cooking the soup base first (for the life of me I can't remember the name for this, but Paul does, of course), before adding the rest of the ingredients. Cooking it long and slow so that the constituent parts break down slowly, releasing their flavour so that the final blending and whisking is hardly required.

He takes great care choosing the right words, making sure that they suit the idea he's trying to convey and the tale he's trying to tell. He writes slowly. I hesitate to say methodically, because I'm not sure that's the case. I think Paul finds writing *hard*. Methodical implies a technical process intricately followed, whereas Paul's writing is, I think, much more difficult than that. He puts his heart and soul into his writing, and when you read his stories that shines through.

Reading his first collection Islington Crocodiles, and re-reading the stories for this new collection, I was struck with how tiring the process of reading his work actually is. That's not a criticism, as in this case it's very definitely not a bad thing. So I tried to figure out why that's the case, and I've come to the conclusion that it's a combination of things. In part, it's because Paul's stories are very richly detailed, both in content and language. The imagery is challenging and in places wonderfuly disturbing, nightmares given voice:

Still, the incessant roar; it was like listening to someone mouthing words they didn't understand with a large cardboard box over their head. Echoic, indistinct and menacing.

And as I said above, Paul's effort and emotional investment in his writing comes through, and the reader will often finish a story feeling as though they've been through the same wringer. That's a sign of great writing.

All of Paul's stories stand alone, but there's also a greater truth, a wider world slowly being formed. It's the world of the Firmament Surgeons, the Autoscopes, Nurse Melt and Doctor Mocking, and all the fantastical, terrible, wonderfully realised horrors and mysteries that they bring. Sometimes it's the difference between sleeping and waking, and in that way Paul taps into all the best nightmares. Sometimes it's not as clearly defined as that, and in these instances we begin to wonder about reality, where it begins and ends, and who really controls it. Since his very first stories many years ago this wider world has been growing, and the sense that there's a war going on—sometimes without our knowing, but often intruding so rudely and catastrophically into the worlds of his characters—is beautifully drawn. It's vaguely Lovecraftian in tone and scope, but a hundred times more effective with Paul's eye for characterisation, and the reader's investment in those characters.

It's *scary*. That's something not so easy to achieve.

I've purposely not written this introduction as a story-by-story description, partly because it's best you discover the stories themselves, and partly because ... well, that can be a bit boring, and it can never do a tale justice. *'All Mouth' is about a guy living in the same building as someone who screams and moans a lot.* It just doesn't cut it.

I think Paul is one of the best short story writers out there. I mean that truly, and I've thought it since before I even met him. I love his attitude to his work, too, and to tell you more about that, I should relate the first time we met.

I'm pretty sure it was at my very first convention in the Midland Hotel in Birmingham. Might have been my second convention. You know how it is, they all tend to blur into each other, but I can remember very vividly bumping into the bar to grab another pint and Chaz Brenchley turning to me and saying, "Tim, have you met Paul Meloy?" This tall bloke held out his hand, and as I shook I said, "Oh yeah, loved your story *The Last Great Paladin of Idle Conceit.*"

Paul seemed very humbled that I'd read and liked it, and he was proud too. As he should be. We went on to chat some more, most of it lost to the haze of the convention, and we've been friends ever since. Over the years I've made no secret to him of how much I admire his writing, and I'm often to be found encouraging him to write more. A selfish act, perhaps, because I want to read more.

But Paul knows his work better than anyone. He's humble but honest, and he *knows* it's good. And he has every right to, considering the amount of time and effort that goes into every short story, every page, every finely honed sentence and image.

This book is something of an event in publishing, and you should be happy. His second collection, I believe it's even better than the staggeringly good Islington Crocodiles. And you can enjoy it in the knowledge that there's more, and quite possibly better to come.

Tim Lebbon

ALL MOUTH

Bridgeman could hear the roaring the moment he walked in through the front door. As usual it was coming from the room to the right, directly off the hall. He closed his umbrella beneath the porch light and shook it with a brisk snap of his wrist. He propped it in the hoop at the bottom of the coat stand and closed the door on the wet late November evening. Still, the incessant roar; it was like listening to someone mouthing words they didn't understand with a large cardboard box over their head. Echoic, indistinct and menacing.

To get to the small galley kitchen, Bridgeman had to walk past the door and go along a narrow corridor made by the stairs, which rose to the left, and the wall to the communal lounge on the right. Bridgeman always found himself skipping past the door, dreading the moment when it might open to reveal the occupant; a man, he imagined, head concealed within its box, stumbling out of the room, roaring, quite mad, his shirtfront wet with rage-sprayed saliva—Bridgeman quickened his pace and tripped down the step into the kitchen. He palmed the light on and the mean 40-watt bulb hanging from a greasy cord above the sink lit the room. His heart was beating with a supplementary nervous flutter.

Work had been a disappointment; Juna had left today, terminating her agency contract with immediate effect following a bust-up with Gary on the factory floor. And Bridgeman hadn't even known she'd been seeing the black welder. Bridgeman had been sniffing around the little brunette for over a week without a shred of success. It was like everything, he mused, filling the kettle and dragging a chair out from beneath the flimsy little table pressed against the wall between the fridge and the draining board: Life had just never opened its legs for him.

He lit a cigarette and waited for the kettle to boil. He could still hear the muted roaring, above the resolute hum of the fridge and the escalation of steam from the kettle. Bridgeman felt jumpy; it was as if the whole house and everything in it was becoming impatient. He stood up and went over to the sink. It was filthy. Nothing left on the drainer but fatty scum, no mugs in the cupboard beneath. Just a tall white tube of supermarket-brand economy scourer and a broken Breville sandwich maker without a plug.

He kneed the cupboard door shut and pulled a mug from the washing-up bowl. It was glossy with fat and covered in bits of spaghetti as if parasitized by monstrous bacteria.

Bridgeman pulled a length of blue paper from a roll lying on top of the fridge. He opened the cupboard beneath the sink again and took out the scourer. He chipped an accretion of chalky chemicals from around the nozzle and squirted a blob of gritty white fluid onto the paper, which he used to rub over the mug. Bits of spaghetti dropped into the sink. He ran the mug under the tap again and was cheered to see the china come up spotless. He dried it on another piece of blue paper towel and lobbed in a tea bag. As he was filling the mug with hot water, the front door banged open and Jase came in.

"Make us a fuckin cuppa, man," he said, striding into the kitchen. "I'm colder than a mother-in-law's kiss."

Bridgeman sighed and looked down at the one clean cup. "Sugar?" he asked.

"Four," Jase said, taking his donkey jacket off and slinging it onto the table. He stood behind Bridgeman, rubbing his hands. "Nice and milky," he added, eyebrows raised. Bridgeman edged past him and went to the fridge. As he opened the door, he heard Jase say, "Fuck it, let's go for a pint!" and then the thick splash of the mug being chucked back into the squalid washing-up bowl.

Bridgeman was about to say something but changed his mind when he caught Jase's expression. There was something compulsive in the other man's demeanour, a horrid kind of uncivilised charisma which Bridgeman found debilitating and frankly impossible to oppose. With his muscular neck the circumference of a cake tin, eyes like knife ticks in a pie crust and unmerciful, thuggish wardrobe, this *mate*, in truth no more than a little-known acquaintance, was the only thing that provided the opportunity to get out of the house and engage in some kind of social contact, however demoralising, against another forlorn night locked in his room with a dog-eared pile of wrist menus.

Bridgeman followed Jase down the hall. Jase walked with a rolling gait, positive of his own loutish magnetism, while Bridgeman felt that he trailed with a gutless gay-boy mince, all self-assurance drained, sapped by his muscular companion. As they passed the door off the hall, Bridgeman almost hoped it would open so that he could finally view the occupant, cordoned from behind the pelmet of Jase's wadded shoulders.

But the door didn't open, although the occupant still maundered within, and they passed out into the night without incident.

"Forgot my brolly," Bridgeman said, wincing beneath the drizzle, but Jase was halfway up the path.

"Don't bother," he said. "We'll go to the Orange Tree. It's only up the road."

Ten minutes later, the lights of the Orange Tree were visible on the horizon. Jase was the kind of bloke who walked ahead. Bridgeman trotted along behind, head down, hands in pockets, listening to Jase as he went on.

"Mate paid for this bird the other night. Pretty little thing, on her knees with her tits out. She goes, 'You can't come in my mouth, I don't like it.' Mate pisses himself and goes, 'For two hundred quid an hour, darling, I expect to be able to come in your fucking *brain*!'"

Dear God, thought Bridgeman. "Did he?" he said.

"Did he what?"

"You know, come in her-"

"Her *brain*?"

"No, her-"

"*Facialed* her," Jase said, and pushed through the heavy saloon bar door into the pub.

Bridgeman followed Jase to the bar. After a moment of standing in silence, Bridgeman asked, "What you having?"

"Stella," said Jase, and wandered over to the fruit machine.

Bridgeman ordered and leaned against the bar. The Orange Tree had always been a lively pub but since the smoking ban it had lost its heart. Whereas previously the bar had been a place at which to sit up on a high stool, do a crossword and enter into shallow intimacies with barmaids, it was now a gleaming counter, soulless as a serving hatch, at which you bought your drinks and headed outside to stand beneath the shelter and complain that the patio heaters weren't working. Smoke had once softened the air; now everything was too sharp under the lights, the generic pub chain décor too *evident*. It saddened Bridgeman, who enjoyed the occasional cigar with a pint, that never again would he be able to sit at a bar and relax into a sedentary, civilised evening, choosing with whom to converse, maybe treating himself to a glass of port with a *Hamlet*, watching the evening unfold from within that hazy, warm, mitigated glow, without having to get up every five minutes to go outside for a smoke. It was like having diarrhoea.

Jase came back to the bar for more change. "Machine's *gagging* to pay out," he muttered. He grabbed his pint, took a long swallow. Then he noticed the large bottle behind the bar, half full of coins, a charitable collection for life-limited children. "Mate nicked one of them once. Walked straight out of a pub with a nebuliser of champagne under his coat. Over a ton in it." Bridgeman noticed how Jase's eyes were already starting to dart around the pub, looking for other people, people who weren't Bridgeman specifically, to come in. *Older* mates. Bridgeman had seen this distraction before, Jase's rapid attention deficit, so he got his question in:

"Who lives in the room downstairs?"

Jase peered at Bridgeman over the rim of his pint glass. His expression became guarded, vigilant. "Some bloke," he said, and took a sip of lager while watching Bridgeman through narrowed eyes.

Bridgeman laughed, suddenly nervous. He hated the uncomfortable deference Jase generated in him. Why couldn't he just talk to the man like anyone else? Something about Jase kept him off-balance, constantly alert to misinterpretation and derision.

Jase put his glass down on the bar and stood, arms dangling, staring at Bridgeman.

"Well-"

"Well, what?" Jase said.

"Well, what's he like? What's his name?" Bridgeman felt weak, girly again. But he persisted, because he wanted to know. "Why does he shout all the time?"

The saloon bar door opened. They both turned to see who was coming in; a bus drove past, bright windows crammed with faces like the cluttered panels of a comic strip sliding through the night, the stormy hiss of its passing drowning Jase's reply.

Bridgeman was about to say something, but Jase had already returned his attention to the fruit machine. Bridgeman observed a whitening of Jase's knuckles around the pint glass. Pub etiquette was about to be violated.

"He's just walked *in*," Jase said through clenched teeth. The words were like bits of static.

Bridgeman glanced over. The middle-aged man who had entered a moment ago had toddled straight over to the fruit machine and was preparing to slot in a quid. Happy as you like.

Jase slammed his pint down on the bar and started across the floor toward the man. In went the quid. Round went the barrels; lights flashed, buttons lit up, options presented themselves. The man stabbed at a Hold button. Bar. Bar. Bar.

Bridgeman watched, enthralled and mortified, as Jase sidled up to the man.

Lost to Bridgeman amidst the merry sound of a cascading jackpot, Jase's remarks nevertheless had a profound effect on the man at the fruit machine. He started to reach for the money pooling in the well beneath the screen and then froze. He turned his head to look at Jase, mouth open. Jase nodded with an expression of great seriousness, and then kicked him in the bollocks.

Jase filled his pockets with the man's winnings, stepped over the shuddering body and sauntered back to the bar. Bridgeman's mouth hung open.

"What?" Jase said. He picked up his pint and drained it.

Bridgeman felt sick. Jase's predilection for casual offences both disgusted and fascinated him. He watched as the man pushed himself to his knees, breathing in deep gulps of air, leaned his elbows on a tabletop and attained a stooped upright posture before stumbling out of the pub.

Despite Jase's recent winnings, it was Bridgeman who bought his next pint (with a vodka chaser and a packet of pistachios); he was too stunned by the sudden violence to point out that it was Jase's round. By the time he'd paid, Jase had wandered off again and was talking to a couple of birds out in the smoking area. No doubt one, or both, of these local lovelies would wind up back at the house, shrieking and clumping about, getting a seeing-to across various items of furniture. Jase brought someone home nearly every night. It mystified Bridgeman how he did it.

Jase behaved like a priapic stereotype. His conversation revolved around whatever cavorted through his head at the time, predictable fantasies about sex and violence, explicit re-enactments during which, Bridgeman imagined, Jase selected mental images from a palette of fantasy beavers—vaginas appearing like ventricles in his mind, like the mouths of red-throated carp coming up to feed—and applied them liberally over the memories of the knackered old growlers, the torn croissants, that dangled in reality up between the spokes of his genuine conquests.

Bridgeman got himself a gin and tonic and a cigar and went outside. Rain blew in beneath the awning and he shivered as a fine spray spattered the back of his hand and beaded his glass. He hunched his shoulders and stood close to the outside wall. He unwrapped his cigar and put it in his mouth. He was about to light the cigar when Jase emerged from the shadows beyond the awning. His close-cropped hair glittered with hundreds of tiny drops of blood, the reflection in raindrops of infrared from the wall-mounted heater above the conservatory door. There was no sign of the girls, which might have been the reason why, when Bridgeman said, "I'm going to have this and go home," Jase walked straight past him without even a grunt of acknowledgement.

Bridgeman shook his head as he watched Jase barge through the conservatory and disappear around the corner toward the toilets. He lit his cigar but only had a couple of puffs before he felt his mood dip and he became enervated by a sense of aloneness. He stubbed the cigar, drained his glass and went back into the pub.

Bridgeman put his glass on the bar and waited for Jase. The entire saloon was empty. Even the barmaid had deserted her station; Bridgeman could hear a faint clonking sound from somewhere, probably a barrel being moved in the cellar. He drummed his fingertips on a bar mat.

The place used to be full of blokes and their laughter, their quick, chin-jutting aggression. Now it seemed only to provide service to a passing trade, people coming in for a quick pint on the way home from work or a couple of builders from the site opposite having a game of pool before knocking off. Jase kept coming, kept getting lucky, but it must only be a matter of time before even he got bored with the thinning pickings.

Bridgeman waited for another five minutes. When neither Jase nor the barmaid returned, he decided that was it, he'd go home.

It had stopped raining when he left the Orange Tree and turned right up the high street. He lit a cigarette and began walking back to the house.

Bridgeman had been living there for three weeks. When things had gone sour with Kelly and he'd found it impossible to live with her any longer, it had seemed easier just to move out, to find somewhere to stay as a stop-gap, somewhere to re-evaluate and get his head together. He still missed her at times, missed coming home to somebody, a bit of decent cooking, a clean flat. No; Bridgeman sucked on his cigarette, flicked the butt into a bush, chided himself for his sentimentality. It had been a fucking nightmare. Always something wrong with her, the anxiety and panic attacks, the headaches, the poxy miscarriage, all that stress over something bad happening to her family, her loved ones, her sense of doom sapping his life, draining him. He remembered the nights she had lain next to him following the miscarriage, sobbing, whispering her fears to him while he had draped a limp arm about her and stared flatly at the ceiling, wishing it would all go away. How fragile he had felt then.

She'd begged him not to leave, promised to get help. Medication, counselling, some kind of talking therapy. Bollocks, he'd said, and left her while she was out visiting her mum. All he'd taken was a rucksack full of clothes, some bedding and his stereo. He'd found the house a few days before, advertised in the local rag. A room in a shared house, communal kitchen, bathroom and lounge. Seventy-five quid a week. He'd gone round on his lunch break and met the landlord. It was a grimy terrace house in a side road off the high street. The downstairs front lounge had been converted into a third rentable room. Each door had a Yale lock fitted and a bolt on the inside for added security. Bridgeman was shown into the back bedroom. It had a pervasive atmosphere of gloom, haunted by the wasted lives that had lodged there on feculent mattresses amongst the cans, bottles and oily containers of long, stotious, malnourished afternoons.

"I'll take it," Bridgeman had said.

The landlord handed him the key and pocketed Bridgeman's deposit and first week's rent in advance. "Rent's due every Monday. Give it to Jase. He's the guy's got the front bedroom. He collects for me."

Bridgeman nodded. The room smelt stale and spicy, like the palm of an old woman's hand. A single sash window looked out over the back yard. Bridgeman could see nothing green in any of the neighbouring yards; just dirt and large plastic toys. A grey-hound lifted its shoe-stretcher head and stared up at Bridgeman while it shat behind a roll of chicken wire in the yard opposite. "Make yourself at home," the landlord said. Bridgeman had fol-lowed him back down the uncarpeted stairs. In the hallway, the landlord said, "Telly in the back room don't work. I'm just wait-ing for someone to hire a skip then in it goes. If you smell gas, tell Jase and he'll let me know."

"Okay," Bridgeman said. "I'll probably only be here a few months, anyway."

The landlord had frowned. "Just make sure you give me plenty of notice. No midnight flits owing me rent. I won't have it."

Bridgeman shook his head. "Of course not, I –"

"I've marked your card, that's all," the landlord said. He but-toned his grey overcoat and let himself out onto the street. "Bins go out Wednesday nights," he said, then turned and walked away.

Bridgeman thought about the day he'd moved in, finding Jase sitting in the kitchen eating inspissated rice straight from the saucepan with a plastic fork.

"Mate needed to store some floor tiles so we stuck them in your room," Jase had said.

Bridgeman remembered how nerveless he'd felt at the time, how that statement seemed to be the deadpan precursor to a whole new species of communication, a series of announce-ments to which he could never formulate a sensible reply.

He reached the house and took out his keys. As he lifted the bunch to locate the street door key, he thought he saw the curtain in the downstairs room twitch. He stepped back onto the path and waited, watching the bay window for signs of movement.

The heavy curtains were veiled behind grubby nets, the runners thick with dusty nodes of cobweb.

After a minute, Bridgeman shrugged and let himself into the house. As soon as the door swung inwards, Bridgeman heard the roaring. He looked at his watch. Twenty past seven. He thought about getting a snack and a cup of tea but remembered the state of the kitchen and changed his mind. His chest felt tight. A line of light flickered beneath the door to his right. The muffled roaring sounded like someone ranting in an artificial language. Bridgeman held his breath. He took a step closer to the door, cocked his head. He could hear the TV but the volume was low. Over the sound of the TV, he tried to make out some words but all he could discern was a loud modulating drone. What would happen if he knocked? Would the occupant answer the door? Bridgeman felt a fluttering in his guts and a vertiginous tingle down the backs of his legs. He had always had a deep-seated fear of nutters, a dread of mental disorder. He had thought too hard about it in his twenties and it had scared him. The loss of control, loss of dignity, the fragmenting of reality and personality, the descent into delusion and paranoia. He thought about Kelly, about her brief, disastrous hospitalisation. She'd come out more of a wreck than when she'd gone in. The roaring continued, drawing Bridgeman back. This bloke was clearly mental. They didn't lock them up so often nowadays, though. He might have been placed there by some charity, left to rave with foul voices roaring in his head, perhaps visited once a month by a nurse with a syringe full of antipsychotics. Bridgeman stepped away from the door. "Mad as a lorry," he said under his breath. He put a hand in his jacket pocket and fingered his mobile phone. He was thinking about calling Kelly for the first time since he'd moved in. He'd changed his number when he'd left because the endless texts were making him anxious, but he remembered her number. Perhaps losing out on Juna at work and the realisation of how fetid his accommodation was had made him reflect on what he'd had with Kelly, what he'd chucked away. Bridgeman pulled his hand from his pocket. Sleep on it, he advised himself. The phone remained in his pocket, and he trod upstairs to use the bathroom and retire to his room.

Bridgeman urinated with the bathroom door ajar, using the landing light to illuminate his ablutions. The bulb was blown in the bathroom and no one had replaced it since he'd moved in. It was as dank and unseemly as an alcove in a derelict bathhouse, Bridgeman thought. How had he ended up in such a shithole? Bridgeman glanced across the landing at the door to Jase's room. He had only seen inside once, hovering on the threshold as Jase took his second week's rent. As Jase counted the notes with painstaking and distrustful labour, Bridgeman had taken in the sight of a moderate-sized room containing a double mattress, portable TV and a multi-gym.

"You're ten short," Jase had said.

"What?" said Bridgeman.

"You're ten *short.*"

"No, I've literally just counted it."

"You're *literally* ten short," Jase had said. Bridgeman could see this turning nasty. He felt suddenly unanchored, frightened. His mouth dried, filled with a cramping mist of adrenaline. He wasn't used to standing his ground. Maybe Jase could consider a reduction in the rent in return for the twelve boxes of terracotta floor tiles still stacked in his room.

"Okay," Bridgeman had said, "Okay. Here." He took a ten-pound note from his wallet and handed it to Jase. Jase took it, folded it and put it in the back pocket of his jeans. He rolled the rent up and put it in his front pocket then shut the door in Bridgeman's face.

Remembering this now, Bridgeman felt the colour rising to his cheeks. He zipped up and washed his hands beneath a trickle of tepid water. He shook his fingers dry; he could smell the bacteria brewing on the hand towel draped over the side of the bath.

He went onto the landing and opened his bedroom door. He switched on the lamp by his metal-framed single bed and dragged the curtain across the window, then turned around and stood, eyes flicking from wall to wall, something akin to panic rising in his chest. What a fuck up. He jumped, startled, when the dog opposite bayed a sudden, nervous volley of barks. He took off his jacket, threw it on the plastic swivel chair in the corner then sat on his bed. He felt like he was staring at the back of his eyes. The room seemed to unfocus, darken. Nothing seemed real at that moment and he was suddenly sure that he had woken up dead that morning. Nothing recent felt like it had taken on any substance at all; he could have been a ghost, frail, immaterial, dead but unknowing. His hands shook. Tears filled his eyes.

"Shit," Bridgeman said in a quiet voice, "this is awful."

He sat like that for a while, dwelling on things, while across the way the dog rattled off sporadic yaps and the sound of lunatic rage rose up from the room below. Bridgeman sighed and took out his phone. When he keyed in Kelly's number, all he got was a voicemail message which kicked in on the first ring. It was a message recorded in happier days, a time before miscarriages and despair, and Bridgeman closed his eyes against the sunshine in her voice.

He made a decision. He pulled his rucksack from beneath the bed and started to pack his clothes. He couldn't stay in the house another night. He'd go over to Kelly's and if she couldn't take him in, then he'd go to his mum's for the night and see what developed in the morning. He breathed deeper, the impulsivity of his decision giving him a sudden psychological boost. He put the rucksack on his bed, pulled off his pillowcase and bundled his duvet into a black bin liner. He put his jacket on and went out onto the landing. All clear. He went back into his room, slung the rucksack over his shoulder and picked up the duvet. He had little else besides his stereo, which he'd come back for after stowing the bags in his car. Before he opened his door, he ground his heel onto one of the boxes of floor tiles stacked against the wall. He grinned as he heard a number of tiles splinter. "Oops," he said.

Bridgeman went downstairs and opened the front door. As he stood in the hallway, he realised that the roaring had stopped. He looked at his watch. An hour and a half had passed since he'd got back from the Orange Tree. Often the roaring would go on until after eleven, then, Bridgeman assumed, whatever medication the crazy bastard was taking probably took effect and dropped him into a synaptic oblivion. Oh well, not his problem any more. God, it would be good to snuggle up in a soft double bed, the only sound to break the silence the rustle of the wind in the trees outside the bedroom window. What had he been thinking of these past three weeks? He allowed himself an indulgent smile as he racked it all up to the understandable phenomenon of male angst and the need for space.

Bridgeman put the bags in the boot of his car, and then went back inside to get his stereo. He had decided to leave his keys on the kitchen table; he had no intention of returning or seeking out the landlord. He was paid up until the end of the week and owed nothing, so this didn't count as a flit. He could have given some notice, but fuck it. That was the way of these seedy lets. He reached the bottom of the stairs and Jase said, "Where the fuck are *you* going?"

Bridgeman cried out. He missed his step and jarred his back as his foot jammed against the bottom riser. He turned on trembling legs as Jase stepped out from the darkness of the communal lounge. Jase's bulk filled the hallway. Bridgeman took a step backwards. What could he say? "I'm moving out," he said.

Jase stumbled as he came toward Bridgeman and Bridgeman could see that he was quite clearly drunk. "You owe me," Jase said. "You're *short*."

Bridgeman backed up the stairs. "Don't be ridiculous, I – "

"I see you standing outside that room listening," Jase said as he started to mount the stairs. He used the banister to steady himself. "Mate don't like spying."

Bridgeman realised with a kind of dumb clarity that Jase must have been skulking there all the time, watching him as he stood outside the mad lodger's door. Jase must have left the Orange Tree before him and beaten him home all along.

Bridgeman reached the landing. "*He's* your mate?" he asked. He recalled the anecdotes, the constant stream of degenerate yarns, and couldn't make the connection between their content, however exaggerated, and the low-functioning mentalist in the room downstairs.

As Jase reached the stairwell, Bridgeman retreated into his room. He went to close the door but Jase lunged across the landing and shouldered it open. Bridgeman staggered backwards and tripped over a pile of floor tiles. He sprawled, reaching out as he did so, and took hold of a shard of terracotta from one of the tiles he had broken earlier. Jase came into the room and stood over him.

"It's time you met my mate," he said.

"I don't want to," Bridgeman said, and slashed at Jase's thigh with the shard. He missed, and Jase knocked him unconscious with his fists.

Bridgeman came to. He was tied to a chair. He moaned and licked his lips but his mouth was so dry his tongue felt more like a gloved finger. His eyes were swollen shut. He was in a lot of pain.

And then he was fully alert, all sluggishness gone the instant he realised where he was. He was tied to a chair, facing the corner like some brutalised dunce, in the room downstairs. His bladder weakened as he heard the sound of something moving behind him. Something crossing the room.

Bridgeman tried to twist his head around, but the back of the chair prevented him from seeing anything more than a peripheral view of the bare grey wall and half of the door. The room stank of sweat and meat and excrement. Bridgeman gagged.

Bridgeman began to weep. Somehow, he knew Jase was outside the door, listening, waiting. Pickings were getting thin, the society he kept was becoming scarce; he needed a boost, it seemed. Needed someone to refuel his flagging invention. The overstated adventures, the embellished capers, needed a top up now and again. How many other hapless lodgers had gone this way? Lonely, lost men adrift in impermanence, ushered into this wretched address, to be picked off by Jase and used to feed the embodiment of his turbid ego?

Bridgeman froze. It was standing behind him, the personification of Jase's fantastic bragging. Bridgeman felt it lean toward him and part of it came into view. From the corner of his eye, Bridgeman could see what made up the bulk of its head. His weeping continued but they were silent tears now as he tried to lean his body away from the thing that stood behind him in that dark and fearful room.

And as the roaring started an inch from his ear, he realised that the thing in the room was, as Jase had said, *all* mouth.

REMEMBER PROSYMNUS

Noel Buck had fallen into a stuporous doze on the train down from Manchester, and when he woke up as the train was pulling into Euston station, he was dispirited to discover his throat was raw, his head throbbed, and every muscle ached like he'd been beaten with rubber hoses. Even his fingers hurt. His skin hurt. He had been incubating a flu bug for the past week, and now it had arrived in force.

He grabbed his rucksack from beneath his seat and stumbled bleary-eyed down the aisle as the train pulled alongside the platform. His throat was so dry and painful it felt like his tonsils had enlarged to the size of fat, noxious plums; their presence at the back of his throat filled his world and every time he tried to swallow, they ground together and made Noel want to be somewhere very far away from his own neck. He needed a cold drink. Coke. *Coke!* His tongue cramped with anticipation. He felt feverish, light-headed, and weak. How did this come on so fast? Noel thought. But it wasn't much of a surprise. He was run-down, had been on the piss for six weeks solid and hadn't had a good night's sleep for roughly a year. His concept of five-a-day was units of alcohol consumed before lunch and nothing at all to do with portions of fruit and veg.

While he waited for the train to come to a standstill, Noel calculated the duration of the rest of his journey home. He reckoned he could make it to the tube, take the southbound to Moorgate, and then change for the Northern line to Morden just about without dying. He would then get a cab to Sutton and collapse in bed for a week. No more booze. Just lots of vitamins, Coke, and cold and flu remedy. Then, when he'd emerged from his sickbed, weak and detoxified, he'd start rebuilding his life with a bit more dignity and focus.

He'd already started the ball rolling. He was on his way back from visiting his son at university. The reason he'd travelled up there was to break the news to Alan about his divorce from Alan's mother, Erica. To his surprise, Alan had shrugged and said, "I know, dad. Mum told me she was leaving you before I came up here."

That night in the student bar, Noel had taken full advantage of the subsidised prices and got drunk. He remembered sitting in a booth talking with depleting eloquence to Alan and Alan's boyfriend—a scrawny little blonde student of dance called Ryan who spent the entire evening making grabs at Alan's knob beneath the table and grinning at Noel with tiny little sharp white, teeth while his son snorted and slammed his knees against the underside of the table again and again in involuntary spasms—about how shit his life had become since Erica had left him.

To make matters worse, at some point in the evening, a very overweight Indian girl called Niloufa had taken a liking to him and had begun a terrifying process of seduction, which ended with ultimate disappointment following a quickie in the ladies' toilet toward the end of the night. It had been, Noel reflected with tedious self-loathing, like trying to hang a manatee on a coat hook.

The problem with further education, Noel had decided when he woke up on the floor of Alan's room in the halls of residence, was that it gave people an unrealistic perspective on their course of life. It gave them a sense of control that was illusive, if not downright delusional. Poncing around with their worthless fucking degrees with it all planned out. Noel's view had been that you got a job, worked hard to pay off your mortgage early, and then spent a long and happy retirement with the fucking *wife*. So much for that, but it wasn't lack of education that destroyed his marriage, nor was it his innate distrust of those that pursued it. Not really.

Irritable and densely hung over, Noel had gathered up his sleeping bag, stuffed it in his rucksack, and let himself out. He'd stopped at the communal bathroom to be morosely sick, and then he'd left for the station without saying goodbye to his self-seeking, overeducated son.

Well, that was a start, he told himself. He knew where he stood. A week in bed with a high temperature might be just what he needed to sweat himself clear-headed again. Noel stepped off the train and made his way along the platform to the concourse leading to the escalators.

He stopped at a booth and bought a plastic bottle of Coke and a croissant the shape and texture of well-wrung chamois leather for a tenner. Then he went to another kiosk that seemed to sell everything and bought a paper bag full of seedless red grapes and a carton of honey and lemon cold and flu sachets. Stocked up, Noel unscrewed the cap on the bottle of Coke and guzzled half of it in one chug. He wiped his mouth, eyes shut in momentary bliss as his raging tonsils were sluiced with the lukewarm cola. He looked at the croissant and decided he'd pocket it just in case he got hungry on the tube, or stuck in a tunnel, or something. He didn't like tube journeys at the best of times. Crashing through those Victorian caves in a big electric cart wasn't his idea of travelling in style.

He traipsed across the concourse and descended to the underground by escalator. His back ached beneath the weight of his rucksack, and he shrugged it off for a moment and rested it on the descending metal step between his feet. He wobbled, his leg muscles suddenly watery, and he had to grab onto the grimy, gouged rubber handrail running alongside the escalator. His brain felt like it had been given a coating of warm, soiled fat. His sinuses felt full of gallons of yellow air and constricted with pressure and bad warmth; it was the kind of bad warmth you might encounter beneath an old hat worn by a pensioner who had died sitting next to a gas fire.

He swallowed some more Coke and watched as posters framed behind sheets of clear plastic affixed to the wall sailed past him. Most of these were defaced or had bits of chewing gum or, oddly, bits of what looked like sandwiches smeared onto them. They advertised shows and sightseeing opportunities. Noel saw a poster advertising *The Woman in Black* and remembered how Erica had nearly cacked herself when they had gone to see that play. Good old-fashioned fun in those days. Now it was *The Thesmophoriazusae* and *The Bacchae* and other old Greek shit like that for Erica and her new man, Dion.

Dion was an artist, a sculptor. He was one of Erica's lecturers at college. Erica had taken a course on Art History, of all the pointless subjects to study, and Dion had mesmerised her with his knowledge and enthusiasm for his subject. It may have been instrumental somewhat in the triumph of his seduction, however, that his many self-portraits and sculptures, arranged artfully around the borders of the classroom, depicted Dion naked and hung like the leg of a milking stool.

Noel remembered a time a month and a half ago when he had decided to surprise Erica at college by pitching up there to take her for a drink after class. She had been complaining that he wasn't spontaneous anymore, so he thought he'd address that misapprehension with an unplanned visit. He'd been held up in traffic, so arrived just as the college was closing up. Erica's orange Volkswagen Beetle was still in the car park, so Noel slotted in beside it and hurried into the college foyer. He looked around for directions and saw a sign for the art department. The corridors were utilitarian and unadorned, pathways through mental endeavour that Noel had imagined would be filled with posters and pottery. Then again, he had to remind himself that this was adult learning and not a fucking infant school.

A notice on a classroom door to his right informed him that this was the art room. Noel stopped outside. There was a small rectangular window in the door, through which Noel ascertained that the room was empty. Then he heard a stifled giggle. It was unmistakably Erica's, and one that she so rarely let out these days. Noel thought of it as her fuck-chuckle, an irrepressible sound she made when she was getting turned on.

Well, he'd walked into the classroom to find Erica and a shirtless Dion standing behind a yucca plant in the corner of the room, Erica supporting Dion's cock on the palm of her hand like the belly of a juvenile stoat.

"Oh, fucking *hell*!" Noel had said, his mind unable to properly comprehend the spectacle before him. He tore his eyes from the sight of Dion's lustrous cockhead dropping against his fly like a gavel as Erica, startled, released it and reached up to re-button her blouse. Aghast, Noel took in the sculptures and paintings of Dion that stood around the perimeter of the classroom: the god-like aspect, Bellerophon chest, and epic loins. In the flesh, he was just as magnificent.

Noel had a moment to register Dion standing with his hands on his hips, head thrown back, waves of thick black hair rolling around his slender throat and across his huge, muscular shoulders, as he laughed. His laugh was like the roar of a lion.

Unmanned, Noel turned and stumbled away.

Erica hadn't come home that night. Noel sat up in a hateful state of rage and impotence, necking the entire crate of stubby bottled lagers he had been saving for an early summer barbecue. Eventually he dozed and came to on the sofa with a hangover of Withnailian proportions—a proper bastard behind the eyes— just as the front door opened and Erica walked in.

She came into the lounge and looked down at Noel. Noel moaned and tried to sit up. He reached out a hand but Erica pushed it away. Noel tried to focus on his wife but all he could see was an image of her naked, her long slender legs glossy with ardent sweat, shafting herself onto a wang of sapling dimensions. Over and over again, and in high definition. He covered his face.

"I'm sorry you had to see that, Noel," Erica said.

"Mmmf," Noel said into his cupped palms.

"It's been going on for months. I'm just surprised you haven't found out before."

"Aw, *Ghod*," Noel mumbled.

"Yes," said Erica, her tone smoothing into one of great admiration, and even with his senses smothered within the humid, breathy cavity of his palms, Noel could discern the change in her attitude. "He is."

Noel looked up at his wife, bemused. He stared at her as she stood amongst the discarded beer bottles as if she'd just appeared, genie-like, from one of them. Her eyes were glazed and her lips were upturned in a smile of saintly radiance. She looked ecstatic.

"Erica?" said Noel.

And then Erica went, "*Oooh*," and her legs wobbled and she clutched at her breasts with spasming fingers while a warm, pink flush suffused her throat and cheeks, and Noel realised, with growing astonishment, that his wife had just come robustly right there in front of him.

He sat back on the sofa and blinked. His headache pounded with pressure the approximate magnitude of an oceanic trench. The room was suddenly saturated with the cloying odour of musk. Erica gasped and stumbled backwards through the bottles. They clanked with hollow good cheer.

Erica looked embarrassed. She stepped over the bottles and stood, still trembling slightly, at the door.

"I – I'm going now, Noel," she said. "I'm going to get some of my things and move out. I think it's best."

Noel had said nothing more to Erica; he just nodded and watched her go. He sat for a while, bathed in what still remained of Erica's gamey aroma, and listened to the sounds of her packing upstairs. It wasn't until the front door closed about twenty minutes later that the thought occurred to him that Dion might have been fucking his wife right here in his own house. And what about Alan? Had he known? Little shit. It wouldn't have surprised Noel at all. Alan had changed so much since he'd come out a couple of months before. All those years playing rugby and bringing home pretty girls, and as gay as a Romanian folksong all along. What a disappointment. He just couldn't imagine... no, his mind closed down at the thought of his son doing those things, just couldn't face it. Not at the moment.

All this replayed through Noel's mind as the escalator descended. When he reached the bottom, he pulled his rucksack back on and stumbled toward the corridor leading to the east-bound platform. What horrible memories he had of that time.

He tottered onto the platform just as the train was pulling in. The carriages were filling up, but Noel managed to bundle onto the train and find a seat. He sat with his rucksack jammed between his knees next to a man reading an Arabic broadsheet to his right and a petite Chinese girl carrying a stack of books on psychology to his left. Noel felt hemmed in by erudition. He sank further down into his jacket and squinted with hot, congested eyes at the row of companion travellers who sat opposite. They looked propped up; they looked like the ill in some prefabricated waiting room, dull-eyed and resigned, all about to get the news that things were terminal and there was no hope.

Something about the quality of the light on tube trains makes everyone look ugly, renders them waxen and pallid, distorts features and blunts expressions. It enhances blemishes and flaws, and makes people appear nervy, disheartened, or cruel. Once,

Noel had sat opposite a young woman in a business suit and watched as huge tears rolled down her cheeks while she stared with a lifeless expression at a point somewhere above his left shoulder and a thousand miles away. Noel had been shocked at such a manifestation of unhappiness. He'd felt the need to make a gesture, show some empathy with a nod or a reassuring smile, and let her know she wasn't totally alone in this clattering transport burrowing beneath the city, but he couldn't even catch her eye. Noel supposed she might have been quite pretty, and maybe when she got off the train and ascended into natural daylight, then she might blossom into something lovely, but down there in the rocking yellow light her brow was too shiny and round, and blackheads darkened the pores around her glistening nostrils like welling pinpricks of anguish.

Thinking about this, and trying not to look at the polished, glabrous head of a fat man sitting opposite, and feeling like absolute shit, Noel fell into an aching, clammy doze.

He was jolted to wakefulness sometime later. He opened his eyes and groaned at the pains in his head and joints. His rucksack had toppled across the centre aisle and the bag of grapes he had stuffed into one of the shallow side pockets had spilled open. Sprigs of grapes had been trodden into the floor.

"You bastards," Noel muttered. He leaned forward, wincing, and gathered his rucksack to him, pressing it back between his knees. He scooped up the little paper bag and inspected it. There were a few dark red grapes rattling around at the bottom, still intact.

Only then did he begin to register the rest of his surroundings. At some point during his nap, the carriage had emptied of all passengers but Noel. He looked left and right to confirm he was alone.

And he noticed the train had stopped in the tunnel between stations.

Noel slumped back into his seat and rested the back of his head against the dark glass of the window behind him. His mouth and throat were dry again, so he took a couple of the remaining grapes from the bag and chewed on them while he waited for the train to start.

He waited. He had a few more grapes. Even chewed to a pulp, they hurt his throat on the way down. He wasn't going near that croissant unless he was starving to death. He ruminated. *Alan*, he thought. His *son*, taking it up the Hovis. He couldn't believe it. What a dreadful disappointment.

The doors to his right slid open with a hiss.

Noel jumped and clutched at the top of his rucksack. The breeze that ran in a cold, desultory river through the underground, pushed and buffeted by the constant passage of trains, gusted into the carriage. It had a gloomy, particulate smell, like cinders from a dead furnace. It rose up into the carriage and filled Noel's nostrils, a sensory extension of the blackened walls that encased the train.

Then he heard a sound. It was a strange, high vibrato, rising and falling in pitch as it became louder. Noel panicked for a moment, and imagined another train hurtling toward them through the tunnel, but the modulation of the sound and its volume made him reconsider after a minute, so he relaxed a little. He remained curious—or at least *vigilant*—though, despite his weakened state, and he got up from his seat and went to the open doors.

He was in the front carriage and so, when he looked out, the top of his head nearly touching the curving, tiled tunnel wall, and peered along the length of the carriage, he could see the train had stopped only about thirty or so yards from the entrance to the next station. He could see light, and he could see, silhouetted against that light, someone walking toward him along the tracks.

The figure was tall and well built, and appeared to be swinging something around his head as he walked with a wide lassoing motion. The unusual roaring sound Noel could hear and attributed to the passage of another train seemed to be coming from the approaching figure, the sound driven toward the idle train by the narrowness of the tunnel.

Noel took a step back, away from the open doors. He shivered, aware of his aching muscles. He wondered for a moment whether he was hallucinating. He ran a palm across his brow. He was sweaty. He had a temperature. He paused and realised the sound had stopped. He felt relieved, and reassured himself that he was probably having a flu-induced—and stress-related, to be fair—moment of delirium, and half turned to go back to his seat and wait for the journey to recommence.

But then, someone said, "Hello, Noel," and a tall, naked figure slid out from the tunnel alongside the carriage and stepped up onto the train.

"Christ," Noel said, and stumbled backwards. He reached for a vertical steel grab rail to his right and used it to swing himself away from the figure mounting the train. He collapsed into a seat and stared up at the man who stood smiling at him; he was composed and magnificent, his head slightly bowed to accommodate the curvature of the carriage, and he carried two things: a piece of wood carved into a spatula shape wound on a length of ancient-looking brown rope, which was now looped round his muscular forearm, and in his left hand, what could only be described as a large wooden dildo.

"*Dion*," whispered Noel.

Dion stepped forward and raised the wooden spatula as if in greeting. Noel looked at it; it was pitted and engraved with curlicues and arcane-looking runes. He recognised it from books he had read as a boy, books about ancient history. It was a bullroarer.

He pressed back into his seat. Dion stepped closer and stood before him. He wasn't entirely naked. He was wearing what appeared to be a large fig leaf. It clung to his groin, held there by a tangle of tendrils that were twined through his pubic hair. It didn't quite cover everything, Noel noticed. He had no choice but to notice; it was at eye level and Noel had a very good view. He groaned and averted his eyes.

Dion threw back his head and roared with manly good humour. His eyes flashed and his fig leaf lifted and fell. Then it lifted and stayed a bit lifted. Noel groaned again and tried to edge away along the seat.

"Noel," Dion said. His voice was melodious, enriched with a profound sensuality. Noel flinched. "Your wife is a *goddess*," Dion said. "She is a woman of great curiosity, beauty, and ecstatic awareness. And for two decades, you have repressed her creativity and desires with your narrow-minded and prejudiced outlook on life. Your only success is your underachievement, which alone is pitiable, but to attempt to drive the passions from your family with your affectless, monotonous reservations is *grotesque.*"

"What are you talking about?" Noel asked. He peered up into Dion's broad, glowing face. Dion sported a shaggy V of hair beneath his bottom lip—a soul patch—an affectation that never failed to create hostility in Noel whenever he saw one.

"Don't stand there telling me what I have and haven't done," he rasped, trying to adjust his posture into something more poised than a subordinate cringe. He still felt awful and his throat was killing him. "Not with *Barbie*'s bush stuck to your chops."

Dion frowned, momentarily irritated by Noel's retort.

"Noel," Dion began, but Noel interrupted him.

"No, you listen to me, you smug bastard," he said. "I don't know what you're doing following me and trying to fuck with my head. Don't you think you've hurt me and my family enough? All I've ever done–"

But now it was Dion's turn to interrupt. He lashed out with the bullroarer and clouted Noel around the side of the head.

"OW!" Noel cried, and slumped sideways in his seat. He reached up and felt blood trickle from his ear. "You vicious cunt," he muttered. His vision blurred with both pain and emotion.

"I'm not trying to hurt any of you," Dion said. He leaned over and put his hands under Noel's armpits and lifted him upright again. His large, lambent eyes smoked with concern. "I'm trying to *free* you."

The side of Noel's head throbbed. Tears leaked from the corners of his eyes. "Free me from what?" he asked. Passivity rippled through his body like a pressure wave; all attempts to resist Dion fled before it, leaving him trembling and spent. Fully in the grip of his sickness, Noel decided to let his delusions have their way with him. Thus, clear-headed to a degree and almost comforted by the full-body encapsulation of his dull aches, he closed his eyes against the vision before him and allowed himself to become a channel for whatever Dion's liberation entailed.

Much to his parents' surprise and delight, Noel had been selected for a grammar school. They had all been expecting him to go to the local mixed-sex comprehensive, but he had achieved high scores in his eleven-plus and had come in as one of the top three most intelligent children in his year. Noel was staggered. He always considered himself to be a bit of a clown.

His parents had been so excited for him. Noel remembered how they had been glowing with a pride and a hope that had nothing to do with smug self-congratulation, but everything to do with bright, surprised joy in the unexpected possibilities now open to their son. This was thirty-two years ago. Punk was dead and Thatcher was embarking on her medieval purge of the working classes. London buses ran with sluggish and unpredictable truculence, and you could buy pulp paperback horrors for just 25p. You could smoke on buses and trains, even on the underground. You could pretty much park anywhere you liked for free. Most cars were shit, but you could drive them as fast as you could get them to go; there were no speed cameras and the eclectic profusion of humps and bollards that now clog pretty suburban back streets like traffic-calming cholesterol had yet to spring up.

Noel had been popular at school for the first two years. He'd made friends; he could be a laugh in class without becoming a fool, and was skilful at tennis ball soccer in the playground. He wasn't the brightest child in his year, but he wasn't the daftest either, and had a raw, languid intelligence that struggled to focus itself academically but would see him through life well enough if he worked hard. He discovered he liked English and biology, but little else. Maths was like trying to pry apart the substance of the universe. Rows of numbers made him anxious and breathless. When the syllabus introduced geometry, he was able to relax a little because the shapes that were drawn on the old chalkboards let his eyes focus on something concrete, less metaphysical. He still didn't really get it, though. He liked the biology labs; large, airy classrooms at the top of the school, their walls lined with long, dark benches displaying murky glass tanks filled with stick insects static as mimes, and clusters of fluttering, stinking locusts.

And so, it had been fine at first. Noel actually believed he might make it in this red brick and marble, rigorously uniformed, Dickensian-desked, chalky, covertly brutal world. He squeezed through corridors at break time and between classes with boys who were, to him, as big as adults—fourth- and fifth-years bulging out of blazers with blue chins and terrible broad backs—and endured bundles in stairwells that took dusty, beery teachers who still commanded a modicum of indulgent respect the best part of a quarter of an hour to unscramble with roars and wading, swinging arms.

He sat at desks stuck tight with chewing gum, looked down between his legs in wide-eyed, silent apprehension at the plump cocks drawn in pen on the seats of the rugged, greasy chairs upon which he sat, the bollocks always sporting a few slashes of cartoon pubes like a cat's whiskers, the fat, bisected glans chucking out a weatherman's snowstorm of correction-fluid jism.

It was a scary place, with teachers swirling about like huge ravens in their university capes in search of intellectual carrion, and science teachers called Doctor this and Professor that. Gone were the sweet little mums who had taught him the time not six months ago in classrooms full of Lilliputian desks and twinkling milk-bottle top collages.

But Noel thought he might survive; home after a bus journey spent head-down to avoid the attention of the marauding boys and girls from the comprehensive, Noel was greeted with a fuss and a fascination from his parents that filled him with both guilt and a drifting sense of midget superiority—borne of his social advantage and the fact that he had started swearing in coarse torrents of libertarian vernacular during football matches at break time.

And then, with a suddenness that left him bewildered, hurt, and afraid, the bullying started. It was a fat little cunt called Stuart Kale; envious of Noel's developing wit and popularity both with his classmates and with some of the more moderate teachers, Kale began a sustained and vindictive campaign of slander and belittlement designed to undermine Noel's self-esteem and leave him isolated and friendless. It worked.

Short and ugly, Kale used the sharpness of his tongue and an outstanding ability to hit every button dead-on when it came to the put-down to destroy Noel's life. In fear of reprisals and, in part delighted by the sight of a wounded victim that was specifically *not* one of them, Noel's classmates turned on him with savage vigour. Noel found himself sitting alone in classes suffering the awful, dense humiliation of watching every chair fill up except the one next to him, the burning shame of seeing eyes

dart away from contact with his own. Breathless with the dis-
honour of it, each of Noel's lessons seemed to drag on for days,
the back of his head swelling, reddening, neck muscles tense and
immovable for fear that he might draw attention to himself and
his terrible, blighted unpopularity.

He travelled home alone, sometimes getting off the bus miles
from his own stop in order to dawdle via the back streets. He
became morose and withdrawn, curled up on his bed cramped
by pangs of loneliness he could hardly stand. What hurt Noel
more than anything was the undeserved nature of the harass-
ment. It had come upon him like a curse, visited by that venom-
ous but charismatic little demi-god, Kale.

Noel spent break times alone in the biology labs. He pot-
tered and read, stared down from on high with dull-eyed distraction and watched the other children playing in the quad. He was
left alone.

After a long year of emotional and verbal abuse, Noel had
become accustomed to his new lonely lifestyle. He was rarely
bullied now; Kale having done such a thorough job of brutal-
ising him that everyone shunned him with callous and unconscious atavism. He found consolation in his routines, and a
vague psychosis played around the margins of his developing
mind, never becoming florid but occasionally enlightening his
forlorn imagination. He hid out in the unconverted loft rooms at
the top of the school. They were tiny, antique, and plank-floored,
the low walls hidden behind shelves packed full of small dusty
books. In these little rooms, ascetic old teachers bestowed upon
a select few a classical education. Rarefied prefects crept up back
stairs and spent shaded afternoons learning Latin and ancient

Greek. Noel felt comforted amongst the books and fancied himself a curator of sorts. At breaks and in between lessons, he sat on a bench beneath a narrow dormer window and read peppery chapters describing pantheons and primordial monsters, odysseys, campaigns, Titans, and heroes.

And then, the following summer, a miracle of sorts.

A new boy joined his class. His name was Pascal. His mother was Italian and he had moved up from Brighton with her when she divorced his dad. Pascal was diminutive, delicate, and olive-skinned. He had large brown eyes endowed with long, feathery lashes. His teeth were bright and white, his lips cute and pouty. He was the prettiest thing Noel had ever seen.

And because he was new, and because the seats next to Noel remained vacant in classes, and because Pascal brought with him a gentle serenity and confidence that enabled him to fit into the society of the cohort without any of the unease and suspicion normally experienced by children joining an established school year, he walked into double history (truly, the longest day of Noel's life), saw the empty seat in the middle of the room, and came straight over and sat down next to Noel.

Noel froze, his eyes wide and his mouth dry. The rest of the class was silent. All eyes seemed to be on Pascal.

Pascal opened his textbook. He looked at Noel and smiled. "Hi," he said.

And that was all it had taken. One shy smile and unforeseen, blessed proximity to this new and remarkable boy.

Noel had fallen in love.

With the proximity came healing. It was fragile, and Noel didn't question it; he was too infatuated with Pascal to analyse the process, but he was aware the other boys were viewing him with less contempt than usual. Pascal had had junior trials for Brighton Football Club, and his delicate skills and light touch with a tennis ball added extra dimensions to his popularity in the playground. Now, Noel found that he was picked for games again, and rediscovered his own touch. The classes they shared, they sat together; those they attended separately didn't worry Noel now. Boys sat next to him again. It was that simple. It was as though a patina of disease had sloughed off him, drawing off any unpalatable residue and brightening his aura, making him attractive by virtue of Pascal's simple acceptance of him.

But it wasn't a *friendship* exactly. Noel, who had become a reserved and introspective boy over the last year, was too aware of the tenderness of his feelings toward Pascal to form a robust familiarity; and Pascal, who seemed in favour with everyone, was just too distant in his novelty and popularity for Noel to try and monopolise or limit him. Noel was happy just to bathe in the gradual, remedial course of his renewal.

But Noel began to notice something else. When he awoke in the morning, warm and snug beneath his blankets, his dick hard and full of sizzling, fuming magnitude, he would roll onto his belly, half-asleep and comfortable, and press his groin into the mattress with dreamy fantasies flourishing behind his eyes, and find that he was thinking of Pascal.

Noel decided these weren't sexual thoughts. He didn't have a lot of experience with girls, but he could summon up the faces and imaginary bodies of the girls from the comprehensive well enough, and replace Pascal's image with the innocent glimpses of thighs and warm mouths that passed for eroticism for a young teenage boy, more than adequate for his immediate, perplexing needs.

But the power of Pascal's *physical* presence was less easy to deny. If Pascal touched him, or nudged him with a knee beneath the desk, Noel would feel his heart rate double and his stomach tingle. And once, feigning tiredness in sociology, Pascal had rested his head on his desk; it was all that Noel could do not to reach out and stroke the tanned nape of Pascal's neck where it ran in a smooth furrow into the soft dark hair at the base of his skull.

Noel started taking himself up to the loft rooms again during breaks. There was a small toilet, walled with large rectangular green tiles and smelling of rusty water and carbolic soap. Noel sat on the toilet seat and had weird, confused wanks. He extruded fat, congested blobs into a cupped palm with the careful, breathless placement of a master cake decorator, followed always by an immediate feeling of emptiness and a pinched ache in his rectum from the force of his release against the unyielding wooden surface of the bog seat.

Then one day, noticing his now regular absences, Pascal asked Noel where he went during breaks. Noel felt a brief stab of guilt and stammered that he liked to take himself off to do some reading in the cool of the loft. Pascal was intrigued. He hadn't realised there was a secret area at the top of the school, and he asked Noel to show him during lunch break. Noel looked into Pascal's pretty, enquiring eyes and smelt rusty water and carbolic soap and said, yes, he'd be happy to.

After the bell, Noel led Pascal up the back stairs. They were accessed by going through a narrow door at the side of the art department. Their footsteps creaked and clumped on the old wooden stairs. There were three small rooms up there, a tiny kitchen, and the institutionally tiled toilet.

Noel led Pascal into the room to the left of the stairwell. It was the room in which he had liked to sit beneath the window and read his arcane books. Pascal took some time looking at the books lining the walls and then came over and sat beside Noel on the narrow bench beneath the window.

"It's good up here," he said. Noel nodded. He could feel the warmth of Pascal's slender leg against his own.

Pascal sat back against the wall and looked around. "It's like a secret place. You could get up to all sorts of things up here and no one would know." He giggled and looked at Noel from beneath conspiratorially lowered lashes. "What do you do up here? Apart from read."

Noel gazed at Pascal. "What?" he said. He was light-headed and breathless; his eyes took in nothing but the movement of Pascal's mouth and the tantalizing hint of the tip of his tongue as it flicked against the back of his teeth.

Pascal turned his body toward Noel and rested his arm against the back of the bench. Noel heard him say, "What do you want to do up here?"

But he might have misheard him.

Noel leant forward and kissed Pascal on the mouth.

If Noel had imagined the bullying at the hands of Kale had been awful before, it was now apparent to him it had been merely a taster when compared to the orders of magnitude by which it increased following Pascal's divulgence to the other boys what Noel had done to him up in the quiet seclusion of the loft. How Noel had enticed him up there and then tried to bum him.

Noel considered the humiliation to be worse because this time he had contributed directly to its source. He felt shame now, whereas before he had merely felt an alienated sense of hurt and bewilderment. He had been able to fill his solitude with fantasies and learning; now, he brooded and cringed with the horror of having brought about his own downfall.

And then, one day soon after, Pascal and a group of boys cornered him in the playground. He had been walking back from the canteen, having waited until it emptied before buying his lunch, skirting the quad by cutting behind the prefabricated huts that held the language laboratories.

Five of them jumped him from between two of the huts, four more followed him into the narrow area between the back of the huts and the fence that ran along the length of the yard. A couple of fifth-formers were standing beneath the branches of a horse chestnut tree sharing a cigarette. They perked up when they saw the gang converge on Noel. They watched with eager, gloating expressions as Noel was surrounded. News of Noel's transgression had percolated not just across his own year, but had travelled like wildfire throughout the whole school. First-years gawped in naïve and open fascination at him; he was the subject of rank graffiti on the walls of the sixth-form common room. Even teachers seemed to ponder his affliction with low regard and the jaded narrowness of expression that was the sole tenure of world-weary and educated men.

Noel felt panic drench his system. He began to sweat, his heart rate doubled, and his legs began to shake. He looked around. Somehow, by way of the contagion that sweeps through a group of organic beings at the hint of a fight, it seemed that the entire school had piled between the huts and were surrounding him, name-calling, pushing, swinging punches. Noel tried to run but his legs wouldn't support him. He was buffeted by kicks and deafened by the screams and taunts.

And then, for a moment, Noel was granted a vision. Perhaps it was triggered by the horror of the moment, or perhaps it was released at last like an abreaction following the years of stress and torment, but for a moment, Noel's grip on reality slipped. Gone was the howling mob and in its place, prowling, snorting, reviled of aeons, the *Hecatonchires* surrounded him, the great primordial beasts of Greek mythology, each with fifty heads and a hundred mighty arms. Noel had read about them during his quiet lunchtimes in the loft, read of their brute strength and ferocity, of their siding with the Olympians in the war for supremacy against the Titans.

Noel summoned the last of his strength and drew a little dignity from those pungent afternoons of sweet escapism and roared a command of his own.

"Fuck the lot of you!" Noel screamed, and collapsed.

When he returned from being off sick, a period of slow recovery that leached into the long summer holiday and gave him the extra six weeks needed for a recuperation of sorts, Noel had already decided what he was going to do with the education system. He spent the next year with his head down, did virtually no work and scraped four O-levels at the end of the fifth-form exams. His parents were distraught, but Noel's heart was hardened. All that promise dissipated before his parents' eyes. There was to be no university education, no degrees, no proud career. Noel quit school and went out to work in a factory. Four years later, he met Erica at a party. They got married, and four years after that, Alan was born.

Hard physical work and a happy family enabled Noel to put the memories of his humiliation behind him. He was troubled by dreams, though. Dreams of being encircled by roiling many-headed torsos and buffeted by the blows of hundreds of fists. He awoke with shouts, entangled in sheets that felt as thin and damp as over-moistened Rizlas. And sometimes he dreamed of Pascal, that sweet and beastly boy who had broken his heart. And those dreams stayed with him all day as a dreary sense of failure and disgrace. And this, these unresolved feelings never spoken of, never counselled or acknowledged, was what had contributed most to his alienation from his wife and maturing son.

*   *   *

"You remember," Dion said. It was a statement, not a question.

Noel was sobbing. "Yes," he spluttered, "yes, I do." All those feelings and memories so long suppressed were raging through his head. He was shaking.

With great tenderness, Dion helped Noel stand up. Noel leaned against Dion's chest. It was like holding tight to the flank of a tiger; he could hear Dion's blood thudding through him, driven with the endless might of an immortal's heart. He wept.

Dion stepped away and picked up Noel's discarded ruck-sack. He rummaged through the pockets and came up with a handful of grapes and the box of honey and lemon cold and flu remedy. Noel stood swaying and watched through bleary eyes as

Dion crushed the remaining grapes in his hand and smeared the juice across his chest.

"What are you doing?" Noel said, but Dion put a finger to Noel's mouth. Noel tasted grape juice. He licked his lips. He watched, a simple fascination expressed on his blotchy face, as Dion tore open the sachets of honey and lemon and tipped the powder over his chest and belly. He ran his palms across his flesh, smearing the powder into the grape juice, making pink and yellow patterns with his fingertips.

"An offering," Dion said. "To a god. For resolution."

Noel looked up into Dion's overwhelming face and smiled.

Dion smiled in return, and pressed something into Noel's hand. Noel looked down, frowned, unsure of the purpose of such a gift.

"Remember Prosymnus," Dion said, and again it was a statement and not a question. Noel nodded, and recalled the story of the young boy who had aided the god Dionysus and then died before he could collect his reward.

He stumbled, and Dion caught him.

The train had begun to move.

The train pulled into the station and the doors hissed open.

A man stood alone on the platform. He was dressed in an expensive tailored suit and had his dark hair cut in a short, salon style. He looked cultured and successful, and confident despite his slight, boyish stature. He worked in the city and had all the trappings of wealth and achievement.

This afternoon, he was travelling a circuitous route home, having been drinking in wine bars in Wimbledon to toast his success at negotiating a deal to provide his company's brand of champagne to the All-England Tennis Club for this year's Grand Slam event, and he was quite drunk. The right education still afforded opportunities in circles such as these; it wasn't what you knew, the man confirmed to himself with intoxicated self-congratulation, it was *whom* you knew that really mattered. He tottered as the train doors opened and he stepped up into the empty carriage. It seemed he had been waiting ages for this train, but he amused himself with his recollections. That huge guy with the little beard under his chin had certainly oiled the wheels at the business meeting. Apparently, he'd been a lecturer at his old university. What were the chances of that? Economics and business studies. Boring, but he was sure he'd have remembered a lecturer as striking as that. Maybe he'd missed those lectures. He had, after all, sailed through the course with the minimum of effort. Life was like that for some, he knew.

And then, as the doors slid shut behind him, and the train began to move off into the tunnel, and as he staggered trying to get to a seat, something clubbed him around the side of the head. He gasped, and fell into the aisle, his briefcase flying from his hand and sliding away along the length of the train.

He tried to get up, but was struck again by what felt like a snooker ball in a sock. He rolled over onto his back, his arms raised to ward off further blows, but none came. Through tearstained eyes, a black agony in the back of his head, the man looked up and tried to focus on his assailant. All he could see was a figure standing over him holding a weapon. A club of some sort. He whined in the back of his throat.

"I have money," he was able to say, but realised very quickly that this wasn't going to be a mugging. He tried to kick out as hands began pulling at his trousers, but was dealt a further blow to the temple and went limp.

*   *   *

Noel stood over the trembling figure and smiled. He held up the weapon he had been given by Dion. It was a large, carved fig-wood phallus. It had some blood and hair stuck to the round, smooth bulb at the top. Noel picked the hairs off and wiped his fingers on his trousers. He looked round, but Dion had gone. He frowned, and then returned his attention to the man at his feet. He smiled again, but this time, there was no good will in it.

"Hello, Pascal," he said. He adjusted the phallus into a suit-able position in his right hand and bent to roll him over.

RECLAMATION YARD

Wet leaves; wet, shiny railings. Sepia mirrors of water under his feet. Thin, leafless trees like streaks of black lightning petrified at the point of impact in the cold, hard rubble of mud at the side of the road.

Elliot stood and looked through the big iron gates. They were old and buckled and flaking with rust. They were chained and padlocked. The padlock looked like a robot's heart, he thought, hanging there, cold and clockwork, waiting to be wound up.

Across the road, Elliot could see Gregory hulking above the trees that bordered the fields rolling away beyond, his great white eyes glowing like vapour lamps from the huge hairy plot of his face.

Gregory saw that the boy was watching and grunted, perturbed, and lowered his massive shoulders and turned and sloped away through the trees.

Others were nearby. Elliot could feel them.

He returned his attention to the gates, or more exactly, to the long, rutted drive that led away from them. It seemed to wind into the very rim of the afternoon, a long road disappearing from sight into trees on a horizon of brown, turned fields. Struck silver by the low winter sun, a range of storm clouds bordered the skyline like a colossal band of liquid chrome, bringing heavy alien rain.

Elliot squinted, and saw Hoffnung, his immense frame illuminated by the cloudlight, slumping from the distant trees, like a great white deflating hot air balloon tasselled by ropes of tentacles, his vast mouth open and crammed with rings of glittering teeth.

Elliot sighed and reached out a small gloved hand and rattled the chain hanging between the gates without much commitment. Far across the field, Hoffnung drifted back into the trees as if alarmed by the chilly sound of the jangling links. The canopy of branches closed around him and he was gone.

Elliot turned. The Rippingales were hanging like tattered lampshades in the air around him. Elliot shrank back, startled by their silent appearance. They were very ugly, but like all his father's monsters, oddly benign. Their eyes bulged with an eager hilarity, and their tongues lolled from their mouths like eels.

Elliot ignored them and walked away.

With fierce grins on their pallid faces, the Rippingales followed him home.

The first time Elliot had seen the Rippingales was the night after his father had forgotten his son's name.

Elliot was lying on his back on his bed, staring at the ceiling. He could hear his mother down in the kitchen, clearing up after supper. The farmhouse was old and deep and crooked, and Elliot's bedroom was at the corner of the house and had a sloping ceiling where the gable slanted down. There was a door behind his headboard that opened out onto a small wooden balcony. Elliot was forbidden to open the door because the balcony was rotted and flimsy but he could kneel on his bed and look out the small window set in the door.

Elliot liked to look out across the fields as the sun set, watch as the day pastelled down to darkness and the moon became defined and the stars appeared. He liked to watch the mystic rhythms of the starlings flocking above the woods at dusk. He liked to watch the house martins dart beneath the eaves, their tiny beaks stuffed with flies. Most of all, Elliot liked to watch out for the hot air balloon.

Distant, spectral, and elegant, it drifted across the outlying fields at twilight, like a hazy planet on a visiting orbit; then, with a sudden far-flung *whoosh*, it would become alight inside, a lovely warm blush of heat igniting its billowing core, and it would rise further and sail away.

Elliot imagined the balloon rider. A girl, roughly his age, intrepid and bright, riding the low sky in a basket beneath a roaring brass burner, hunting monsters. The balloon sailed most evenings, even in the rain, and once Elliot had watched it flush like an ember in the distance through a blowing squall of snow. What must it have been like up there? Like a trinket in a snow globe, lifting into the cold white static of the air. What would she hope to find out there? Something humped and freezing, somnolent beneath a new-laid drift; a strange creature to rescue, or to fight? Elliot realised he had never seen the balloon return, only soar away. Did it come back at night? In the early hours of the morning? And when it did, was there slung beneath it a great net, its contents snarling, coiling, its weight dragging the balloon down like a quick-setting moon?

Elliot sat up and knelt at the end of his bed.

It was dark and if the balloon had flown today, he had missed its ascent. He decided he would stay awake tonight, all night if he had to, and watch for its return.

Elliot was ten in a week. He had asked for a telescope for his birthday, something he had seen in a catalogue. It was an Infinity Deluxe 76mm Newtonian Reflector kit. It was a small blue telescope described in the brochure as *playful-looking*. It was ideal for beginners, apparently, but Elliot wasn't really interested in astronomy. He wanted to be able to see the balloon better, maybe see who was piloting it, and maybe see what cargo it returned with.

But for now, he had to squint out across the dark fields, through the spectre of his own reflection, and wait.

While he waited, he thought about his father.

They had been eating their tea. Just Elliot and his mum and dad, around the kitchen table. There was a small green china vase in the middle of the table filled with a sweet-smelling spray of freesias, his mother's favourite flower. Dinner was lamb and red pepper stew. Mum had baked bread fresh that afternoon. Elliot watched as his father tore a strip of dark crust from the edge of a thick slice and dunked it in his stew. His dad was quiet tonight. He ate slowly, chewing every mouthful a great deal before swallowing, a slight frown creasing his brow. Elliot looked up at his mother, who sat opposite. She was looking at her husband. Elliot realised there were two types of worry, both evident there on the faces of his parents. One, a worry about something internalised, something perplexing that needed thinking over; that was the look on his father's face. The other was a worry about some*one*; this, much fresher on his mother's face, much more vigilant and alive.

His father looked up, and his expression regained some vitality of its own.

"What do you think of this stew, Roger?" he asked, looking directly at Elliot. There was a crumb of bread stuck to his chin. Unnerved, Elliot sat and stared at his dad. He watched as his father's expression changed again. This time, his top lip trembled, and Elliot could see a sudden anxiety in his eyes.

"Rodge?" his dad said in a quiet voice, and reached a trembling hand across the table. "The stew, Rodge. What d'you think of the *stew*?"

And then Elliot jumped, and dropped his fork. His mother burst into tears.

Roger was the dog.

The balloon returned while Elliot slept.

It hung above the farmhouse, its purple fabric billowing, its gas burner hissing. Like a colossal lantern, it bathed the house and yard with soft amber light.

Elliot had nodded off watching the horizon. He stirred and rolled over onto his back. The unfamiliar light flickered against his eyelids and he awoke. For a second, he was disoriented. He was still dressed in his shirt and jeans. He'd never slept in his clothes before and he felt clammy and uncomfortable. His jeans had ridden up and were creased tightly in the crack of his bum. He shifted and sat up, pulling at his waistband. He turned, then, and looked out the window above his headboard.

A year after Elliot was born, his father wrote a book. It was the only book he ever wrote, but it became quite famous and, to his delight, he sold the rights for it to be turned into a short film. The film had never been made, but his father still got cheques every year because the company that bought it wanted to keep it *optioned.* Elliot wished they'd hurry up and make it.

The book was called *Junction Creature*, and his dad had illustrated it himself; it was full of strange, dark, wonderful pictures of people dwarfed by huge creatures, people on tiny boats being menaced by forests of tentacles, woods and mountainsides home to unwary trekkers being stalked by wolves the size of lorries and monsters as high as pylons approaching from the distance. There were things in shrouds with glowing eyes and rows of terrible teeth, which hung still and ominous in the periphery of little children.

But even though the pictures were scary, there was something about the creatures that filled Elliot with wonder rather than fear. They meant no harm, these beasts. They wanted to coexist, not intrude.

Junction Creature was different.

Elliot's dad had never drawn Junction Creature. He was too awful to put on paper. Junction Creature had lived forever in the dreams of children; he was the darkness that made them grow up bad, and sometimes they didn't grow up at all. Sometimes they disappeared, or were taken.

Junction Creature needed just one more child and then he was free. He chose a girl called Lesley, because Lesley always had incredible dreams. Not all good dreams, though; sometimes she had the kind of nightmares that woke her screaming, clutching at the dead night air around her, petrifying her stone cold in the pure consciousness of *being* but not knowing who she was or even *what* she was for a time after. Lesley had powerful dreams and Junction Creature wanted them. He wanted them to fuel his escape, to reach the velocity necessary to burst from the sleeping heads of everyone and ruin the world.

Junction Creature hated hope. Hope made him sick. He would prowl the outskirts of pleasant dreams and lift his leg and pee on their perimeters. He would encroach, and whisper, and scrawl the brightness with deep, smoking wounds from his claws.

He had become so powerful, and the world around reflected this. There was so little hope now. People had no beliefs, no rock to stand on. Just contemptuous, elegant equations and the pursuit of their own desires driven by fear and hate.

Junction Creature loved hate. Hate was rich as dung, as high and sweet and rotten; it had a *proper* taste, a savour pungent enough for something as deep as the universe and as cold. And fear was the mother-sauce that confected the hatred into something fit for a god. Junction Creature gorged himself when he found bad dreams, and hollowed them out and poured in his own filthy lies. They set like concrete in a mould, and the dreamers found waking an unbearable thing, and they took to staying in bed or neglecting their families or took drink, or tablets, or both.

What were the other monsters? They were the old nightmares of man, the primitive fears that kept him alert and fired his imagination. They were the old symbols, rebukes, and principles that kept him humble and outward-facing, that shook him but never destroyed him, that warned but never caused hopelessness. They were frightened now. Frightened of Junction Creature, and set about making it their business to warn people one last time of the terrible danger they were facing. So vast they were but unnoticed, a vague awareness, a flicker on the outskirts.

Needing to walk with man in his waking world, now that their heads and their dreams had become inviolable vaults of self-interest and despair.

And how Junction Creature loved *despair*.

With claws like sexton's shovels, he'd scoop despair in clots and smear it on his gums, rub it in his blazing eyes to make them sting and burn, and run with its unrelenting blight, and he'd throw back his head and roar.

Hate was good. Fear was even better.

But *despair*.

That was the end of everything.

Elliot hadn't bothered trying to see where the light was coming from through his tiny window. He pulled on his trainers and ran through the house, his heart hammering and his mind white-washed with panic.

He flew down the stairs, not caring if he woke his parents with his clattering and clumping, and banged through the kitchen to unlock the back door. Roger, the limping and antique whippet, staggered up from his basket and weaved across the tiles to join Elliot outside.

Elliot stood beneath the balloon. The bottom of the basket hung only a few feet above the chimney pots.

Her face pale, expression grave, blonde hair fine and moving in a draught from the great brass burner, a young girl peered over the lip of the basket.

"Hi, Elliot," she said.

Elliot lifted a hand and waved. His mouth hung open.

"I've brought you something," she said.

Elliot stood with his arms hanging limp at his sides. He felt like his knees might buckle. Then Roger started barking. He gave out three hoarse *woofs* and began padding around Elliot's legs, his grey muzzle wrinkled, showing his few remaining teeth. He seemed agitated and trembled more than usual.

Lifting from within the basket, like ragged, miniature copies of the balloon above, the Rippingales, all eight of them, rose into the air and surrounded the farmhouse.

Elliot recognised them from his father's book. They grinned, thin white lips peeled back from enormous teeth. Their tattered shrouds dangled, hiding whatever bodies and limbs they might have beneath.

There was a sudden *whoosh*, much louder than Elliot had heard from across the fields before, of course, and it made him startle and cry out. The balloon glowed, lifted, and began to move away.

Roger was lying on his back, growling and rolling in something. He was drooling.

"Wait," Elliot called, but the balloon continued to rise.

Then the little girl's head appeared again and she called down, her voice almost lost now.

"What, Elliot?"

"What's your name?" was all he could think to ask.

"Lesley," she said. "Now I have to go."

Elliot opened his mouth and then closed it again. He watched as the balloon sailed away. Roger was lying at his feet, panting, his eyes shut. Elliot nudged him with the toe of his trainer. No response. Roger was either terrified or elated. Either would probably be enough to kill him.

Elliot looked up at the farmhouse.

The Rippingales had gathered together in a clump of heads just to the right of the door that led off the flimsy balcony into his bedroom at the corner of the house. They gazed down at Elliot with macabre, swollen eyes.

Elliot dragged his gaze from them and bent and picked Roger up. He stank of something decayed plastered to the thin fur on his back. Averting his face, Elliot carried him inside the house and dumped him back in his basket.

Then he went and washed his hands in the Butler sink beneath the kitchen window, and went back upstairs to bed.

Weeks passed and his father's behaviour became more erratic and strange. When he was at school, Elliot knew, his parents visited doctors.

Elliot was very frightened. He loved his dad, his kind, quiet, gentle father, who drew marvellous pictures and shared good, sweet time with his son. He knew something was wrong, and he feared, above all things, that it might somehow be his fault.

Elliot wasn't a bad boy. He wasn't spiteful or remote or sneaky, and he tried, really *tried,* to please his folks of his own will, because their life was fine, and Elliot felt happy and safe within it. But without information to the contrary, or reassurance, or hope, Elliot wondered, and worried. What might he have done to disturb his parents so?

And as his father became forgetful, and his mother grew drawn and distant and fretful, Elliot saw more of the creatures his father had created.

They lurked in bushes and copses along the lane that led to school. They floated at the edge of his vision and drifted at his back as he walked home alone, beneath the low, darkening clouds of those mid-autumn afternoons, his books pressed beneath his right arm, the peppery October smells of bonfires and fallen leaves in his nostrils. They stood massive and abandoned amongst the high trees of the woods, and attempted concealment amongst the barns and buildings of the farms and factories, spread out through the countryside near Elliot's home. They didn't frighten him, and a part of his mind even suggested to him he was imagining them, but their shadows, and their smells, and their glimpsed expressions all combined to form the idea—despite Elliot's inability to define an intent, a *purpose* for their presence—that they were as real as he was, at least as real as his father was perhaps, and that as his father became more eccentric, so his creatures became more *evident* to Elliot. It was a clever insight, but Elliot had been given some time to come to it, and he was a bright boy.

Elliot lived, went to school, walked, ate, and slept, with the constant unusual companionship of his father's monsters, and he didn't speak of it to anyone. If anything, they reassured him, and perhaps *that* was their purpose. Like the characters in his father's book, the unacquainted folk, perceptive only of something uncanny on some impatient yet courteous approach, Elliot let them be.

The night after his encounter with the Rippingales at the big, buckled gates, Elliot went to bed early. He knelt on his bed and peered through the eyepiece of his new, blue, Infinity Deluxe telescope. He fixed it to his headboard with a bracket supplied with the kit, and spent long hours looking through it at the distant fields. And so far, he had seen nothing more of the balloon. Again, he wondered whether he had just imagined the whole thing. Since the night the balloon had appeared over the house, and the Rippingales had lifted diffidently from the basket to bring in the reign of his father's monsters, Elliot hadn't so much as had a glimpse of Lesley or the balloon. Now he had the kit, it was a massive disappointment to him. All he could see, with a sweep of the chunky little telescope, was a damp, dark panorama of trees, fields, and the high, rising sky excessive with cloud.

Elliot sighed and lay back on his bed. He closed his eyes and was soon asleep.

Elliot woke up with a start. His heart was hammering, and his eyes were wide and staring into the dark. He groped above his head and caught hold of the curtain covering the little window in the balcony door. He yanked it back and sat on the edge of his bed in a cold blue lozenge of moonlight.

Something had woken him from a deep sleep. It burrowed into his dream and pulled him up from its depths; the dream was still vivid, a disorienting overlay of emotion still tugging at his mind.

It had been a strange dream. It had been in black and white, like one of the old movies his dad loved to watch, or like his sketches—all shadow and shading, like an old photograph. Elliot had been walking a path in some woods toward a small stone cottage. There was a rough plank door and a window to the right of the door that reflected the blackness of the night. There was a narrow verge of earth surrounding the cottage, and it was planted with pumpkins. In the dream, the pumpkins were grey like cement, and their thick stalks looked like lead pipes. As Elliot watched, the door opened, and a fat man dressed in a tight black sports jacket, a wing-collar shirt, necktie, and sporting a bowler hat emerged. Elliot recognised the man and felt the dream suffuse with an eerie and delightful sense of well-being and joy. The man was Oliver Hardy. Elliot knew this because his dad had recently introduced him to the delights of Laurel and Hardy films. They sat together and laughed until tears filled their eyes at old videos of them, videos his dad had kept for years. He told Elliot one day that he had a treat for him, something he had been saving to share with his son, and he had shown Elliot the videos, all neatly labelled: *Pack Up Your Troubles, Babes in Toyland, Block-Heads, The Music Box, The Flying Deuces*, and lots more. Elliot loved them immediately.

Ollie stood looking down at the pumpkins. He wiped his brow with a white handkerchief, and bent and pulled one of the pumpkins from its bed and lifted it to his chest. Then he turned and went back inside the cottage.

Elliot drew close to the cottage and found himself inside. There was a single room with bare white walls. There was nothing inside the room but a cold pot-bellied stove and a pine card table and a narrow-backed chair. There was an oil lamp hanging from a hook attached to the flue rising from the top of the stove. A fat flame guttered inside its smutty glass bowl. The floor was bare earth, pressed flat and hard as concrete by the years it had been packed underfoot. Sitting on the chair was another man, smaller, with a bow-tie and loose-fitting double-breasted suit. He also wore a bowler hat, narrower than Olly's and with a flatter brim. His face was white and sad. Before him on the table sat the pumpkin.

A shadow moved across the window outside. It was large and slow and moved like a bus going past. There was still no sound.

Elliot looked back at Stan Laurel and saw that Stan was looking out of the window. He was crying. The pumpkin was gone. There was something else lying on the table. Elliot couldn't focus on it. He knew what it was, but he couldn't remember what it was called or what it might be for.

There was a sound from outside, breaking the phantom silence of the dream. A scraping sound, and a low, revolting snort.

And then, Elliot was awake and sitting on the side of his bed and could hear the sound again, the sound that had woken him up.

It was coming from downstairs.

Elliot got up and went to his bedroom door. He opened it a crack and peered out into the hallway. There was a lamp on downstairs. It lit the landing with a twisted funnel of pale lemon light.

Elliot strained to listen, but all he got was a clear sense of something very deliberately not making any noise. There was a presence there, down in the house, something big, and still, and now intolerably silent.

Elliot opened the door and stepped out into the hallway.

Elliot's parents' bedroom was opposite his, thirty feet away at the other end of the narrow passage. Their bedroom door was open. Elliot padded across and peered in. He could make out the shape of his mother, curled beneath the duvet, but next to her, the duvet had been folded back in a lumpy triangle and his father's side of the bed was empty.

Elliot went to the stairwell. There was something blocking the hall beneath the stairs. Elliot started down and then stopped, his hand gripping the banister rail. He was looking down onto the back of some kind of enormous creature, with a ridge of spine knotted like a length of battleship chain beneath a bristled hide, and bulging flanks, and a great head pointing down the hall toward the front door. Elliot knew who it was.

It was Coates, and Coates was a wolf and a boar; and he had a great grey fleshy snout with nostrils like sleeves going up into his head, a wolf's muzzle with long, jagged teeth. Coates had tiny red eyes and big, muscular, impatient jowls and large pig's ears unfolding on either side of his head. He had a chest barrelled like a lagged water tank, and his front legs ended with hooves and his back legs were sprung and long and powerful as a jackal's.

Coates.

Elliot edged to the bottom of the stairs. His eyes were wide and his breathing was shallow. Coates was massive. Elliot had felt his presence in the woods around the house before, seen the dark lumbering evidence of his movement through the trees, heard his racking snort in the darkness outside the house on occasion, and thought he'd heard the flinty sound of his hooves clopping on the cobbled lanes that ran through the outlying farms. But he'd never seen him this close.

Coates' eyes glowed. His snout twitched. Elliot rounded the banister and stepped into the hall to stand before the beast. Elliot could just about see above the coarse hackles that ran along Coates' spine and he could see that the kitchen light was on beyond the hall. Coates' girth filled the space; there was no way past him. Elliot stepped closer. Coates' snout twitched again, and Elliot was thinking he could probably slide both arms right up into Coates' cold, slippery nostrils, almost to the elbows, and feel around in the quarries of his head—not that he'd want to! He was just considering Coates' *scale* when Coates snorted again, this time blowing a thick, glutinous sheet of mucus from his snout that covered the front of Elliot's pyjamas.

Elliot stumbled backwards, horrified. It stank. It stank like old sodden towels in an old man's house, greasy and bacterial, and he gagged as the stench clouded up into his face. Coates grunted and shifted his weight onto his back legs, then sat down on his haunches. He regarded Elliot with silent impassivity.

Elliot scowled up at Coates.

"Get out of my way!" he said. "What the hell are you doing here anyway?"

And then Elliot heard another sound, a scrape and a clump and a crash, from the kitchen. And then he heard a voice, his father's, full of emotion: "Outside! Stay *outside*!"

"Dad!" Elliot called, standing on tiptoes and trying to see past Coates' great head to the rectangle of light at the kitchen door.

Coates edged backwards, his flanks bristling against the walls on either side. Frustrated, Elliot clenched his fists. "Right!" he said, and turned, determined to let himself out through the front door and go around to the back of the house and get into the kitchen that way. But then he stopped, because his mother was coming down the stairs.

Her eyes were half-closed and she stumbled down the stairs holding onto the banister. Her nightdress was twisted, the collar exposing one shoulder. She reached the hallway and saw her son. She glanced toward the kitchen. She was clearly disconcerted by seeing Elliot.

Elliot looked back down the hall. Coates was gone.

"Mum?" he said. "I heard Dad."

His mother walked ahead and stood in the doorway to the kitchen. She reached out and took hold of the doorframe with a trembling left hand. She let out a soft cry of anguish and turned to Elliot, who was following up the hall behind her.

She held out her hands. "Please, Elliot," she said. "Go back to bed. Please just go back to bed."

There was another crash from the kitchen and Elliot and his mother both jumped. Elliot wanted to see, wanted to know what his father was doing, but before he could say anything or before his mother could tell him again to go back to bed, his father walked into sight. His mother turned. She cried out again and stepped into the kitchen.

His father was naked. His chest, throat, and face were streaked with some kind of thick, black medium, and it took Elliot a moment to realise that it was paint, or ink, that smothered him like a terrible burn. His father's eyes were huge, staring, and full of unquenchable fear. He raised his hands and Elliot saw that they too were coated, and webbed between the fingers with the stuff, as if his father had been scooping it in handfuls from a tin.

Elliot could smell it now, the flat chemical odour of it, and despite his mother's request, he stepped forward and peered into the kitchen.

The windows above the kitchen sink, and the glass in the door leading out to the back yard, were covered as if a screen had been drawn down, in a thick coat of paint. He could see arcs and swoops and prints in the paint where his father had applied it with his bare hands. The paint was on thick; it dripped with all the languor of a black, satanic candle.

Elliot's mother stepped between Elliot and his father. She embraced him and led him away, across the kitchen, and gathered a linen tablecloth to wrap him in, to cover his stark, blackened nakedness. Elliot watched from the doorway, transfixed by fear, by horror, by sadness. By a sudden sense of complete loss. He couldn't speak.

Elliot's father stood like a prophet, a doomsaying mystic bound in a sacred robe, his face and hands visible, black with paint, after writing blocks of unadorned judgement upon the glass. He gazed around the room with fear-filled eyes.

Elliot's mother reached for a cloth and ran the taps. She gripped the cloth with both hands, her back still to Elliot, and squeezed it beneath the running water. She turned to her husband. She held the cloth out gently, to clean some of the paint from her husband's face, but he recoiled, his backside bumping up against the edge of the dining table.

"No!" he said, his voice loud, distressed.

Elliot's mother paused, did not advance. She remained by the sink.

In a quiet voice, she said, "I need to clean up, darling."

"No!" his father shouted again. His voice was fractured with fear, almost a scream. "Don't touch them! Don't touch the blackouts!"

Elliot turned and ran back up the stairs.

Elliot lay on his bed and listened to the sounds from downstairs. Tears welled at the corners of his eyes, and he closed his eyes tightly in fury at them; they ran down his face and felt cold and unwelcome in his ears. He sat up and rubbed at his face, dug the wetness out of his ears with his fingertips.

Shortly after he had returned to his room, he heard his mother using the telephone in the hall. Her voice was low but he could hear the emotion in it, the distress. His father had gone quiet.

And then others arrived. Elliot went to the door and listened. It was a doctor, he was certain. Who else would come out in the middle of the night following an urgent and whispered phone call? Elliot heard more murmurings, a calm voice asking questions, and his father muttering replies. And then someone else came to the house, and Elliot heard voices at the front door and the shuffle of coats and shoes, and then the door closed and he listened as a car started and drove away.

Elliot tiptoed to the head of the stairs. He became suddenly aware that he had developed the habit of creeping about his house, fearful and alert, and he scolded himself and squared his shoulders. He went downstairs.

In the lounge sat their neighbour, Audrey. She was sitting on the sofa facing the fireplace. She was staring at the cooling embers, her hands clasped together on her knees. When Elliot walked into the lounge and approached her, she jumped and looked at him with an expression of alarm. "Oh, Elliot, you surprised me. I thought you'd be asleep." She made room for him on the sofa and they sat together, both looking into the grate.

"I'll put some coal on if you like," Elliot said. "It's cold."

Audrey nodded. She looked sad, Elliot thought. He got up and put a scoop of coal onto the embers and placed a log from the stack by the hearth onto them. He blew on the embers and watched them brighten, flicker, and come to life.

"There," he said. "Better." He returned to the sofa and sat down next to Audrey.

Audrey smiled, but Elliot had already detected it was the kind of smile that preceded poignant news, and braced himself, sat ready for the information he had been dreading.

"Elliot," she said, "Your dad's had to go to hospital. Mum's gone with him, of course. She asked if I could stay with you until they get home. Is that okay?"

Elliot nodded. Audrey was nice. Her husband was a farmer and had let Elliot watch a calf being born one evening a couple of years ago. Elliot had been amazed by the sight of it sliding out of its mother, like a bundle of wet, black overalls being pulled from a washing machine.

Elliot settled back onto the sofa and watched the fire. His mind drifted and he found himself thinking about a day a year or so ago, when he had gone with his dad to the yard at the end of the lane that led from the rusty gate now padlocked with a robot's heart.

It had been cold, Elliot remembered, but they were wrapped up in coats and hats and scarves. They had taken the car, an old Hill-man Avenger estate that smelled of Roger the whippet, and gone along the lane until his father indicated and turned right onto the rutted track that wound into the trees at the bottom of the field. Unknown to Elliot, behind the wood was a large yard, full of barns and sheds and lean-tos. They were all piled high with junk, or what looked like junk; rusty machinery and old tools, pottery, ironmongery, baths, sinks and taps, radiators, fire surrounds, moulded plaster fittings, grates, ceramic doorknobs, long elegant hinges. Elliot was fascinated.

They parked behind one of the sheds and got out.

"Don't wander off, mate," Elliot's dad said.

Elliot's breath came out in puffs of steam. He reached up and his father took his mittened hand, and together they began to explore the shabby wonders of the reclamation yard.

Elliot's father explained that a reclamation yard was a place where people could go if they wanted to buy replacements for old stuff that had broken and needed to match its surroundings, or to collect and install things for nostalgic reasons. It was like an antique shop, but more practical, he said. Elliot asked what *nostalgic* meant. His father told him it meant longing feelings about the past. Elliot understood. That year he had started at his new school. He sometimes *longed* for his old classroom, with its tiny chairs and desks and simple, happy books on racks behind Mrs. Healey's desk. Maybe he would find something here to help him remember it.

They went into a barn and Elliot's father began looking at fire surrounds. Some were wooden and some were plaster, some were iron and ornate and some were decorated with patterned and coloured tiles.

Elliot's father chose one, tipped it toward him, and tested the weight of it. It was a big iron surround, painted black with a deep bevelled mantelpiece. He turned to Elliot.

"What do you think? To replace the old one in the lounge?"

Elliot nodded. It was quite impressive. "It's great."

"Right, that settles it. Let's get it over to the car."

Elliot helped his dad lug the surround out of the barn and across the yard to the car. It was heavy, but his dad took most of the weight. Elliot held onto one of its flanks to contribute a little, to please his dad. They both made extravagant grunting sounds as his dad put it down and leaned it against the side of the Avenger.

"Better pay up," his dad said, and Elliot was suddenly oddly taken aback. He blinked. Wasn't all this junk free? His dad must have caught his expression, because he laughed. "You'd be surprised how much a lot of this stuff goes for, Elliot," he said.

Elliot *was* surprised.

They went back across the yard and found a hut occupied by a man in a dirty blue boiler suit and mud-speckled motorcycle boots. He was sitting in a faded deck chair, smoking a pipe and drinking a mug of tea. Inside the hut were bookcases filled with small items, oddments that didn't really fit any of the other categories outside. While his dad paid for the fire surround, Elliot had a poke through the junk on the shelves.

There were tins and badges and medals, polished brass bullet cases and memorabilia. Elliot was unimpressed. And then he saw the kaleidoscope.

It was about a foot long and made of brass. Elliot picked it up. It was quite heavy. He turned it in his hands and heard the sugary rustle as the loose and delicate beads inside moved and settled. He lifted it and peered through the small eyehole in one end and pointed the kaleidoscope at the overcast sky. The object chamber was full of pieces of multicoloured glass, and as Elliot turned the kaleidoscope in his hands, they jumbled and caught the light and reflected off the canted mirrors to form endless, beautiful fractal patterns.

There was a price tag tied to it with a piece of white cotton. It was twelve pounds. Elliot bit his cheek.

"What you got there?" his dad asked.

Elliot held the kaleidoscope up. Dad took it and examined the price tag. He looked at Elliot and raised an eyebrow.

"You want this?" he asked.

Elliot *did* want it, but didn't really know if he should ask. But before Elliot could say anything, his dad said, "You should have a souvenir. I'll give you a tenner for it."

"Huh?" said Elliot.

But his dad was talking to the man in the boiler suit.

The man looked thoughtful for a moment, and then said, "Why not?" and took the ten-pound note his dad handed to him and stuffed it in his bulging breast pocket.

"Great," his dad said, and handed the kaleidoscope back to Elliot.

As they walked back to the car, his dad said, "You've got a good eye for a bargain, son."

Elliot held up the kaleidoscope and smiled. He felt very happy. It was a strong, deep feeling, beyond mere gladness at the events of the day, or the good time spent with his dad, and it felt almost supernatural, something utterly benign eddying through him, greater than everything else all put together. It was joy Elliot felt, but didn't fully comprehend.

As they drove away, the fire surround stowed in the back of the estate, Elliot looked back at the reclamation yard and wondered to himself whether this was the sort of day where *nostalgia* came from.

Elliot awoke with a start. He felt disoriented for a moment, and cold. A thin grey light was coming through the blinds at the window. He felt the presence of someone in the house with him and heard sounds coming from the kitchen. He had fallen asleep on the sofa, he realised. Audrey had been here. She had put a throw over him, but at some point, he had kicked it off.

Shivering, Elliot got up and walked to the kitchen. He remembered what had occurred that night and hoped very much that his parents were back. But when he went into the kitchen, it was Audrey he saw kneeling on the mat by the back door with a big bowl of hot soapy water and a rag, trying to clean the black paint from the glass.

She had already wiped most of it from the windows above the sink, but Elliot could see the panes were smeared and gloomy, like grey smoke somehow got into the glass. The putty around the edges of the glass and the sill remained black, too stained to remove with only water. They would need repainting.

Audrey heard Elliot approach and looked up. She had rubber gloves on. They had been his mother's yellow washing-up gloves, but now they looked like mechanic's hands. The water in the bowl was as black as sump.

Audrey gave Elliot a weak smile. She looked very tired. "It was emulsion, luckily," she said. "Comes off with a scrub."

Elliot watched as Audrey resumed cleaning the last pane of glass beneath the door handle. As the paint washed away, Elliot felt a stab of unease. Whatever his father had been intending to do, however peculiar his method, Elliot knew his father was trying to protect them from something. A part of him wished Audrey had left it all alone, despite it being unsettling to see, as he knew his father never did anything with paint or ink that didn't have some important meaning to him.

As Elliot was thinking about this, he heard the front door open. He ran out into the hall, suddenly hopeful this might all be over.

But it was his mother, and she was alone. Her eyes were very red and she was trembling.

"Oh, Elliot," she said, and he ran to her, and she held him, and they both cried for their dear man.

Even though his mother tried to explain to Elliot about pre-senile dementia, about how suddenly it struck and how quick its course was and how it had affected his father in such a terrible way, Elliot couldn't believe something so impossible could happen to his father.

There was no cure, she told him. And he would get worse until one day, he wouldn't know them anymore.

Elliot was devastated.

His father had been admitted to a ward at the psychiatric hospital in town. Because of his condition, he had to be nursed surrounded by people who were old, at the end of their lives. Elliot couldn't stand it. He only visited his father there once but his father became so agitated that Elliot had to be taken away. It had been awful, and Elliot couldn't get the image out of his head of his father pacing the stinking corridor, rubbing his hands together like they were terribly cold and shouting at the nurses who tried to comfort and contain him.

Elliot couldn't understand why his father was so distressed. One of the doctors tried to explain to him, in her own kind way, that his condition caused him to become confused and disoriented, and they used lots of techniques and designed an environment to settle and reorient people who were upset in this way. But Elliot didn't think she was right. His father wasn't disoriented. He was terrified of something.

And then one afternoon, some weeks later, they had a phone call from the hospital.

Elliot stood next to his mother as she listened to what they were telling her. "Right," she said. "Okay then. Thank you for letting us know."

When she put the phone down, she stood and stared at the receiver for a long moment before turning to Elliot.

Elliot felt hot tears sting his eyes. His stomach felt suddenly very empty, his head very light. "Mum?"

"Your dad's been very disturbed today. They had to sedate him. He's asleep now, but he's hit some nurses. They're struggling to cope with him, Elliot." What she left out, what she felt Elliot didn't need to know, was that his father managed to get hold of a marker pen from somewhere and when they found him, he had been colouring in all the windows in his room.

"When can we see him, mum?" he asked.

His mother looked at him like he was mad. "You can't see him like this, Elliot. It's not fair on you."

Elliot was undeterred. "I want to see my *dad*!" he shouted.

His mother's face fell and she reached for him. "I know. Of course, you do," she said. "We both do, but he's too unwell. Maybe when he wakes up, he'll feel more settled. I'll phone the ward this evening and see."

Elliot nodded. He let his mum hug him but broke away quickly and ran upstairs to his room.

But his father didn't settle. If anything, he was worse when he awoke and had to be sedated again. Elliot lay curled up on his bed and stared at the wall. Outside, through the fields, the lanes, the long narrow droves between the farms, and across the yards, past hoppers and sheds, pens and barns, something high and black and formless gathered itself up out of the earth and began to walk.

Elliot moaned in his sleep, rolled onto his back.

The mass moved like smoke and all through it, drifted eyes like remains, as if torn from the sockets of beasts and thrown in binfuls to roil in a slick of filthy sea.

Elliot began to dream.

He was back in the cottage in the wood, and he was standing on the packed mud floor before the table on which lay the *thing* he knew but couldn't name.

He watched as Stan Laurel picked it up and held it out to him, his simple face white and sad. He looked at Elliot with watery eyes.

Elliot reached out and took it from him, seeing it, feeling it in his hand, but still unable to recall what it was.

He looked up, but now he was alone.

And the glass in the window was suddenly darkened again by the passage of something large moving past it. The floor began to shake, and cracks appeared in the packed earth. Elliot stumbled across to the door and threw it open.

Something slid around the side of the cottage, just out of sight as he turned to look, but it left an impression of speed in the night air. Elliot froze. He didn't want to see what made the air move like that, what shaded it with such a swirl of angry particles.

But it had moved so fast, it was around the cottage and at his back before he could even turn and face it.

As Elliot cried out in his sleep, the Rippingales huddled outside the house. Their lidless eyes rolled and their tongues lolled. Others joined them, below in the garden. They paced and pawed and whined. Amongst the trees the giants stood, their faces solemn, grave and long-suffering.

In his dream, Elliot turned to face the dark thing awash with raw, bleeding eyes.

Elliot fell back through the open door of the cottage as the thing lunged at him. He knew what would happen it if got him; he would be consumed in there, in that terrible moving blackness, and nothing would be left of him but his eyes, floating, wide, unsocketed, and seeing nothing but nightmares for all eternity.

He slammed the door and listened to it hiss, an inversion of sound, something exotic; *dark* sound.

It pressed against the walls and made them tremble.

Elliot took three short steps backward, toward the middle of the room, and stopped. He had walked into something. He turned and found himself looking up at Oliver Hardy. Ollie smiled, his eyes crinkling. He did a thing with his tie, where he took it in his fingers and fluttered it beneath his chin, a sweet, almost bashful show of delight.

Outside, the thing hissed a crackle of black static again and Elliot felt the walls *bend* inward.

"We know all about *this*!" Ollie said in his broad New York accent. "Don't we, Stanley?"

"Yes, Ollie," came a small, wavering voice from behind the big man. Stan peered around Ollie's shoulder. He saw Elliot, and he smiled.

Elliot smiled back. Some of those feelings of well-being were beginning to come back to him. He remembered the times he'd spent with his father watching *The Boys*, as his dad always called them. The fun and laughter.

The pressure on the walls seemed to lessen. "Stand to one side, son," Ollie said, and gently moved Elliot using the splayed fingers of his left hand against Elliot's chest. "Come, Stanley."

"Yes, Ollie," said Stan again, but there was steel in his voice now.

Elliot stood and watched as Stan and Ollie walked across to the door, Ollie with a determined swagger, Stan at his side but not in his shadow.

They turned and smiled, lifted their hats, and then they went outside.

Elliot awoke and sat up. His dream was vivid in his mind. As the door closed behind Stan and Ollie, Elliot saw them change. They seemed to become things of light, burning filaments that flared, *glorified,* and flew into the heart of the darkness that surrounded the cottage.

He glanced over his shoulder and saw the pale shades of the Rippingales assembled outside his window. He knelt on the end of his bed and looked out. He saw the gathering of his father's monsters, those things the size of trucks steaming and crowding in the yard and those beyond, like sentinels, with their great faces, pelted, imperious.

And coming across the distant fields toward the house, alight with orange vapour in its billowing throat, came the balloon. And then, beyond, beneath, coming in great tiers, and slabs, and terraces, the darkness chased it.

Elliot ran downstairs. He had fallen asleep fully clothed again, so only stopped when he reached the hall to grab his coat. He went to the back door, and stepped out into the yard.

There was a moment when he heard a great murmuring, and then they all fell silent. Elliot heard nothing but the outlying whooshing of the gas burner beneath the balloon as it drew closer and began to descend. He stepped out from beneath the porch and started walking through the beasts that gathered there. Some nuzzled him, some just stared with huge, damp eyes, and Elliot knew in his heart it hadn't been these his father attempted to blot out with his window paint.

As he walked, the Rippingales floated along just above him. They formed a circle, a ragged carousel of grins. The beasts parted before him, backing away slowly on hooves and claws. Elliot could smell them, their warm, horsey, manger smells.

Elliot stopped and looked up. The balloon was now overhead, its basket at the height of the roof of the farmhouse. As he watched, a furled rope ladder appeared at the lip of the basket and dropped, unrolling with a snap, its bottom rung only a few feet from the ground.

Elliot felt the beasts around him begin to draw away, to gather themselves in a circle around the rim of the yard. He reached out to take the ladder, now almost in a trance, aware of little else but the thought that he must climb up, and get aboard, and together he and Lesley might fly into battle with that sliding black monstrosity and try somehow to defeat it for his father's sake. But before he could put a foot on the ladder, it was pulled from his grasp.

"Elliot," he heard from above, and he was startled, and suddenly filled with delight. "Go back inside! Now!" He stepped away from the ladder. He wasn't meant to climb up.

Someone was climbing down.

It was his dad.

"I'm okay, Elliot. I feel…fine for now." Elliot and his dad were sitting opposite each other at the kitchen table. Elliot watched his father carefully. The hope he felt was so fragile, he felt it as a sensation drifting throughout his body, the way a fine, briefly sunlit mist might dampen blades of grass in a meadow. It was a very delicate emotion, and full of trouble.

The balloon had gone, piloted by the little girl up into the low white clouds that hid the moon. They had stood for a moment in the kitchen doorway and watched as it rose from view. And then they had gone in, and his father indicated for Elliot to sit down with him while he told him what happened.

Lesley had come for him, broken him out of the hospital. Together they ran down the corridors and out into the grounds. The balloon was waiting there, tethered by a rope, and they climbed in and off they had flown.

There was a nurse on duty that night, a horrible fat thing with bright, tangled orange hair. She prowled the corridors carrying a huge glass syringe. She was the only nurse on the ward that night, and Elliot's father had never seen her before. As they ran past the nurses' office, Elliot's father saw the staffing board pinned outside the door. The names of the nurses he knew, the men and women that usually staffed the ward at night, had been scrubbed out by what looked like angry scrawls from fingers with sharp, dirty nails. And written in red, large, ugly letters, beneath the words *Nurse in Charge*, was the word: MELT.

Elliot's dad took a moment to think. His eyes became distant and he drummed his fingertips on the tabletop. Elliot had seen his dad do this before, when he was making up his mind about something. Before he became unwell, Elliot's dad was a man who always thought before he spoke. *Words have power, Elliot*, he used to say.

"Something happened to me when I was a boy. About your age, Elliot," his dad said. "I've never told anyone because it was so awful, but I wrote about it, in *Junction Creature*."

Elliot's eyes were wide, his face grave. His father was about to share a secret with him, honour him with a disclosure that might make sense of the past few months. Outside he could hear muted sounds: hooves, claws, circling, guarding. Elliot's father noticed his son's expression and looked toward the window.

"They'll protect us for a while longer, son."

Elliot nodded. "Tell me, dad," he said.

Elliot's dad's best friend had been a boy named Sandy Jaffe. Sandy was short, and thin, and slightly disturbed. He had weekly appointments at a child psychologist's office and spent an hour talking about his thoughts and experiences. This was wild and exotic and quite mad, to Elliot's dad, at the time, and his ignorance of anything therapeutic or beneficial about the treatment—in its place was an image of Sandy lying on a couch in some kind of laboratory, being probed by a severe and humourless man in a white coat—made Sandy a profound and fascinating friend. Sandy's parents had money and this wealth, accumulated as a reward for hard work and long hours in both their careers, had consequently led to Sandy feeling neglected. So, he had developed an anxiety disorder, and still wet the bed.

Elliot's dad was aghast at first, but the bold confession of Sandy's nocturnal enuresis came a year after they were already firm friends, and Elliot's dad was generous-hearted and a boy you could trust, so it went no further and their friendship didn't suffer for it. In fact, it made Elliot's dad feel even more protective toward his friend, and their bond grew stronger.

There was a railway cutting at the bottom of a meadow near to their village, which ended at the mouth of a tunnel that bored through the surrounding hills. The boys liked to play there, or sit at the top of the cutting and watch for the trains to pass.

One overcast afternoon, they were rooting around in the pebbles at the edge of the tracks at the tunnel mouth. They had a good view up the line for about half a mile so they could hear if a train was coming, and likewise they would hear a train thundering through the tunnel a good minute before it arrived.

That day, Sandy seemed especially distant. He stood staring into the tunnel, his fluffy blond hair moving around his ears in the constant breeze that evaporated from the tunnel mouth. It smelled of cinders, that breeze, and the throats of cold fireplaces. He was wearing a blue plastic Mac and odd translucent brown galoshes he said he inherited from his granddad.

Elliot's dad picked up an interesting-looking piece of metal. It might have been a hinge, or some kind of mechanism fallen from an ancient locomotive. He walked up to where Sandy was standing to show him.

"Look at this. I reckon it's a piece of gearbox. Or part of the braking system of an old steam train. What do you think?"

Sandy didn't reply, just stood staring down the tunnel.

"San?"

Sandy turned his head and looked down at the rusty piece of metal. "It's the flush off an old bog," he said. His face was pale, paler than usual. The overcast sky and gloom of the tunnel mouth seemed to smudge his features, made him appear indistinct, like some papery mannequin glimpsed propped up in the twilit window of a darkened charity shop modelling third-hand galoshes. The sun was low, somewhere off behind the hills, and they stood in lengthening shadow in the chimneystack scent of cold tunnel air. It was probably time to go home.

"You okay, San?"

Sandy looked up. Elliot's dad couldn't identify the expression he saw on Sandy's face. It was complex, beyond his repertoire; Sandy looked defeated, suddenly very tired. "Not really," he said.

Elliot's dad reached out a hand, an automatic gesture, to comfort, to engage his friend, but Sandy stepped back into the darkness beneath the tunnel's crumbling brick arch. "I'm having really bad dreams," he said. "*Really* bad." Sandy was used to answering difficult questions, and learned in therapy sessions how to express his thoughts. Elliot's dad was used to Sandy's sudden mood swings and intimate revelations, but now, this early evening, Sandy seemed to have collapsed into himself with greater velocity than usual. He took a step further into the tunnel. The dusty draught from the depths at his back became a gust that rattled the plastic flanks of his Mac. It carried a new smell now, something like iron and dry, lifeless earth in which nothing could grow.

Instead of reaching out for his friend, Elliot's dad backed away. He felt suddenly awfully afraid. Not of Sandy, nor his broken expression, but of what was behind him, coming at pace through the tunnel toward them, and of what it carried that gave off that cemetery smell.

Elliot's dad put his hand to his face, covered his mouth and nose. Not just to block out the smell, but also to suppress the scream rising within, pushing up through his chest with the force of his fear. His sides cramped as adrenaline was released and his mouth went dry, and the skin on his back, buttocks, and thighs cramped with a convulsion of electric gooseflesh.

His spine arched, and his eyes widened, pupils dilated to draw in more of the failing light, and he turned and fled, leaving Sandy where he stood, his best friend, with that thing at his back.

A thing that engulfed him like a wave of tar, passed over him, and took him away; the abductor's god, the devil-in-dreams, aswirl with carrion-eyes; *Junction Creature*.

And as he ran, Elliot's dad felt the pressure of the thing as it pressed outward like the skin of a balloon filled with hate, a dark, reaching diaphragm belling out from a voracious gut to try and swallow him, too. He tore up the line and jumped the rails. He hit the slope of the cutting and turned an ankle. He part-crawled, part-staggered up the incline and made the top and was flying, despite the pain in his ankle, and did not look back. He heard that thing inside his head, dragging smouldering claws through his innocent soul. He knew if he fell, or turned back, that eye-filled thing would be there, welling up out of the cutting in a clutching, overfolding mass. Elliot's dad didn't look back, and he didn't fall. He ran home knowing his friend was lost, and he was right; Sandy was never found. His best friend was gone.

"It all happened so quickly. Poor Sandy." Elliot's dad sat with his head in his hands. "I can still see his face in the gloom of that tunnel. He looked hopeless. And I left him. I didn't even try to help him. I've never forgiven myself."

Elliot said, in a quiet voice, "But you wrote about him, didn't you?"

"Yes. The little boy at the end of *Junction Creature*. The one Lesley saves in the final battle. That was my way of saying sorry to my friend, of trying to go back and help him. But there's more to it than that."

Elliot remained silent, waiting for his dad to continue. He could see how strained his father looked, and how that strain was communicated in his voice, in the tension and effort of his words.

"It wanted me, too, Elliot. After it took Sandy, I started having dreams as well. Awful, dark dreams, full of paralysis and dread. I thought it was shock, you know, and grief, but it was much worse than that. Whatever had taken Sandy had come for me. I had seen it, *felt* it, and it was undeniable, its presence, in my nightmares. So, I started drawing, trying to create my own guardians to protect me. And it worked. It hated my hope, you see. I made those creatures so real, gave them so much of my *self*, and created a world for them to take me to. I projected everything I was into them and spread them out across the landscape of my dreams so that wherever I was, when that thing came for me, I could call on them and they would be there.

"And then I had you, and the dreams came back with a vengeance. A terrible force. And I knew that if it couldn't have me, if it had failed to destroy me as a little boy, it would come for you."

Elliot's father sighed, a deep, shuddering, hollow sound. There were tears in his eyes.

"I was terrified, and so I wrote *Junction Creature* and put all my hope in *that,* because I wanted you to be able to see, to share my guardians, my great, magnificent paladins. But I don't think it was enough. When I started to get ill, I panicked. I thought so many dark thoughts: Was it a punishment for leaving Sandy to that thing and running away like a coward? Or was it the thing itself, rotting my brain, destroying me from inside? Or was it trying to take me from you so it could get to you without my influence obstructing it? I'm still not sure. Or maybe my illness came first, a stroke of bad luck, and my condition called to it and brought it back. Whatever is going on, I need you to fight this thing with me. Now. Tonight. And finish it off while we still have some protection."

As his father spoke, Elliot had been losing focus on the kitchen, the house, and all the strange sounds outside. In his head, he was back inside that cottage in the woods, where he had met Stan and Ollie. He could hear his father plainly, could comprehend what he was saying, but his stare must have seemed blank because his father reached a hand across the table and gently shook his shoulder.

"Elliot? Do you understand?"

Elliot nodded. His focus came back, and he looked at his dad.

"I know what we need," he said. Elliot felt sudden excitement rising in his chest, a beautiful epiphany. He had remembered what the object was that Stan had been holding out to him in the room of that cottage in the forest. It was so obvious now that his dream would offer up a symbol of happiness and simple fun. Why hadn't he been able to recognise it before? Dreams frustrate, but sometimes they withhold in order to protect.

"My kaleidoscope! We need my kaleidoscope!"

Elliot jumped up and ran for the stairs. His father called after him, "Don't wake your mother, she's exhausted."

Elliot took the stairs three at a time and skidded around the banister onto the landing. He was about to run to his room but stopped, and gasped. He took a step in the other direction, toward his parents' room, toward what sat wedged in the open doorway.

Coates.

Elliot approached the beast. It sat on its haunches blocking the door completely. Its stillness was immense, a presence so powerful Elliot could hardly bear to go too near. But he drew closer because he knew his mother was asleep in that room and he had to know she was safe, and as he did so, Coates opened his eyes and looked straight at Elliot, and Elliot nearly shrieked. He stumbled sideways, one hand over his mouth, the other grasping for the banister that ran along the hall above the stairwell.

But he wasn't afraid. He could see past Coates' massive shoulder—in fact, Coates seemed to shift his bulk slightly in order to give Elliot a sliver of a view into the room—and he could see his mother asleep beneath the duvet, her face quite peaceful, and Elliot knew with great certainty that she would not wake up tonight until this was all over.

Elliot backed away, and Coates watched him with eyes that no longer glowed with the crimson gale-beaten flames of a brazier burning in a wilderness. Those flames had abated; the fierceness had been replaced with something equally unassailable, but much more expectant and controlled.

Coates' eyes were Elliot's father's eyes, blue and clear and intelligent, both human and utterly nonhuman in Coates heavy, hackled head.

Elliot turned and ran to his room, leaving Coates undisturbed, fuming, and impregnable, protecting his mother from the devil-in-dreams. He went to his bedside cabinet and pulled open its drawer and grabbed the kaleidoscope, and was out and down the stairs, glancing once back along the hallway at Coates and hearing, as his feet thumped down three at a time again, 'Go', both a deep, warm, hearty snort, and a voice somewhat like his father's; a blessing from Coates that echoed in his head and put steel in his bones for the fight ahead.

He skidded into the kitchen and held out the kaleidoscope for his dad.

Elliot's dad held up a hand. "It's yours, Elliot. You were meant to find it. Only you can use it. Do you know what to do?"

Elliot looked at the cylinder in his hand. He sat down at the table next to his father and held it up to his eye. He glanced at his dad, shrugged, and then did the only logical thing one might choose to do with a kaleidoscope.

Elliot put it to his eye, pointed the object chamber at the light, and turned it clockwise so that the coloured beads fell into a new and complex formation.

Elliot slowly lowered the kaleidoscope. He blinked, and then looked up at his dad.

They stood together beneath the sloping corrugated roof of one of the now-empty barns that looked out across the reclamation yard. Elliot perceived the outlines and suggestions of the great beasts of his father's imagination as they gathered beyond, and in the shadows and corners of the abandoned buildings, and amongst the trees and in the shelter of the overhangs and narrow brick alleys between them. Elliot could hear the slow steam-engine sound of their collective breathing, like something huge and oiled paused impatient and sweltering in a siding behind a derelict station.

Elliot's father took his hand and they stepped out from beneath the shelter of the tin roof. Elliot allowed himself to be drawn to the centre of the yard, where they stood beneath the clear sky. His father's hand was warm and rough. Elliot squeezed, and squeezed his eyes shut, too, against the sudden prickling of tears.

"The Boys," his dad said. "You could tell, couldn't you? Just by watching them? They were angels, Elliot. Of a kind."

"I know, dad. I think they saved me once, in a bad dream."

Elliot's dad nodded, his face alight with a beaming smile. "How wonderful," he said. "I wanted to give you something good to remember if you needed it, when you thought of me. And you've used it so well. We have the same gift, then. You can draw on your good memories to help fight for you in your dreams. That's why I was so frightened when I started to get confused and forget things. If I had no memories, that thing could just break right through and hurt you."

Elliot continued to squeeze his dad's hand. "But your monsters, did I call them out, or did you send them?"

"I don't know. I think maybe both. At the right time."

"And The Boys? Stan and Ollie?"

"All yours, Elliot. Same with the kaleidoscope. Same with this place. There's age here, memories, resonance. It's a good place. I can put memories here, keep them safe. The kaleidoscope was your way back here. I couldn't do it. I was too weak, but you can bring us both."

Elliot let go of his father's hand. Out beyond the perimeter of the yard, he heard what sounded like a storm tide racing in across a vast continental beach of bones and broken shells. A drenching, planetary clatter. It was all the sounds of eager pursuit, of Junction Creature's pindown, cornering, questing howl. It was dark sound, an inverse wave that felt like it was being sucked from the delicate ventricles of his mind and out through his ears, planted in his head and drawn out like a rusty chain rattling through a foundering ship's side.

"What do we do?" Elliot asked.

"We use our authority," his father answered.

"Authority?"

"Yes. We have rights over this thing. We have what it hates. Our hope. Come on." Elliot's dad took his hand and together, they walked across the yard toward the gates. Elliot held the kaleidoscope tight in his fist, the glass beads in the object chamber hissing against the mirrors with each step. Chhh chhh chhh.

From out of the shadows of the barns and spaces between came their monsters. Gregory was there, the biggest, the strongest, his great eyes blazing like arc lamps high on a crane's cab; Hoffnung, gentle and retiring, a hundred teeth bared, each the size of a refrigerator door; and the Rippingales twirling in their shrouds; and a whole congregation more at their side. Horns, antlers, spines, stings, plates and manes, they bore their phantasmagoria unto the scrutiny of moonlight, and their tension sang like a hymn against the thing that crawled toward them with its cargo of stolen eyes.

Elliot's father squeezed his hand. "Now, son," he said. "Here it comes."

Elliot remembered his father's story, of what happened to Sandy, and the fear he felt. And understood it well.

The thing that slid off the glimmering field and through the gates brought with it a dread so revolting that Elliot was overwhelmed with the urge to turn and run, and run screaming. Only the warm presence of his father and the creatures at his back held him fast for a second while his mind raged, and that was enough, just enough.

Elliot watched it cover the distance between them and then rear up like dense, polluted surf. It hung, a wave that couldn't muster the gravity to crash, and its eyes, those other's eyes, shoaled to the trembling rim of its membrane and gazed out at them.

With one arm, Elliot's father embraced his son, pulling him to his side. His other arm rose and he pointed at the thing before him.

And everything that stood behind them, everything drawn there by Elliot and his father to fight their corner, every monster of his father's imagination, drove past them in thunder and dust and fell upon Junction Creature with teeth and claws and pounding hooves. Passed through its abhorrent crust and tore at its insides, bit down on eyes that swirled and gawped and burst in strings of blackened humour.

Elliot wept against his father's chest. The monsters were dying. Each one that bit and rent was consumed somehow, even as the dark thing shrank back and retreated.

One of the Rippingales turned slowly in the murk to look at Elliot, its eyes mournful and its teeth red. It grinned more widely than ever, then grew faint and was gone.

"Dad," Elliot moaned. "They're dying."

Elliot felt his father squeeze him tighter. "I don't think it's death, Elliot. Not for them. I think they're seeds, seeds in its flesh. Planting hope in Junction Creature's guts. It'll send it mad. It'll dement it." And then his father laughed, the breath of his hilarity warm on the top of Elliot's head.

And then his father said, "Look!" and stood, releasing Elliot so that he could stand himself and look around.

Coming from the doorway of a small hut set back from the rest of the buildings, a discrete grey construction not much bigger than a tiny cottage, almost hidden by trees at the rear of the yard, walked two men.

They smiled when they saw Elliot, and lifted a hand each.

Stunned, Elliot raised a hand in response, the hand holding the kaleidoscope.

The men approached, their suits and bowler hats black and immaculate, and one, the smaller of the two, Stan Laurel, continued to smile his simple smile and took the kaleidoscope from Elliot's hand.

"Stand aside, young man," said Ollie, and his eyes crinkled with mirth, and he waved, a delicate fluttering of his fingers, and together he and his friend walked up to the trembling flank of the devil-in-dreams and they plunged the kaleidoscope into it.

They stood together as the membrane bucked, trying to throw out this thing, this sudden, horrible vector of joy, and their faces were grim now, and Ollie thrust his arm through and gripped the object chamber and twisted it with a great and effortful turn of his wrists.

And then they let go. They stepped back, pulling their arms from the dark, trembling flank, and watched as the kaleidoscope drifted smoothly off into the heart of the thing; it looked like a battery, or

some kind of power cell, glowing golden, burning so hot with bril-
liant fuel.

Stan and Ollie turned to Elliot. Their good cheer and sense of
well-being were still evident, but their expressions were grave.

Ollie said, "Turn away, Elliot."

And Stan said, "Goodbye, Elliot."

And Elliot did turn away, to be held tight in his father's arms, as
sudden and apocalyptic light erupted.

They were alone now. Standing together at the edge of the
yard. There was silence; a *strong* silence, to Elliot's ears. No more
sounds of alien thunder, of unknowable shores.

All the monsters were gone. Elliot looked around, but knew
he had seen the last of them. His heart ached a little, but then he
looked up at his dad, and saw the peace on his face and thought
it was very much worth the sacrifice, even to have his dad back
for a while longer.

They held hands and started to walk up the lane that led to
the road and the padlocked gate. They would have to climb over.
Elliot didn't mind.

Had Junction Creature taken his father's sickness with him,
or was this a respite, a remission? Time would tell. But for now,
dad was back and that was enough.

They walked and after a short time, they talked; they talked
of hopes and fears, obscurity and certainties, of the future and
of the now.

Elliot's dad admitted he would like to try and write another
book. He had the idea and felt inspired. It would begin with a
man alighting from a train in an abandoned station. And Lesley
would be in it, in her hot-air balloon, and she would meet this

man and together they would defeat Junction Creature for good, using instruments of brass as he and Elliot had. It would be good for him to write it, he said, and to draw again.

Elliot agreed, and looked forward to it. But he was thinking about now, and what they would do when they got home.

"Shall we watch a film, dad?" he asked.

His dad smiled, "Yeah. That would be great. You know what I fancy?"

Elliot didn't really need much time to think. It would be their favourite.

"*Pack Up Your Troubles*?"

"*Pack Up Your Troubles*! Of course."

They reached the gate, and Elliot's dad hoisted him up and over.

JOE IS A BARBER

Joe is a barber.
He works at Tony's.
It's in a cellar
Beneath a recording studio
On Denmark Street.
You go down some stairs
And it's seven pound twenty a haircut
No appointment required.
Tony trains his own boys.
Their uniform is powder blue shirts and pink ties.
They wear their shirt sleeves down
With cufflinks.
Joe's cufflinks are little scissors.
Tony's are dice.
There are four barbers working for Tony.
They are all alike.
They're wannabe Tonys

With a bit of clubland charisma.

They'd all fuck your girlfriend

And brag about their brown wings.

They're the kind of lads who are polite in a copper's way

When he's got you bang to rights.

You have to watch your banter.

If it's not up to scratch

You might notice an exchange of glances

And a smirk.

They'll think you're a bit of a wanker.

They are all world-weary and cynical.

At their young age they think they've seen it all.

Tony is hard but fair.

He stands behind the barbers as they cut away

Staring at the backs of heads like a judge.

"Scissors all over," Joe says.

"Clippers at the back?"

Tony is watching.

He starts off indifferent

And has to be satisfied.

It's high-pressure stuff.

Tony wouldn't look out of place

As an extra in an East End soap

Or a police drama.

He has a big, plain Londoner's face,

Not handsome but women find it sexy;

It's the potential for violence.

It's a face that takes badly to drink

And will grow red and bulky as he ages.

Joe's small talk is patented.

"What do you do then?"

"Lived round here long?"

A few questions, then a bit about himself.

A few opinions and, if you fit in, something mildly phobic:

Tony doesn't mind the occasional

Foreigner or *queer*.

If it's essential. If you're careful.

This chat can make men feel uneasy.

Where else but certain bars do strangers

Talk with such intimate superficiality?

And eye contact reflected back from glass

Makes even crude talk bashful,

Oddly shy.

Joe does a good cut.

Nothing fancy.

You don't go into Tony's and ask for highlights.

Joe was bullied at school.

He was anxious in the showers,

Too watchful.

Nobody likes that.

Tony helped him.

Tony helps them all.

Joe's quite good looking.

His eyes are grey and clear,

His skin is soft and clean-shaven,

His hair is short and gelled spiky on top.

The pink tie goes with his eyes.

All the boys have business cards

On a little plastic shelf beneath their mirrors.

Joe has a way of looking at you,

When he puts his face alongside yours

When the cut is done,

When he holds the mirror up behind your head,

"You have a nice nape,"

Joe says in a professional way.

You tip well and this time

Joe presses his card into your palm

As he takes the tenner.

It's got his mobile number on it.

His private one.

Now you wish you hadn't called it.

Because you're back in the barber shop

In the cellar

In Denmark Street.

And it's late and the clubs have all shut

And you shouldn't have come back down here with Joe.

You're still naked

But you're tied to the chair and it's tipped back

On its chromium base.

Joe stands with his back to the mirror.

Behind you Tony watches, like a judge.

Starting at your feet, Joe says, "Scissors all over?"

He looks up at Tony.

"I'll try not to take *too* much off."

DIRTY BLACK SUMMER

Jemma Dolsen said it best: You can always have the life you want. You just have to take it from someone else.

I first met Jemma Dolsen at a holiday camp in Somerset. I had just turned fifteen. It was the last holiday with my parents I remember enjoying. A year later I felt for the first time that mean disconnect from them children experience on the brink of adolescence. Everything felt jaded. I was bored with them, and they, I think, with me. I was morose and predictable. What had been sweet up until then—the beaches, the quiet harbours, the activities put on by the camp entertainers—was now tacky, soured by hormones that demanded more colour, more *edge*.

The following year, we didn't go away at all, but endured a fractious summer at home irritating and despising each other. After that, my parents left me at home and went away for long weekends together until I was old enough to be left for longer and then they disappeared abroad for two boozy fortnights a year.

I was sitting on the kerb at the side of a path lined by small, neat whitewashed chalets. A sloping football pitch lay before me, running away to a cliff edge overlooking a glittering strip of

Atlantic. I could hear people playing in the pool behind the main building. Their exultations sounded like the screams of gulls trapped in a burning cage.

I looked up as a shadow slid over me.

"Alright?" said a tall, blonde girl. I recognised her. I had seen her around the camp over the last few days but hadn't spoken to her or even made eye contact. She had looked bored, traipsing around with her parents and older brother, going from dining room to games room to bar. I thought she was probably older than me—it turned out she was fifteen too, but a few months off her sixteenth birthday, so it was no surprise she looked under duress.

She was striking. Not pretty, but certainly attractive. I was too young and unsophisticated to understand the subjective nuances of what made someone attractive, but I knew I liked the way she looked, and at fifteen, that was enough. I also think that it made her easier to talk to. If she had been simply pretty, I might have shown my nerves and blown it. She had a large nose (and perhaps it's not surprising, when I reflect on it, that throughout my life I've always been attracted to women with large noses). She had green eyes and a wide mouth with a slight sullenness to the fullness of her lips. Her blonde hair was cropped short and looked glossy with some variety of waxy product.

"Hi," I said, and Jemma Dolsen became my friend.

It usually took a few days for the kids to start making friends and pairing off, making those often shy, tentative initial introductions, so when Jemma spoke to me, I felt the pall of speculative isolation lift with a sense of familiar relief. The possibility of spending a week alone without making a friend was a real fear for quiet kids like me.

I've thought about that process—if it *is* a process; it feels more like an event at the time, when you recall it—of bonding, of friendships forged, many times over the years. Not even at school, where primitive hierarchies and savageries still remain, are friendships so quickly and openly made than when on holiday as a child.

I was in the army for twenty years, and even there our camaraderie took time to develop.

No, it was here, on a budget week's holiday that the fastest bonds were made. Was it because of that brevity, the knowledge that time was short? The end of a holiday might as well have been the Apocalypse for friendships made there. It was all over. So: make it fast and make it matter.

We wandered around the camp and I still remember the conversation. Names first: "I'm Jemma." "I'm Steven." And then: "We're from Leeds." Me: "We're from South London." Then: "Want a game of pool?" Me: "Yeah."

Over pool, Jemma offered me a cigarette. She had a battered pack of ten JPS. I was both shocked and thrilled. I refused, of course. That level of rebellion was nowhere on my radar yet, but Jemma didn't mind. She lit up with a match and blew a mouthful of grimy-looking smoke toward the rafters.

"Those'll kill you," I said. I took on a long red and watched it rattle in the jaws and roll back into baulk.

Jemma grinned and pointed the glowing tip of the cigarette at me.

"Nah," she said. "I'm going to live forever."

We agreed to keep in touch, as is traditional at the end of the holiday. I didn't expect it to last, but Jemma was a determined correspondent and I received a letter in the post less than a week after we got home.

I wrote back after a few days. It was more of a list than a letter—it took me a while to get the hang of writing in a way that was conversational, even interesting, when the only prompt was the blankness of the remaining paper waiting patiently to be filled.

After a while, our letters to each other became less frequent but they still remained a part of our lives over the next year.

A few weeks after Christmas, I got a letter from Jemma full of the excited news that they were returning to the holiday camp again that year, and the question: Was I going?

I wanted to see Jemma again, but my parents were struggling. Dad had been threatened with redundancy at the factory and mum was drinking pretty hard again. Home was lousy and the photo Jemma sent me, of her in a bathing suit with the sun high and behind her on a beach somewhere *there,* someplace spent happy on warm sand during the week we had met, was a heart-sinking torment to my adolescent imagination. I could see a glimmer of shining sand between her legs, a salty, twinkling wetness, and I closed my eyes.

I'd been in an ambush in Northern Ireland. My friend had been shot by a sniper and died in my arms in a rain-lashed road-side ditch three miles outside Enniskillen. I remember the puff of blood discharging from the back of his head as the bullet took him in the face. His arms shot out at his sides and he stood for a moment, his eyes wide and full of such terrible, knowing fear, and he collapsed, and I caught him.

I was his mother then, holding him as he died. As she had held him at birth watching everything shining in his eyes, filling him, I was her, watching it all go away again, nurturing him as all light came up out of him forever.

In my dream, Jemma Dolsen takes me down to the playground at night, the last night of our holiday. I can hear the sound of a barn dance in the clubroom. The strings of coloured bulbs are alight around the open-air pool. She takes my hand, and her long, strong fingers feel cool and remarkable entwined in mine. She laughs, and pulls me on. We run, and the sea beats at the cliffs in time with the blood pounding in my head. The moon is out, full and pure, and Jemma's hair looks silver in its light.

We come to the fence at the bottom of the football field and stop. Jemma turns to me and, to my surprise and delight, she hugs me. I stand there, awkward, even in dreams, and feel the warmth and weight of her. Her face is pressed against my neck and I slide my fingers cautiously into the short, waxed hair at the base of her neck. It's like nothing my fingertips have ever encountered, something exotic, glamorous, and forever memorable. I can feel her breath on my throat, and there's something so happy in her at that moment that when she lifts her face and looks at me, her chin raised, I am almost reluctant to kiss her in case it takes us beyond innocence.

But I do kiss her.

The last letter I got from Jemma was a miserable thing.

She was disconsolate that I wasn't going to be at the camp that year. It was going to be intolerable without me. She would be lonely, heartbroken, lost. She missed me, she said. Did I love her? she asked.

We *had* fallen in love, probably very quickly, but had never admitted it to each other. Yes, yes, yes, I said in my letter. Admitting it at last made my head feel full of warm, expanding air. I felt a lightness in my being that was wonderful, and also frightening. A rich, fragile happiness, unleashed from my store of emotions at a deeply troubling time of my life, never before felt but *there*, waiting to be triggered.

I wanted to speak to her, to hear her voice, and a sudden nostalgic ache gripped me. It was strange, but we hadn't spoken on the phone at all since last summer. I wasn't given to using the telephone in the hallway, not really liking the weight of the handset and the heavy curled wire. I wasn't one to *chat*. The phone was something I didn't really consider. It was my parents' thing, and it was predominantly silent except for the occasional call in the early hours to tell us a distant aunt or uncle we had little to do with had died. We just wrote our secret, occasional letters and sent cards and rarely, a photo. I had two photos of Jemma, one from the beach and another, of her standing beneath an apple tree in her back garden (I assumed it was her garden). It was taken on a gloomy day, but she looked good, radiant. Her hair looked an inch longer. I could see it curling behind her ears and she had a fringe that feathered across her brow. She was holding a daffodil, so it had been taken recently, perhaps especially just for me.

But now I wanted to talk. I added our home phone number to the bottom of my letter, and asked for Jemma's in return. I sent the letter, feeling both sick and erotically charged with a swaggering *adult* sensation, and hoped very much that she would call.

But she didn't, and I received no more letters from her.

No email, no Facebook, no mobile phones and obsessive tex-
ting available to us back then. Just the unreliable post and that
drab black phone that never rang and crouched on the side table
in the hall like the trophy head of some peculiar lantern-jawed
beast. I gave it a week for my letter to arrive with Jemma. An
arbitrary number of days, but that was about the timescale for
correspondence in my experience. By the fifth day, I was hoping
for the phone to ring, but by the seventh I was *waiting*. What an
all-consuming wait that was; I didn't leave the house other than
to go to school, in case I missed her call. And hoping, hoping for
that letter back, with a number for me to take the responsibility
of the call away from her. Jemma wasn't shy, but she might be
amorous enough to let me take the lead.

And coming in from school, wanting to see a note by the
phone: *Jemma rang*. Or my mother saying the same, *You just
missed her, she left her number…*

But no call, and no letter.

The next few weeks dragged by and I experienced a heartsick
anxiety that made me restless, sleepless and nauseous. Terrible
doubts assailed me: Had I offended her? Had I scared her off,
sickened her? Was I pathetic? Perhaps my first letter had been
lost in the post and never arrived.

I wrote her another letter. Calmer, attempting insouciance,
laddish charm, self-deprecation. And then I wrote another on
the heels of it that I wished I hadn't sent, because its tone was
pleading, and I hated myself for sending it. Now I was in a world
of confusion, the tone of my letters uncomfortably varied and
increasingly desperate.

I vowed to stop writing them altogether, to apply a little dignity and let it go. Fuck it, it was just a chick.

I couldn't leave her photos alone. I kept looking at them, my heart squirming, throat tight, my mind a mist of immature fantasies and ideas. I felt abandoned. A resentful anger kept surging through me. I was furious with myself that I hadn't had the nerve to kiss her that last night, that I'd only pecked her cheek and disengaged from the hug and stood staring out over the dark sea with eyes that were unfocused by astonishment at what I'd just declined because of some self-defeating scruple, the fear of doing something that was as pure, and as normal, and as *essential* as anything I might do in my life.

And I'll always remember her expression as I turned: A smile *and* a frown, perplexity and disappointment, but typical of Jemma, her generous mouth giving me some benefit of the doubt; and her confidence, too, pronounced in that slight smile: that she might get me next time.

But there was no next time.

I dream again of that last evening. She hugs me. I feel the shock of it through my body. Her legs are bare, slim; she is wearing cut-off denim shorts. She kisses me and I feel her sigh of pleasure and relief, a small warm gust across my tongue. I trace the curve of her waist, down, to the smoothness of her thigh. Jemma ends the kiss and looks into my eyes, her chin raised, her hand on mine; and then she pressed her cheek against mine and whispers in my ear and uses her hand to guide mine, and this time the feeling is more than exotic, it is life-changing. My fingers are not in her hair this time.

But I never touched her, never even kissed her. The innocence I tried to preserve had tormented me for much of my life, that milestone I stumbled on and existence veered, took a new road, the wrong one, I know. I would have been someone else if I'd just kissed Jemma and gone where my dream takes me even now.

You can always have the life you want.

Jemma said that to me, one afternoon late into our one week together.

You just have to take it from someone else.

The lunch meal was over and we were playing table tennis, waiting for the evening entertainment to start. *Pock pock pock* went the little airy ball.

Jemma's brother was watching us from where he sat on a low stool over by the Pac-Man machine. He was taking quick sips from a bottle of Cresta. His name was Billy. He was tall, skinny, and unappetising. Where Jemma had a generosity of features, his were mean; a small, pointed, upturned nose, thin mouth, and pale, close-set eyes. His hair was reddish and thin, and he would be bald on top by the time he was twenty-five.

Billy watched us, but he watched us *individually*. Not as someone watching two people together playing a game, but alternately, watching me, and watching Jemma. His expression changed with his focus of attention. Billy didn't like me, and his quick sips became more pronounced at the neck of the bottle when his consideration was on me and slowed to a repulsive, ruminative suckle when he was gazing at his sister.

Jemma had the art of ignoring Billy down to perfection. It was like he didn't exist to her. He made me edgy and self-conscious. His presence was like a dark streak of something unpleasant smeared on the wall in my periphery. Mostly, we were able to avoid him, but today he had found us and decided to stick around. Needless to say, it affected my game.

"Twenty to three!" Jemma crowed as the ping-pong ball clipped the edge of the table and shot off beneath the pool table.

I went to retrieve the ball, glad of a moment to duck out of Billy's line of sight.

"What do you mean?" I said, as I flicked the ball over the net to Jemma.

"Twenty-three," she said. The ball was already nestled on the slightly cupped palm of her hand, ready to be served. "Game point. Or are you trying to cheat?"

"No," I said. "What you said about having the life you want. What do you mean?"

Jemma closed her hand around the ball. She tilted her head and smiled that effortless and enigmatic smile.

"If you want something, have it. But that usually means you have to take it, and that *always* means someone else doesn't get to have it."

A philosopher would have taken this statement apart, but at the time it sounded exciting and risky, and to a fifteen-year-old boy, plausible. And those "haves" and "takes," well, it sounded pretty hot when Jemma said it. And when I look back, and remember how I felt when she said it, how suddenly aroused and exhilarated, that a girl I was with had such naughty wisdom, I think fuck philosophy. What is it anyway? A self-defeating religion that sheds nothing but weak, flickering light, snuffed by action, and which peters feebly against the colossal tectonics of the emerging self.

At the time, though, I missed the enormity of it. That was a day before Jemma offered her mouth to kiss, to have the thing she wanted, and I couldn't let her take it. Had that rejection been enough to crush her nascent certainty before it had even had a chance to be tested? Did that explain the half-smile, her brave confusion? Am I being *philosophical*? See where it gets you?

Do I tell you of the years that followed? It would be soap opera. My mother's alcoholism, my father's suicide. All done better on the television, to be honest. Tawdry, sly deaths. My time in the army, an honourable discharge followed by my own unending, cheap script; a storyline I acted out with detachment like the longest-running character in a sidelined drama nobody else cared to watch. Alcohol, drugs, and destructive relationships. Yawn.

I got a job as a security guard on a factory estate in South London. I got fired for falling asleep dead drunk on the night a gang decided they'd rob the safe from the office of a storage firm. I was lucky not to be prosecuted for complicity, for turning a blind eye. The fucking noise they must have made.

I spent some time on benefits—and to be honest, that was a happy time. Just me and my drink on a busted sofa in a one-room bedsit. I still think fondly about that sofa. It held me like a mother as I slept and suckled.

The system found me out eventually and I had to find employment again. I worked in a charity shop, sorting bags of shit in a back room. I hated the stale, old-woman stink of it and walked the day I pulled a pair of used verruca socks from a bin bag. I'd found my limit, and no shame in that.

I decided life might be more suited to me up North, so I gave up my tenancy, packed up and drove my clapped-out Polo to Leeds. I'd saved some money, not much, but enough for a few weeks of bed and breakfast, which felt comforting enough, and I always figured I could look up some old army mates if things didn't work out as quickly as I'd like. I'd kept in touch with a few, so I knew I was welcome to crash if I needed to. A couple of them even offered me work—more security stuff, but it was there if I wanted it. Again, another comfort.

And of course, we had the Internet now. I was nearly fifty for fuck's sake. How did that happen? I'd done a few computer courses to keep Social Security happy and had an account I could use in the library. I was supposed to use it to look for jobs, but I'd discovered Facebook while uploading CVs and joined it for shits and giggles.

I looked up a lot of my old mates. I joined an ex-services group, but got sick of all the death notifications. A lot of motorbike accidents and suicides. *Stabilis*, boys.

And of course, I'd searched for Jemma.

Or Jemma Clarke (Dolsen), as her Facebook page revealed.

If you want the truth, I hadn't thought about Jemma for a long time. The tiresome pangs and regrets had subsided a great deal in the monotony of army life and there had been plenty of girls to take the edge off any pubescent memories of lost opportunities, and later, there had been substances at hand to dull whatever lingered.

But I'd been clean for a few years and the last woman I'd been with had been over five years ago. I'd started to think a lot about the past again.

I was surprised at how much anger still remained.

Her profile picture was one of those flags from a recently terrorised European country. France, I think. Jemma was standing in solidarity with them. Currently, Jemma was France. Sending prayers and happy thoughts. She hadn't bothered filling in any of the personal details: schools, jobs, religious views, contact info. All that deep state data-mining shit. Good for her.

I clicked on the icon and her page opened up.

My hand gripped the mouse as though I was hanging onto a rock at the edge of a cliff to stop me plummeting into an abyss. My vision swam and my heart rate notched way up. I closed my eyes and took a breath. Clicked "photos."

And there she was.

I don't know what I was expecting. A girl, unchanged? A gulf of decades denied? A memory somehow still innocent and untouched, *unfucked*?

I felt a miserable rage as I looked at her life. She had a husband. He looked like a nice guy. Beard, glasses, good hair. And kids. Two of them, by the looks of the pictures. Girls. Grown up now. Good-looking. Happy. It's all rosy in the ether.

She was lovely. The generosity of her features had aged well. Her hair was short and still blonde, her eyes wide and bright, her mouth heartbreakingly full. I gazed at her face—a face I had dreamed about for so long, but not seen since that one frozen week in time we had shared—until my eyes clouded with tears and I had to turn off the computer because I couldn't stand looking at her any more.

They talk about alternate realities, the multiverse, and here it was in all its deceitful glory. The life you could have had.

And I heard Jemma's voice, for the first time in years: You can always have the life you want. You just have to take it from someone else.

I slept in my car for a couple of days when I first arrived in Leeds to save money, until I started to smell myself and decided it was time to find digs.

I got a room in the cheapest place I could find that wasn't a drug den and settled in. I got in touch with one of my mates and we met up. He was doing well, had his own security firm. It seemed to be the default choice of business for ex-servicemen around here. I agreed to a few nights work, cash in hand. We drank.

I asked a couple of favours.

Stabilis.

I still remembered Jemma's old address in Leeds. It was imprinted on my memory like a hallmark on a silver bar of questionable purity.

I did a drive-by one morning, the pressure of my curiosity too great to ignore. It was not for closure. It was to open something, something that itched deeply and wanted gouging. The Polo idled at the kerb outside a small council house on an estate in South Leeds. The small front garden was tidy. The brickwork looked newly pointed. I wondered if one, or both, of Jemma's parents were still alive, still lived there. I thought about her brother, Billy. What had come of that creep? I'd looked him up on Facebook, my new recourse to intel, but there was no sign of any Billy (or William) Dolsen that fit what I knew of him.

I put the Polo in gear and drove away.

The nights at the factory were long and tedious, which was just what I needed. I thought about Jemma. I used the computer in the security office to look on Facebook a lot.

That grinning, bearded twat of a husband. I clicked on Jemma's friends list and found him. Fuck my life: Neville. Neville Clarke. I hated Jemma a little bit more just for that. I dwelled on things, made calculations judging by the apparent age of her kids. I couldn't avoid the thought: Was he her first? Had be bimbled into her path in her late teens, all unaware of what his gilded little destiny held for him? Had he been the first to stick his hand up her skirt, undress her, marvel wet-lipped at the smoothness of her thighs, the fresh tightness of her, close his eyes and lie back as she took a cock in her mouth for the first time? Fuck.

I shoved myself back off my chair and stood up. I was shaking. The factory was silent, the big steel doors shut tight against the night. But I wished for an intruder tonight. I wanted to kick the living shit out of someone.

Two days later I got the call. My mate had the address I wanted. It had been a long wait, but I had kept myself amused. I was drinking again, but only on my days off.

People of my generation didn't usually move far from where they grew up, especially girls—unless they married a travellin' man—and Nev, it appeared, was a homebody. As I'd hoped, Jemma was still in Leeds.

I packed a small bag—just a small one—and set off to see Jemma.

Big Nev—I was calling him that now, for some reason; I think I just knew, somehow, he had an effortlessly big old happy dick—had provided well. They had a very nice semi-detached cottage in the expensive part of the city. A big landscaped garden looping around front-to-back. A double garage with what looked like a recently added extension over it. A conservatory. Top drawer.

I got out of the Polo and walked up the block-paved drive. I reached the front door.

The doorbell had a red button set in a circular ceramic surround. It made me think of the sudden, membranous hole that appeared in my mate's forehead when he took a bullet in Ireland. How he had sought to give the rest of his personal eternity to me as a gift. I did not take it; after all, he did not have the life I wanted. I just witnessed the end of his. It could so easily have been me lying there. A matter of a few feet. Maybe it should have been me.

I pressed the bell.

"Hello, Jemma," I said.

Jemma Dolsen—because that was her name—frowned and smiled. It was perfect. That expression of mild perplexity and half-concealed pleasure that had captivated me so long ago. I loved her so much.

"Hello," she said. She held the door half-open but I could see that she was in her dressing gown, some yellow silk thing that reached down to just above her knees.

"It's me," I said. "Steven."

We sat at Jemma's kitchen table. It was a big table, set in the centre of a big kitchen. The tabletop glowed in the sunlight streaming through the conservatory windows. It looked expensive, that table. The price of a car, maybe. One I'd drive anyway.

I thought Jemma might be mortified to see me. But there was nothing awkward in the way she stared at me across the table. She seemed genuinely pleased to see me. It disarmed me. Had I wanted to frighten her? See something other than that self-assured curiosity on her face? I realised I was a freak, a creep, sitting there in grubby clothes, my boots leaving dirt on the wide white floor tiles, my hands clasped on the bag in my lap beneath the lip of the table. Why wasn't she more confused? Why the hell had she let me in?

"Nice house," I said to break the silence.

Jemma looked around the kitchen as if seeing it for the first time. She pursed her lips and then sat forward, resting her elbows on the table.

"It's so good to see you, Steve," she said.

My fingers unlaced, gripped the fabric of the bag.

"You don't seem surprised to see me," I said.

Jemma laughed.

"Of course, it's a surprise. A lovely surprise. I never forgot about you. A part of me always imagined meeting you again. Have you had a good life?"

"Not really," I said.

Jemma's expression changed to one of regret. There was no pity in it. "I'm sorry to hear that."

"You've done alright."

Jemma seemed about to speak, but paused. Again, she glanced to the side, acknowledging her surroundings. She pushed her chair back and stood up. Her dressing gown revealed the tops of her breasts, small and neat and tanned, maybe from foreign holidays or sunbed sessions, cupped in a lacy white bra. I didn't look away. I pressed the bag down harder into my lap.

Jemma came around the table and stood beside me. I closed my eyes and let out a sigh I had no way of suppressing when she put a hand on the back of my neck.

"You didn't write back," I said, and realised, with an abrupt loosening of all previous inchoate intentions, that I was crying, and had come here only to do so.

Jemma let me weep. Her hand remained on the back of my neck, and she spoke quiet, sweet, kind words, and then spoke of things that made me cry harder, and draw on everything I had in me not to howl. Eventually, my grief subsided and I sat staring at the tabletop, my eyes glassy and unfocused. I thought about what Jemma had said as I had wept.

She stopped writing when her brother found my letters. They enraged him. Whatever feculent ideas he had harboured for years sluiced over, and he raped Jemma. Violated her one afternoon when their parents were out, in the shreds of my final letter, strewn across her bedroom floor. And he had done it again, a week later when he found the letter Jemma was writing to me. And Jemma told her parents, who probably knew what their son was capable of, and he was put away.

"He's not allowed anywhere near me, or my family," Jemma said. "But he still lives here, in Leeds, on licence."

"Does Nev know?"

Jemma shook her head. "He was never interested. He's moved out. We're getting a divorce."

Neville Clarke, Jemma revealed, was an arsehole. He had Occamed the gift of being uninteresting down to spectacular and elegant new equations. He was a wafer, an indistinct presence in Jemma's life. A parsimonious, unadventurous, obsessive-compulsive little man. And now we were being frank, he had never been able to satisfy her either. I didn't laugh at this, not after Jemma's soft disclosure about her brother, but a small part of me, a hidden compartment where mental antimatter generates dark emotions, was greatly pleased to hear this. Their marriage suddenly didn't surprise me.

"What's in the bag?" Jemma asked.

I put the gun on the table.

Jemma had retaken her seat opposite.

"Whoa," she said as the pistol hit the shining oak with a single, heavy clunk. That table had been crafted to absorb the faint tittering sound of fine china, and the heaviest metal it had been groomed for had been silver cutlery. The gun was an affront to the table's pompous utility. Fuck this table.

"Is that a silencer?"

"Suppressor. Yes."

"Whoa. Were you going to kill me?"

I sighed and looked at the gun.

"I don't think so," I said.

Jemma's eyes were bright and full of mischief. "Nev?"

I shrugged.

Jemma laughed, a sound so accepting of the preposterous, that I laughed, too.

"I think I was going to blow my brains out in your lovely, pristine, sunlit kitchen." I said.

You can always have the life you want. You just have to take it from someone else.

Jemma made me a promise.

Come back, she said. After.

She did not touch me again. There had been no embrace, and no kiss goodbye. Still no kiss. Her colour was high, her eyes shining with excitement.

I drove to the address she had given me.

It was a flat on an estate on the east side of Leeds. It wasn't too bad. Tidy verges and a few shops doing business in a small parade. Nothing boarded up.

I parked a few roads down and walked the rest of the way.

I walked up a flight of concrete steps and knocked on the door. It was painted blue. There was a fan of pebbled glass mounted in the door, and I watched as the silhouette of someone made his way down the hall.

A chain rattled and a bolt was drawn back. The door opened.

"Hi, Billy," I said. The gun was already up, pointed at his chest.

I really wanted that kiss.

Stabilis.

ELECTRIC BREAKFAST

onsider this, you zombie-hugging schlockmeisters: Horror is in what never happens. Hell is an absence of events. Time is a weight on your chest like an anchor, fastening you down into that seat in the window of the low-cost cafe, the nicotine-sticky sofa in your barren, lino-tiled flat, the disinfected orthopaedic chair in the acrid lounge of the residential home. You find yourselves here, under this weight, and wonder with slow processes how this could possibly be. When did people stop seeing you? When did friends go away? Were there ever friends? How did you let slip the chances to make a family? How did your personality develop such fractures down which dark eddies of regret, acrimony, and panic rush foam like runoff from a lonely, canted moor; all this confusion hastening through your fragile, honey-combed ever-hollowing heart to well like black reflections from your shuttered eyes?

You realise the Judgement has already come. You've stood before God, some aeon ago, and His Christ never knew you. And now you're in Hell, and it's never going to change and this is it and it's all over and you're filling days.

Which is where we find Daniel. Three courses of outpatient ECT already in the bag and labouring under the perplexity common to those receiving such treatment. He's had his electric breakfast, and now he's shuffling through a gloved fist full of change to find the money for a proper all-day fried one.

The cook is a large, heavy man in a striped apron. There's a gleaming splash across the fabric where some pan has ejaculated a molten wad of fat.

Daniel drops four pounds in change onto the counter, which will get him a semi-decent fry-up and a cup of tea. The cook snatches it up and puts it in the large pocket at the front of his apron. He sneers at Daniel and holds an off-white mug beneath the nozzle of a stainless-steel urn and presses a lever above the nozzle. A jet of steam is followed by a stream of boiling water, and the powder in the bottom of the mug is reconstituted into half a pint of fawn-coloured tea.

Daniel takes the mug and stirs three loaded spoonfuls of sugar into it. He looks up at the cook but the cook is busy at the stove, cracking and frying small, cheap battery farmed eggs on the griddle in batches of six.

Daniel turns and walks over to the table in the corner by the window, which looks out onto the street. The tabletops are red Formica with rounded corners. There's the benchmark triumvirate of condiments: salt, pepper, and a red plastic bottle of ketchup. And a fag burn the size of a thumbprint. Daniel sits in the white plastic chair closest to the aisle and this he *can* remember—with a deep sigh of nostalgia: Times past when he was able to sit here all day rolling and smoking his emaciated cigarettes, grinding them out in the little tin ashtrays, drifting and stuporous with medication and the consolation of his flat, slow thoughts.

You weren't happy though, were you, Daniel? Not really. Because sedation is not a cure. Denial is not reframed cognitions. No, you need to feel the sharpness of your condition; you need to feel your mind filling with the black waste blown back from the memories you have and the emotions they generate.

That's why they stop your tablets and plug you into the mains. It gives you superhero powers; the electroconvulsive therapy has done something to your DNA. It's mutated it and now you can do tremendous things.

So, when the door to the café explodes inward and the dead pile in, you're up in an eye blink, lashing out with implausible speed, cutting them down with a handful of knives from the cutlery tray. Red paper napkins seesaw and flutter like wound dressings. You and a couple of builders push them back and manage to barricade the door with an upended table and a couple of chairs. One of the dead whacks its face into the plate glass window; the glass stars and starts to bow inward like a shattered windscreen. You spin around because you've heard a gurgling shriek. There are more of them at the back door, and the cook's gone down beneath a pile of them. You're over the counter and amongst them. Legs and arms fly up and clatter against the cupboards. The place is filled with the tragicomic stench of the dead's miscreant bowels. You're killing the dead.

You've never found werewolves, zombies, vampires or their ilk forbidding. Exciting, but not frightening in a way to induce horror. You can fight monsters, the externalisation of primitive fears; you can hole up in a building with companions and weapons and hold them off; you can consult manuals and apply the well-documented and effective traditional methods of silver bullet or holy water. You can shoot them in the head.

You can't fight depression like that. It's inside already and it's not amenable to force. It's a cunt and it kills you slowly. It's a chemical possession, and the exorcism rites are callous and undignified, speculative and imprecise.

You shake your head and blink. Of course, it's not the dead. You'd drifted off a bit and when the labourers from the site down the road came in, you made up a little adventure. You have no powers. You have no gifts.

It's the Polish boys; sometimes they're quite friendly. One of them gave you a cigarette once. They sit and talk in vigorous, interrogatory ways, their broad, dusty fingers jabbing around their manly, consonantal words. They love their puddings. They carry bowls filled with piles of crumble coated in thick, steaming custard back to their tables like wise men bearing gifts of breath-taking importance. They prise off huge, syrupy chunks with their spoons. They laugh a lot and their voices are always raised. You think that if happiness could be personified to walk with men, it would look like a large Polish workman with a bowl full of crumble.

Daniel sighs. He doesn't know what to do with his hands. He wants to smoke. Since he started the course of ECT, his mind has wandered, unable to focus on anything for very long. They want to cure his depression.

Do they know how fatal that can be? Daniel is afraid, because as the memories return, he remembers the thing that came to his room in the small hours, when he was a boy, with its huge woman's face and flying hair, its wide, screaming mouth, the soaring terror of it. He doesn't want to remember what it said, the curses it placed on him, the words of power that fragmented his hopes. He was only six but this devil-in-dreams was no respecter of age. In his dreams, wherever Daniel went was sullied by the taunts and derision of this unbearable thing. *I'll take every good memory you have*, it told him, *and render them worthless. You'll find no comfort here.*

And in the waking world, it dogs him as depression, an everlasting retardation of every aspect of his life.

Daniel tries to describe the sound of it.

Like an immense block of metal dragging across a concrete floor in the darkness of an underground chamber. The scream and scrape of it. Tortuous, inexorable, tectonic. The pressure and determination of it, like a vast hoof sliding down some steep chthonic cliff of shale, the weight of the creature above and the creature itself unknowable and unruly.

Daniel thinks of those pretty places he visited with his parents on sweet budget holidays as a child; sun kissed harbours and soft, sloping beaches; little streets with whitewashed shops full of bright paintings and seaside toys.

Now it rains all the time and children carry knives. Winter lasts nine months and the snow has no enchantment; it's the grating dazzle of a million optic fibres thrashing in your face. Your parents are dead. None of your dreams came true.

Daniel wakes with the thought: *They will hurl against me stones like crags.*

And he remembers how the thing came to him last night. Again, the sound; then the visitation: This time, the face was at his window. The mouth black with ink that poured from between its rippling, fuming cuttle fish lips. It's the enormous head of a woman, some harpy/medusa/wendigo hybrid. The expression is fiercely accusing, the eyes huge and dead. Because it is dead. It's dead because he poisoned it with the ink flowing from its mouth. The ink from the quill that scratched out the story of his life, which read

Now daddy is dead stay and look after me don't make me ill don't leave me what will I do I only have you now

So, do you remember looking up at your father as you stand together by the seafood stall on the promenade? The sun is high and warm and the concrete is wide and white beneath your sandals. The sun flashes off the low waves sliding up the beach and you squint a little. Your dad is wearing a compact blue straw trilby hat at a rakish angle and he's smiling as he holds out the small paper cup. He's offering you his tub of whelks. You peer into the tub and wrinkle your nose at the piquant smell of vinegar and white pepper. Your father impales one of the strange dead white things on a two-pronged disposable wooden fork and holds it out to you. It smells like the inside of the caves you were exploring earlier down by the rock pools: cool and green and slaking. Some of the old boys standing around the stall with their tubs of cockles and jellied eels are watching you. They smile and make good-natured jokes as you open your mouth and set your teeth around the whelk. It's chunky and weird and folded up like a dead thing's inner ear. Peppery fluid bathes your tongue; you close your eyes and bite. It crunches like cartilage. It's like biting into a knee. It's delicious.

Do you remember the man you found dead at the side of the road? He was lying on his back on a verge with his hands clawed at his chest. He was gone, so far forever fucking *gone* and the worst thing was, he looked like he knew it. The last expression fixed on the flesh of his face was astonishment.

Daniel tried the church once. Hoping for light.

He saw healing; his heart griped with his own need. He left each Sunday weak with guilt. People took him into their homes, fed him, anointed him, loved him; Daniel left feeling the throb of dark fury like some new humour pulsing through a system of vessels hitherto undiscovered.

A young man in his twenties with long hair and a leather jacket stuck it out with him. They used to go to the café together and talk, but the boy seemed more perplexed than comforted by his belief.

So, they drifted away from that scrupulous hope and Daniel found himself alone again, with his endless, unprovoked memories.

What can a man alone do?

You would like to go home. There was a place, once, where you felt safe. You could wander for days through its arcane, green tiled corridors, along its roads and pathways, across its allotments and pitches, and not be disturbed. Your life was ordered yet liberated by an absence of responsibility. In here, even the most disturbed could rage without duty, the most soporific could edge their way from room to room and never be called to account.

But it all ends, of course. Like some unforeseen quantum breach, it's over. The old boys die off in sheltered housing; day centres where you dined on Christmas day with your carols and economical turkey dinners and fragile little paper crowns are closed; the long wards that grow out from the hospital like fractal arms are reduced to nothing by bulldozers, and housing estates are built with access to golf courses and country parks.

Daniel's father killed himself when Daniel was twelve years old. Men kill themselves in violent, demonstrative ways. His daddy shot himself. It is hard to shoot yourself with a shotgun; attempts often go wrong. If the shotgun is placed beneath the chin, the barrel can slip. This is what happened to Daniel's daddy. He was in hospital for three weeks. Daniel wasn't allowed to visit him. He was expected to die, his mother said. But how can a child *expect* his daddy to die?

Daniel wonders how a woman can drive a man to kill himself, which is often the way of these things. To create such conflict in a man's head that death, the end of *everything,* is seen as a viable decision to take.

Children of parents who commit suicide are at a higher risk of killing themselves later in life, Daniel's psychiatrist told him once. They develop fewer *inner resources* to mount appropriate stress responses, he said.

Daniel saw a man kill himself when he was on an acute psychiatric ward in his twenties. People who are suicidal in hospital are put on observations. Sometimes that means that a nurse will have to follow a patient everywhere, even into the toilet, so they can't harm themselves on impulse. Daniel wonders about that impulse, too. To elect to put yourself into a place before all else existed, the nothingness before the Creation, to leave your body and slip your mind through a slot before time. Daniel tries to imagine death as a moment of going back. There might be pain, but who remembers pain after they're dead?

Psychiatric wards are usually well risk assessed. Windows are small and locked, there are no handles or hooks from which to hang one's self, and everything has a rounded bluntness to it. But the man with the nurse saw an opportunity and took it. He showed very good resources, Daniel thought.

There were two low metal-framed chairs by a coffee table in the corner of the television lounge. Daniel was sitting with a cup of tea watching a programme about antiques when the man walked into the room. He glanced over at Daniel and, in that moment, Daniel knew that something lethal was going to happen. It was in the man's eyes and the emptiness of his expression. He had made his mind up to slip everything back through that slot in time. Daniel opened his mouth but the nurse walked in and said, "Game of cards, John?"

The chairs had metal arms with thin strips of wood screwed to them for rests. The man bent over, put his head between the seat cushion and the armrest, and then threw his body up and over the seat, breaking his neck. Daniel wonders whether there was a moment as the weight of his body had arched over his head, the moment of no going back before the slot opened in his head and everything rushed into it, that the man had thought, *I wish I could undo this act?*

Daniel holds his head and closes his eyes as the memories burn through his brain. He pictures them leaping between the synapses, gathering momentum and mass, throwing themselves at his mind's eye like suicides in front of trains. The thing that visits him in the night tells him he'd be better off dead. It shows him his past, and every good memory he should have is tainted by its dismal, overwhelming influence. It coats everything in the dull black ink that pours from its mouth.

So, he makes a decision.

Daniel leaves the café and walks up the high street toward the railway station. When he arrives, the train is pulling in.

Daniel watched some videos once on a website of people ending their lives by jumping in front of trains. A camera was mounted high up in the cab and afforded one the same view as the driver. They were all filmed at night. At first, there was nothing but the tracks racing off beneath the train, and then a figure would appear, bright white like a little ghost, lit by the glare of the train's headlamps, standing at the side of the track, and then with a hop they were gone, extinguishing their torments in an instant. What upset Daniel most was their lack of hesitation. They were about to pack their minds off into that space behind the slot, and they didn't waver; they did it like they were stepping off a kerb.

The train takes Daniel out of town and into the countryside. He dozes in the sunlight that warms the carriage. When the train enters a tunnel, Daniel jerks awake. He feels a moment of panic. He was dreaming that the world outside was bathed in a thin, green gruel of light and everywhere the dead walked. He was the last man alive; everyone else had gone through the slot.

Daniel slumps back in his seat and wipes his chin. He dribbles now the medication has stopped. It used to dry his mouth.

The ECT is helping Daniel by lifting his mood. It's a strange and controversial intervention. Nobody really knows how it works. It's well known that the most dangerous time for depressives, when they are most likely to kill themselves, is as the mood first starts to lift. Energy and motivation return. And the realisation that this thing has robbed them of so much life, that there will be no more opportunities. It's too much for some to bear.

Daniel closes his eyes again and tries to remember something good. If he can just hold onto one thing, then maybe it might carry him out of range of this nightmare visitation, might provide some sort of asylum from its contamination.

Daniel thinks of that day by the seaside. It's just him and his dad, on the seafront. Nothing bad has happened yet. He's six and his daddy is there and it's sunny and warm, and the shops are full of the kind of toys he's never seen before in the town where he lives on the outskirts of London. There are buckets and spades and little nets on sticks of bamboo; there are bags full of small polished stones and pieces of quartz; varnished conch shells and plastic lighthouses filled with layers of multicoloured sand; there are blown glass dragons and dried seahorses and rascally postcards. It's so much fun there in that soft light.

Daniel's train gets in as the starlings are gathering to flock above the pier. He alights and walks through the ticket office. It's unmanned and cheerless. A narrow, broken vending machine leans against the wall by a shuttered newsagent. When Daniel came here as a boy, it was noisy and alive. Posters showed impossibly azure skies over golden beaches. It was a time of heavy, charismatic old coins before everyone was apportioned up into decimals. Daniel finds this kind of nostalgia exhausting. There's no end to it. *What was is no more nor shall it ever be again,* the mocking voice of the thing in his head murmurs, *it's all gone.*

Daniel walks out onto the street. He turns left and his feet carry him down to the front. He looks out across the bay. He hasn't been here for forty years and the weight of memory nearly crushes his heart. He feels so much more than he wants to, and tears well in his eyes and spill down his cheeks. Inside, he howls but nothing more than a whimper escapes him. He closes his eyes and his hands grasp the flaking railings before him.

It's too hard for him. He doesn't have the inner resources to continue with this. He turns and walks up the hill to the station, the grey sea seething up the pebbles at his back. He is resolute.

He doesn't stop until he reaches the edge of the platform. He is alone. He can hear the London-bound train approaching, so he walks along the platform to the place where it slopes down to rough cindered ground. He can hear the electricity like a remote storm in the rails.

Daniel steps onto the tracks and picks his way across to the far side. He looks up. He'll not risk hesitation.

As he watches the train rumble toward him, Daniel realises that he can hear the sound that terrified him so much as a child. All those years of trying to describe it, trying to place it in some kind of context, and here it was.

Daniel can describe the sound perfectly. It's the squealing hiss of a train's emergency brakes. He has a moment to look up and every memory he's *ever had* comes back and they are all sweet and bright and coloured and he can see the face of the woman screaming as the ink flows back into her mouth.

Daniel thinks, *What have I done?* And then everything slows to a standstill. He squints as the sun reflects off the window in the cab of the train; he could reach out and touch it, it's three feet away from him. He can smell the machine.

And then, something opens up in the air in front of him. It is a vertical line of light; time and the locomotive strain against this uncanny deferral, but Daniel finds he has enough of the former to step closer and look into the light. There's someone standing on the other side. Daniel narrows his eyes again and begins to smile. The smell of diesel and hot metal has receded. All Daniel can smell now is the sea. The figure on the other side is a man. His face is in shadow because a forty-year younger sun is up there high in a blue sky behind him. The man is holding something out to Daniel. Daniel can smell rock pools and pepper.

Can love make a moment last forever? Daniel thinks.

He goes through the slot to find out.

DOGS WITH THEIR EYES SHUT

When I was little, mum and dad used to take me to the Reservoir End Dogs' Home. Because I was adopted, as a joke sometimes they'd tell me they were going to leave me there to be rehomed. Or put down.

We'd drive there in my dad's white Hillman Minx. Once there, we'd do the same old thing. Wander round the pens, stand for ages staring at the poor, ramshackle hounds, not saying much to each other, and then go and have a cup of tea in the cafeteria next door. It was customary, once a month at least. I think I just adapted to it in the assumption that it was standard family routine: school, clinic, therapist, dogs' home. It wasn't boring, just something we did. It comforted me, gazing at the spectrum of dogs on show there. One cage had three elderly greyhounds tottering about in it. They looked like identical slices of one fatter dog. Other varieties just looked depressed, or anxious, or plain nasty, rheumy-eyed and untameable.

I remember one time, there was this little brown puppy. It was in a pen all on its own, curled up on a pile of grey blankets. It didn't have any toys or bones or anything to comfort it. It looked up at us as we gathered on the other side of the chicken wire. One of its eyes was sticky. It thumped its tail and got to its paws.

I knelt down and put my face near the fence, my fingers holding onto the wire either side of my head. The puppy padded over to me, across the cold, uneven concrete floor of its pen, and looked into my face with one big brown eye and one half-closed, manky one. "Hello," I said and waggled my fingers. The puppy squirmed, backside in the air, tail wagging like a little brown finger. It did a little bit of wee, then inched forward and nuzzled my fingers. It licked my palm.

"Ahh," I said, and looked up at mum and dad. Maybe this would be my lucky day. I imagined the journey home, my new puppy curled up on my lap in the back seat while I fussed over it and thought of different names for it. We were already bonding.

Then mum said, "Oh, no!" and I turned back in time to see my puppy being sick in the narrow gutter that ran along the edge of the pen beneath the wire fence.

I was removed. The next time we went, there was a ferocious-looking old Alsatian with one ear pacing about in the shadows at the back of the puppy's cage. I thought I might ask one of the hard-faced girls who worked at the home what had happened, but they always looked a bit remote in their blue tracksuits so I didn't bother. I like to imagine that the puppy was taken home by a nice family who had a warm house with a big garden, but it was more likely that it had been destroyed. It hadn't looked well.

The dogs' home is gone now. There's a large static caravan park there today, Reservoir End Caravan Park. I live there in a nice two-bedroom caravan. It's bright and clean and has a neat wooden veranda and a big white and lime green striped awning, which pulls out over it. It's got a proper toilet and shower,

L-shaped lounge/diner, and Sky TV. The site allows pets and has its own social club. The social club is a converted static caravan owned by Colin Dack. God knows how he got a licence for it, but these places are a law unto themselves. It's in the middle of the fens and the closest seaside town is Invidisham-next-the-Sea. Colin Dack has his own business on the side, teaching people to drive cars pulling caravans. He has a plate on the back of his car, which says Colin Dack's Caravan Courses. One night, someone added *for cocks* in marker pen underneath, which Colin has never entirely managed to erase.

I like living here. When my parents died, they left me a bit of money, the old terrace house in Sudbury, and dad's Hillman Minx, which he kept in mint condition in the garage and is now a bit of a classic car. I sold the house but kept the car. I drive it into town for shopping and when I take my dog Bix to the coast for a good run on the beach. He sits up next to me on the big old bench front seat, his frondlike ears blowing around his slender muzzle like scarves in the breeze from the open windows.

Before I sold the house, I thought I might like to get a dog. So, feeling nostalgic, I decided to drive out to the old dogs' home at Reservoir End and see about finally getting my pup.

As I drove up there, through the hot, monotonous fens—the tiny comma-sized thunderflies that rise innumerable from the fields during harvest time sneaking underneath the brittle seals around the windows and blowing through the air vents irritating the skin of my arms, my scalp, my ears—I thought back to those family days out.

My parents had moved up to Sudbury in the early seventies from the East End of London. The opportunity for a pastoral retirement appealed to dad, who had lived amongst the bomb-sites of East London and the plotlands of Basildon while he was growing up. Although they overlooked a huge, smoking conur-bation, the shacks and meadow lanes of the Plotlands gave dad a taste of country life he held fast to as he grew up.

Once he was out of London, the proximity to the country-side and its long, looping, untroubled byways overwhelmed him, and at every opportunity we'd be loaded into the Minx and taken on long drives through villages and fens, stopping at pubs or farm shops, sometimes making it as far as the coast at South-wold or Great Yarmouth.

It was on one of these outings that we discovered the Reser-voir End Dogs' Home.

Mum spotted it first. "I haven't noticed that before, Jim," she said. She pointed at a large metal sign shaped like a greyhound, which hung from the branch of a tree growing beside a farm track.

Dad slowed down. I sat up in the back and looked out of the window. I heard the *tink-a-tink* of the indicator and we pulled off the road and onto the track. The suspension on the Minx was negligible, and I was thrown about like a molecule in a cloud chamber as the car thumped through potholes and surged up verges. Dust rose either side of the car and obliterated my view. And then we were in the clear and dad was pulling up outside a long, single-storey prefabricated building positioned at the end of a slim concrete car park. We were the only visitors, it seemed; the car park was empty. We got out and walked over to the entrance. I could hear the restless sounds of the dogs in their pens out the back: yapping, whining, scratching.

We went through the glass double doors and into a small foyer. I remember the smell, like old jumpers soaked in weak disinfectant.

There was a man standing behind a desk facing the doors. On the wall behind him were hundreds of photographs of dogs. He looked up and smiled as we walked in. Then, for an instant, he appeared startled. He looked at me for just a second or two too long and then returned his attention back to my folks with that grin again, except this time it looked a little strained. It's a strange thing to remember, but it makes sense now when I recollect it.

I wandered over to the part of the building designated the "gift shop." I loved these sorts of places. There were posters of dogs, postcards of dogs, books about dogs, ceramic models of dogs, rubber dogs, dog-themed crockery. It was great if you liked dogs. I picked up a *Ladybird* book about exotic breeds and had a thumb through it. Then mum and dad came over.

"The man said we can have a look around," Mum said. She looked quite excited. "Do you want that book? You can have it if you want." She took the book out of my hand and went back to the desk. "We'll have this," she said to the man behind the desk. He rang up the amount and smiled at me. This time, it was a genuine smile, without any trace of the surprise he'd shown a moment earlier.

Mum shoved the book at me and we marched out through a door at the back of the gift shop and into a wide yard surrounded by wooden pens. "See if you can spot some of the dogs in the book," she said.

"That's about exotic breeds," Dad said. "These are all mutts."

"You never know," Mum said.

I went from cage to cage, my little hardback book open in my hands. I thought I'd spotted a Pharaoh Hound, but Dad said it was just a dodgy old whippet with a fractured skull.

I continued to look around and soon realised that my mum and dad were no longer in the yard. I was being bothered by the bureaucratic yapping of a tailless Jack Russell, so I closed my book and went back to the door which opened into the gift shop. I pushed the door open and went in. Then I stopped.

I stood behind a tall carousel displaying postcards, and listened.

Mum and Dad were in deep conversation with the man behind the desk. They all looked excited. The man was pointing toward the gift shop, clearly thinking I was still outside. Dad stood back and shook his head, but Mum slapped him lightly on the arm and looked into his face. I could hear her voice, fast and breathy, and Dad's expression changed, softened. He looked at the man behind the desk and then began talking again.

I couldn't make out what they were saying and so I crept forward. As I tried to edge around the carousel, I set it spinning with my elbow, and the sound of the cards rattling alerted my folks and the man behind the desk, and they all stood to an awkward attention.

"Hello, love," Mum said.

"Did you spot any exotic breeds?" asked Dad.

I walked up to them, my book beneath my arm, my eyes narrowed. "They're all mutts, Dad," I said.

The man behind the desk said, "Sometimes we get quite posh breeds in. Had a *Shiba Inu* in once. Whatever that is." Nervousness made his last syllable bray into a laugh and his eyes widen, as if he'd just remembered something of moderate importance.

I looked at all three of them. They looked very suspicious.

"Ice cream and a drink?" Mum said.

"There's a café next door," the man said.

"That's decided it, then," said Dad.

Mum grabbed my hand and we left. I looked back over my shoulder. The man was smiling at me. It was a very nice smile, full of love.

I suffered from nightmares as a child. My parents were good people, composed, understanding and of generous dispositions. But as I already mentioned, I was an adopted child and whatever dark neuroses roused me screaming in the night were something hidden in my past and predicated by my nature and early experiences. My parents found ways to calm me, familiarity and repetition being good tactics, and the visits to the dogs' home provided a soothing diversion and assurance.

I saw a therapist once a week from the age of six. My nightmares had become so bad that I was terrified of going to sleep. Something vast and swarming, with great and terrible rims, that swelled inside my head until I couldn't breathe with the malevolent, absorbing pressure of it. Doctor Mocking, my therapist, was a kind man, and he helped me discover ways to understand this thing—he called it the devil-in-dreams—and gave me special words to say to weaken its hideous strength.

Sadly, Doctor Mocking died, but I *know* I see him in dreams. He's there in the background, a figure of encouragement and strength, and sometimes he whispers those words to me again and I remember them when I need to.

Each time we went to the dogs' home, Mum and Dad would end up standing with the man behind the desk, conversing in low tones, casting the odd glance in my direction. I got to increase the size of my book collection and had a nice set of key rings and pens and pencils growing in my bedroom at home. I was becoming a bit of an expert on dogs.

Unfortunately, I never got to have one of my own. Over time, the visits became more obligatory, and I'd sense the frustration that made my parents hurry me up. Then Dad got ill, and two years after we first discovered the Reservoir End Dogs' Home, we stopped going and never went again.

So, that was the first time I'd gone back, or thought to go back, since then. I drove the same roads Dad had driven in the old Minx years ago and noticed how little the countryside had changed.

I followed the country lanes, flat fields either side stretching to the horizon, until I came to the rutted turn-off for the dogs' home. I slowed the Minx and looked for the old sign. It was gone, and in its place, a small wooden sign nailed to a fence, which read: **Welcome to the Reservoir End Caravan Park**.

I turned the Minx into the drive and found it had been levelled and surfaced and edged by wide, tidy verges planted with shrubs. I drove the short distance to where the car park and entrance building for the dogs' home had been and pulled up in a landscaped parking area, which gave access to a number of narrow boulevards bordered by static caravans of various sizes and colours.

I got out of the Minx and stood in the sunshine having a look about. To the left of the car park was a small booth selling ice creams and drinks, its wooden sides and pointed roof garlanded with brightly coloured rubber rings and buckets and spades and lilos. Next to that was a shop selling groceries, cigarettes, and alcohol.

I went over to the window in the side of the ice cream booth. A good-looking girl was sitting on a stool reading a magazine about cars. She was wearing a green sleeveless T-shirt and cut-off denim shorts.

"Hi," she said, and put the magazine down on a shelf next to the stool. "Can I get you something?"

I asked for a Coke, then asked if she remembered the dogs' home, and how long it had been gone.

She frowned. "No idea," she said, "but if you go down to the social club, Colin'll tell you anything about this place you want to know."

She pointed to the boulevard directly in front of the shops. "Down there, on the left," she said. "Colin Dack's Social Club. It's open all day."

I thanked her and went as directed until I came to a large, cheerful-looking caravan painted Carolina blue and decorated on the outside to look like a fishing boat. It had portholes painted on the slatted wooden sides and nets and orange floats nailed across it. The door was open and the plastic strands of a fly blind rattled in a slight breeze.

I went up some steps and poked my head through the blind. It was cool and shady in the social club, and I could see a string of coloured lights twinkling in the corner.

I was about to walk in when a voice said, "I wondered when I'd see you again."

I stopped dead on the threshold, blinking. My eyes adjusted fully and then I laughed. "I don't believe it," I said.

Balder, older, sporting a long grey beard and sideburns, Colin Dack was the man who had worked behind the desk in the dogs' home when I'd been a child.

Colin sat me at his bar and poured me a drink. It was a very nice ale, dark and hoppy, called *Old Blackout*. It was almost a stout, it was that dark.

Colin was excited to see me. He told me those days working at the dogs' home were very happy ones for him. He was a great dog lover and sometimes missed the racket of the place and the affection he received from the animals.

"I don't miss skidding around in all the shit," he said. "Hell of a lot of that. But that's what we had the girls for after all." His eyes sparkled and he grinned, showing both rows of teeth missing most of their premolars.

As it turned out, the dogs' home had closed shortly after we'd stopped going there. It didn't get any visitors and couldn't stay open. The site had been bought up and developed by some businessmen from East London, and Reservoir End had been reborn as a caravan park. Colin told me that he had been one of the first to buy plots on the site. He owned three caravans: the social club, his own caravan to live in, and a third just along the next boulevard, which happened to be for sale.

Colin told me that he had been renting it out to an old friend who had recently moved to Dartford. It needed a bit of work, but it was a good size. I said I'd like to see it.

Colin took me round to have a look. It certainly had potential. I liked the veranda with its white and lime green awning pulled out to shade it.

I asked Colin how much he was asking for it. When he told me, I made him an offer straight away.

"You'll want to know about the dog," Colin said.

I sold the house at the height of the market. It went quickly, and for a large amount. I'd done a lot of odd jobs over the years but had never really been able to settle on a career, and now I had the opportunity to live off some pretty substantial savings and let things idle for a while. I was happy to get away into the countryside. I wanted a quiet life; stress made me unwell and caused the nightmares to come back.

After meeting Colin and agreeing to buy his caravan, I spent most days up at Reservoir End, sitting in the bar, or doing work on the caravan, or tidying up the postage stamp garden at the front. When the sale went through, I packed up the Minx and moved the remainder of my stuff over to the site.

The other reason I spent so much time up at the park was Bix.

When I made my offer to buy Colin's caravan, he explained that there was a codicil. His friend had left in a great hurry, full of important things to do, and had made Colin promise to look after his dog, Bix. Colin had promised, but found that once his friend had left, Bix wouldn't leave the caravan.

Colin had tried everything to entice him to come out, but Bix just lay curled up in the corner of the bedroom on his cushions and refused to budge. Colin fed him and put paper down for his business and spent time fussing him and talking to him, but Bix couldn't be browbeaten, lured, or charmed into leaving.

"I've known Bix for years," Colin said. "Loveliest dog you could ever meet. Stubborn little bath bun, though."

I asked whether Bix seemed depressed. Colin shook his head. "Nah, he's happy enough. Seems like he's waiting for something to happen, like he doesn't want to miss something. He goes as far as the French windows in the lounge and has a nose. He looks up at the sky, and then he goes back into the bedroom and curls up in the corner. Wags his tail and gives me a lick when I go in. He's not low. Bet my life on it."

I was going to ask something else, but I noticed the way Colin was looking at me. He was restless, shifting from foot to foot. The thin plastic soles of his flip-flops kept gritting on the tarmac of the road outside the caravan. He was wearing a faded yellow T-shirt with a palm tree on it and a pair of old white denim jeans cut off at the knees. His sideburns were very bushy and very grey, and his long, thinning hair was pulled back over his scalp and held in a ponytail by a green elastic band. He was looking at me the same way he used to look at me when I was a boy: apprehensive, tense, slightly eager, and, if I'm honest, a bit in *awe*.

"So, whoever buys the caravan gets the dog?" I asked.

Colin was beaming. He clapped me on the shoulder. "That's the solution!" he said. "I'm glad you thought of that!"

I smiled, and then we both jumped at a loud volley of barks. We turned and looked up the steps that led onto the veranda. Still barking, nose pressed against the glass of the French window, tail wagging like a strip of willow in a hurricane, Bix was giving me a welcome.

"Well," said Colin, "that's the most noise *he's* made for weeks."

I asked if I could go in and say hello. Colin took me by the wrist in his bony left hand and dragged me up the steps and onto the veranda. He squatted down and put his face level with Bix's. Bix was mostly obscured now by clouded breath and smeared saliva, but I could discern two warm shining eyes peering out at me above his panting chops.

"We're coming in," Colin said, "Bix, step away from the door."

Bix backed away and Colin straightened up and slid open the door. We went in.

Bix had removed himself to the doorway to the bedroom. His head was cocked and his tail still wagged, but there was a more cautious air to him now. He was a fine dog. Tall and slender with a barrel chest just showing a hint of ribs. He looked rather like a greyhound, but was taller and had feathering on his ears, tail, and the backs of his legs.

Bix walked over and stood looking up at me with those soft, golden eyes. I reached down and stroked the silky fur behind his ears.

Colin told Bix my name, and we were introduced.

Later, after I'd met Bix, I went home and dug out some of my old books. I found that *Ladybird* book of exotic dogs and went through it until I found a picture of a dog like Bix. In fact, it was like looking straight at a photo *of* Bix.

Bix, it had turned out, was a saluki. Opposite the picture was a page of information. I read on. Salukis are sight-hounds. They use their eyes rather than their nose for hunting and are used by Bedouins to bring down gazelle. They're intelligent and reserved and sensitive and are faster than greyhounds, but have no interest in racing. They are short-haired and their coats are white, cream, black or light brown. (Bix was tri-coloured: black with white tips to his ears and a tan patch on his rump the size and shape of a strawberry).

I closed the book and sat in my dad's old armchair in front of the gas fire in the lounge and closed my eyes. Then I opened them again and set the book down on the coffee table, on its bottom edges, open like a photo frame, with the picture of the saluki facing me. I smiled. I'd finally got my dog.

I closed my eyes again and, as I often did, fell asleep in the chair.

And had my first dream of Lesley and her adventures in Quay-Endula.

"Had any more of those dreams?" Colin asked me as I sat at his bar reading the paper. Bix lay at my feet, sprawled out with his back legs tangled amongst the legs of my stool. He stared up at me and his tail thumped twice on the scuffed red lino-covered floor. The only other person at the bar was Eddie D. Eddie didn't say much, but Colin told me he was a retired comedian who had moved to Reservoir End a few years earlier to get out of London. He didn't come into the social club that often, but when he did, he drank a lot and sometimes got talking to Colin about favourite comedians and comedy routines. Drunk, Eddie still had good timing and delivery. He was pleasant enough and always treated Bix to a packet of crisps. It made Eddie smile to watch Bix ploughing around on the lino with his nose shoved in a packet of Salt 'n' Vinegar, and I certainly wasn't going to deny Eddie that. He just seemed very sad.

Since that first time, asleep in my dad's old chair, I had dreamed of that pretty girl with a vivid and almost narrative-like regularity. Each time she matured a little, and explored her new world and made friends, embarking on adventures and fighting great and terrifying machines as she protected her loved ones. I felt like I was watching a life unfold and become complete. I seemed to be channelling her experiences rather than creating them through my unconscious. It was thrilling and unearthly and the dreams left me feeling elated and, sometimes, intensely nostalgic. I had told Colin about them and he had been enthralled. In fact, Colin seemed more excited by them than *I* was.

I told Colin that I had dreamed about Lesley last night. He was eager to hear the latest. I kept him up to date with her adventures at least once a week.

Bix made a soft huffing sound and sat up, his eyes never leaving mine. I smiled and stroked his head. Bix, too, was always interested in hearing about Lesley.

I closed my eyes, still with my hand resting on Bix's head, my fingers working into the fur behind his ears, and told them some more of Lesley's story.

*   *   *

Lesley thought the violas, cellos, and violins looked like the desiccated cores of strange, enormous fruits. There were tall, thin, pallid men wearing black dinner jackets playing horns and tubas, sousaphones, and trumpets, squeezed together into a corner like an assembly of pallbearers thrust through plumbing. She could hear a piano playing a slow run of sombre chords and, somewhere toward the dusky rear of the salon, a counterpoint of tympani and the wooden pop and clatter of a glockenspiel, a sound that always made her think of unstrung puppets tumbling down timber stairs.

Above the flung-wide French windows, a narrative was being performed on the balcony. A fat man, costumed in a velvet jacket and a tri-corn hat, was leaning over the iron railings shouting the story at the crowd massed in the street. It was a quotidian performance, but the content was compelling and delivered with brio if not finesse, and so the crowd was responding with increasing interest. The small courtyard onto which the French windows opened was only broad enough to allow for three filigreed round metal tables, two chairs of equally delicate iron cushioned with disks of green silk no thicker than a gramophone record perched beside each one.

"*I awoke cellars-deep in a mineshaft,*" the man on the balcony roared. "*All around me gilded cages swept up on shelves; each bound in granite and crammed with a child.*"

It was an old legend, one Lesley had heard many times before as she grew up in Quay-Endula. How a killer had come to one of the mining towns during the last days of winter. He was known here as the Flyblown Man, but other Quays had their own names for him: The Cager, Rainscissor, others more obscene still. There were pictures of him in books, depicted as a figure scratched against tree lines, brittle and rangy, each hand carrying oblong cages. His face was never visible, veiled always by a swarming ball of blowflies.

The town had awoken to discover the children gone. All but one, a lad named John Stainwright, who had suffered a nightmare of such vivid horror that he had crawled into bed between his sleeping parents on the night of the abductions and thus, by luck, had avoided being taken from his own bed. The next morning, he had gone back to his room to discover his bedding torn to shreds, the whole room icy from the wind that blew in through the open window above his wash stand.

John's father and the rest of the townsmen searched the forest all day until, with a cry that inked the dusk with a thousand rising starlings, a man found his boy, curled up dead in a cage that hung from the branch of an elm. More cages hung from the branches of surrounding trees, and as the men stumbled through this horror—some dropping with their grief, holding their heads, screaming, at the roots of the trees which held their babies, some reaching up through the branches to try and bring the cages down—they were funnelled toward the workings of the mines where they found, as if on display, the remaining children exhibited on shelves cut into the seams of the coalface.

Lesley skirted the edge of the crowd and strolled across the square. As she passed a stall, a man shouted her name.

Lesley turned and caught the apple he threw to her in her left hand.

Aaron the stallholder was beaming. He was skinny and ugly but utterly unmindful of his looks, and delighted in charming women with an appealing confidence and apparent innocence of intent that had resulted in the acquisition of a number of fine-looking companions over the years. Lesley knew the bawdy talk around the square, rumours of what he had stowed beneath his apron, but she'd never been wont to find out for herself. Aaron was her friend and Lesley had her reputation to consider.

And she was off to meet with Phyn.

Phyn Dakker, her second in command. Handsome, grave, loyal Phyn who tried to teach her chess during downtime in the Attachment, and who never grew impatient, but looked at her with his cool grey eyes and sighed when she swept the pieces off the board or picked up her king halfway through a game and dropped it in his ale, laughing as it bobbed like an ornate fisherman's float in the foam.

"Thanks, Aaron," Lesley said.

"Are you hunting today, Lesley?" he asked.

"Maybe," she said. "I'm meeting Phyn to find out."

"Lucky Phyn. You take care, my angel."

Lesley took a bite of the apple. "Always," she said.

Lesley stood outside the Attachment and looked in through its ground glass window. The Attachment was their favourite tavern in the Old Town. It had twin bars; one selling drinks and the other, opposite, providing food. All kinds of cold meat and bread beneath glass cases, pickles, cheeses, roasted vegetables, jars and pots of oils and spices stacked on dark shelves lining the wall behind the bar. It was a fine delicatessen, proudly run by Krait; his brother, Enoch, across the marble floor, took equal pride in his concern. The polished mirrors above the bar were unspeckled and were perfectly angled to reflect the line of gas lamps that hung from the high ceiling. Hundreds of bottles of exotic spirits depended from their optics, displaying labels as fascinating to read as lurid book covers. The bar top was mahogany and glowed like a massive block of deep red heat in the gaslight. All along the bar were the hand pumps, constantly foaming and chuckling with the flow of good strong brew. At the back of the room stood a piano and Lesley could see Phyn sitting on the low stool in front of it, head bent in concentration as he played.

"Hello, Phyn," Lesley said. She caught Enoch's eye and held up two fingers. Glasses were placed beneath taps and golden Crusader was poured for them. She heard a rather stagy cough and turned to her right. Krait was standing behind his counter. He smiled and raised his eyebrows. "A slice of venison pie," Lesley said. He smiled, delighted, and lifted the top of a glass case. He reached in and pulled out a thick wedge of pie, wrapped it in translucent, greasy paper, and put it on the counter in front of her. There was a deep but unspoken competitiveness between the brothers. Sometimes, in quiet moments, they would stand like gunslingers, facing each other across the marble floor, one anticipating the other's move, measuring up the possibility of custom and which of them would respond the fastest.

Phyn stopped playing. "Hello, Lesley. Are you well?"

"Of course, I am, Phyn. Don't I look it?"

Phyn coughed and stood up. "Thrusting," he said. "Shall we sit at the bar? I've got news of the ship."

Lesley took her pie and sat next to Phyn on a stool at Enoch's bar. Their pints sat waiting like two upturned golden bells. Crusader really was a heavenly brew. Lesley unwrapped her pie and tore off a piece of glazed pastry. It was sweet, salty, and buttery. A pink chunk of venison slid onto the paper, soft and succulent as Turkish delight. She scooped it up and put it in her mouth.

"You hungry?" Lesley asked. She nudged the pie toward Phyn with a fingertip. "Help yourself."

Phyn shook his head. "I've been well looked after here. It seems that everyone knows about the ship and wants to ensure we're well fed before battle. Krait wouldn't let me sit at the piano without ministering to my appetite with slices of lamb as thick as bibles. If you paid me at all, I'd be a rich man. Nobody wants to take my money today."

"Anna sends her love," Lesley said.

At the mention of her little sister's name, Phyn's face lit up. A smile was a rare sight on his solemn, concentrating face, but he grinned and looked more dashing than ever. "How is that dear girl? I haven't seen her for such a long time."

Lesley couldn't be jealous of Phyn's love for her sister. She had been so hurt and frightened once that she could trust any man was a wonder, and the ease with which she had taken to Phyn was nothing short of miraculous.

"She's fine. She's off playing down at the wharf today. I think she wants to see the ship for herself."

As suddenly as levity had brightened his expression it was gone, replaced by the frown of concern she knew so well.

"Don't worry, Phyn. Good Lord, she's got Bronze John with her. How could she come to any harm?"

Phyn seemed relieved. Then he became businesslike and said, "You know there's increased Toyceiver activity in Quay-Fomalhaut. We've lost six ships this year, despite our efforts. A spy said Contraption Beach is crawling with Toyceivers and piled with wrecks. He said it looks like Hell's dockyard."

Lesley nodded. For the last five years, ships had been appearing at sea. Sometimes they received advance warning and were able to bring a vessel in to the Quay-Endula docks, but predominantly they were pirated by Toyceivers and wrecked on Contraption Beach. The Toyceivers stripped the wrecks to make their Uproar Contraptions, monstrous battle machines, and used them to invade and destroy the Quays. Lesley knew war was coming to Quay-Endula, but she would make it as difficult for them as she could.

The ships they saved were usually devoid of any crew. Sometimes they found bodies. Once they boarded a boat and found a crewman cowering in the corner of the engine room. He was babbling, but eventually calmed enough to tell them that a great metal frame appeared above the ship as it cruised the *Atlantic* and a shaft of light engulfed them, pulling them from the world and into the Quays. The creatures that swarmed from the light as they went through had slaughtered everyone else. As everyone stood transfixed on the decks, looking up at the vast, unearthly frame drifting above them, he had fought panic and hidden himself away. As he closed the door to the engine room, he heard the screams of his crewmates echoing throughout the ship.

Phyn continued, "Our systems indicate that a ship should be breaking through. We've got a good bearing. I suggest we drink up and get the crew together. We need to make the best of our advantage."

Lesley nodded. "How's the *Rogue Angela*?"

"Oiled and ready. Grode and Fyco have been on her all morning doing checks."

"Ok," Lesley said. She drained her glass and placed it on the bar. She stood up, brushed crumbs from her green tunic, and turned for the door. Phyn followed.

The *Rogue Angela* was in dock, anchored alongside the sunken tenements of the Waterlogs. She was a corvette, a small, fast escort ship, heavily armoured and with a single cannon mounted on deck in front of the bridge. Around her bows ran a brass rail that allowed the big harpoons to be maneuvered into position manually, rattling along on heavy greased chains. On the stern were the depth charge racks. Her funnel was black, the rigging whitewashed, and her ironclad as grey as the shadowed waters that buoyed her.

Phyn and Lesley walked along the wooden walkway lashed to the sides of the tenements just above the waterline. Between the gaps in the planks, she could see the tops of great sash windows and the dark flooded rooms behind them. Scum and flotsam gathered at the edge of the water against the brickwork. The windows they passed at eye level were grimy and cobwebbed. What little light entered illuminated rooms full of machinery, pumps, lagging and great, unfathomable turbines—cylinders and dials, green glass portholes and lattice vents—which either no longer served a function or perhaps never had. They were just another obscure feature of Quay-Endula that Lesley had never had a chance to fathom; this was her place but some-times the symbols were too ambiguous, far beyond her ability to interpret. Some of the rooms above were full of salvage, gear they could use to refit the *Rogue Angela* or some of the smaller vessels in their scanty fleet. Above these, in the topmost rooms were the dorms and communal rooms they used for planning and strategy meetings, and for rest between engagements.

Overhead the afternoon sky was dark, and the floodwaters of the artificial canals between the tenements were becoming choppy in the wind that was funnelling in off the sea.

They reached the roped gangplank and stepped aboard *Rogue Angela*. As Lesley's feet touched the deck, a loud voice shouted, "Captain on deck!" and she heard the shrill whistle that announced her arrival on board.

Two men stood to attention by the ladder that led up to the bridge. One was Grode, all seven feet of him, stripped to the waist and zebra-striped with engine oil. His huge, bald head was stippled with beads of perspiration. At his side, Fyco fidgeted and made the piping sound between his teeth again. Grode stared down at him and nudged Fyco in the side of the head with the back of his fist. It was a gentle nudge, but it was forceful enough to cause Fyco to drift sideways in a moderate stagger. He looked up at Grode with an expression of enormous love. Grode looked heavenward and returned his attention to Lesley.

"All ready, Captain," he said. "Would you like to inspect her?"

"You do the preliminaries, Phyn. I want to check the compass."

Phyn nodded and went off toward the stern with Grode. He would check the cannon, harpoons, and machine guns mounted on the deck, ensure they were operational and loaded. Then he would go down to the engine room and let Grode reassure him of *Rogue Angela's* efficiency and working order. Then they would start the engines and they would prepare to sail.

Lesley went up onto the bridge with Fyco.

It was a comfortless, utilitarian room with an all-round view. There was a large wooden wheel and a rank of dials facing the front of the ship. A map was spread out on a table to the left of the wheel and in the centre of the room, mounted on a slim iron pedestal, was a compass. It was unlike a normal compass, as it had no cardinal points. It was a metal disc with a needle shaped like an arrowhead held in place by a delicate brass spindle. Normally the needle was static. You could spin it with a finger but it would be no more responsive than a loose clock hand, slowly coming to rest under gravity at a random point. It was not magnetic nor was it designed for standard navigation.

This was the Incursion Compass.

Whenever a ship was about to appear at sea, it began to agitate. Only slightly at first, then with increasing excitement. It would tremble like an adder's tongue, then begin to make a slow circle of its plate. Finally, it would settle on a position and remain there, still trembling, indicating the point at which a ship would come through.

Lesley's father had given it to her the last time she had seen him.

"This is one of only two Compasses that still exist," he said. "Your godfather has the other. This is your Instrument, Lesley. When the time comes, you'll know what it's for. It will tell you."

Lesley looked up into her father's sweet, tired face. "It looks like a sundial. It's heavy."

"Responsibility has no atomic weight; its burden is spiritual."

Lesley held the disc in her hands. It was flat and smooth as a plate. The needle affixed to its centre swung downward in a loose arc as she tipped it through ninety degrees.

"How does it work?"

Her father shrugged. "It's not my place to guess, darling."

But Lesley found out, with the purposeful directions of Phyn, exactly what this compass—this *Instrument*—was for. Its sole and specific purpose was to indicate the position of the ships that were hauled through by these monstrous frames. Once it started to agitate, Phyn would summon Lesley and a crew and they would assemble to strike out for the designated position in the hope of intercepting the ship before Toyceivers could pirate it.

Lesley noted the direction in which the needle was pointing and nodded to Fyco. Fyco stood to attention and saluted.

"Let's head out," Lesley said.

*　　　*　　　*

Three o'clock on a late October afternoon is my favourite time to be sitting at Colin's tiny bar drinking a pint. There is a stillness over the caravan site, the lowering autumn sun lighting the westward-facing sides of the mobile homes in pastel ranks. It pours through the slats in the blinds at the windows of the clubhouse and makes the smoke from our cigarettes loom like ghosts of drunks shouldering to the bar; a time to reflect not ungenerously on one's life, perhaps a sweet and dusky reversal of three in the morning, the witching hour, when anxieties are deepest and shadows most risky and alive.

Colin's bar is a perfume counter salvaged from the demolition of an old department store in Invidisham-next-the-Sea. It's a narrow right angle of shiny wood, which fits perfectly into the corner of the social club. You walk through the door, batting aside the multicoloured plastic strips of the fly blind, and there it is, Colin's pride and joy, lit up with a jolly string of Christmas lights all year round and providing seating space for a couple of high stools. Colin has attached beer pumps and a Coke dispenser and put out some heavy yellow glass ashtrays and beer mats he found in an antique shop. There's optics and crisps and peanuts on the wall, and Colin can make you a toastie or a burger with ingredients he keeps in the fridge behind the bar.

The wood of the bar has captured a million different scents over its years standing in the perfume department of the store in Invidisham-next-the-Sea, and it gives off an alluring history of soft, seductive odours. It struck me once, leaning against that fragrant wood, that people who buy perfume over counters like this on those bustling, pungent department floors, spritzing and inhaling, testing and contrasting, must be *happy* people. It's just not something you do if you're dejected. This bar top was a record of a hundred thousand people, enthralled in the flush of a new love or the electrifying *frisson* of a secret affair, feeling good about themselves and wanting to feel even better. It made *me* happy too, bathed by the drowsy memories of that contented, joyful multitude.

It was one of those afternoons I loved. Outside, the sky was clear and the air was musky and cold. I could smell bonfires and fallen leaves. Bix was asleep at my feet in a scattering of broken crisps. He was lying on his back with his paws in the air lightly snoring.

Colin had made his own pumpkin lanterns and was putting one on each of the little tables in the bar. He was intending to have a Halloween theme night on the last Saturday of the month and wanted to get people in the mood.

"These'll go mouldy in a few days," he said. "I always bloody do this. Get ahead of myself. Now I'll have to do another lot."

I thought they looked fun. Colin put the last pumpkin lantern down on the bar next to my pint. "There you go," he said. "Knock yourself out."

The pumpkin was about the size of a slightly deflated orange football with slitted eyes, an isosceles nose, and a wide, jagged-toothed grin. I tilted it and reached inside the cool, hollowed-out skin. There was a tea-light sitting at the bottom on a mat of fibres. I took it out and lit it. Then I dropped it back into the pumpkin and sat back to enjoy the affable glow flickering from within.

Colin brought over a glass full of tawny liquid. There were slices of lemon and lime, mint leaves, and chunks of apple floating in it.

"Punch," he said. "See what you think. I'm trying out a few recipes for the do."

There was a wood-burning stove in the corner of the clubhouse by the stage. Colin went over and threw a few logs in and lit the firelighters. He soon had a blaze going. He came back around the bar.

"Glad you like it," he said. Then he arched his eyebrows and said, "And how's Lesley?"

I laughed. Bix awoke with a start and lay there looking up at me with bleary eyes.

Colin just seemed to know. It was uncanny. I'd only dreamed of Lesley again last night, and as before on all other occasions, the dream was vivid, intensely memorable, and followed on exactly from where I had previously left it.

I told Colin I had more of her adventures to tell; it had been the most exciting dream so far, and I had been looking forward to telling it.

*   *   *

They followed the direction of the needle. The corvette *Rogue Angela* ploughed through the waves, her small crew busy about her decks. Everything was checked and rechecked, tested, calibrated, and moved into position.

Phyn entered the bridge.

Lesley was leaning over the Incursion Compass, lost in thought.

"Lesley?" he said, drawing close.

"Oh, Phyn," Lesley said, stepping back from the pedestal. She laughed and shook her head. She ran the slender fingers of her right hand through her short blonde hair. "I was thinking about my dad," she said. Then, briefly, she looked perplexed. In a whisper, she said, "About my dad." She looked up at Phyn, and then laughed.

Phyn, usually so serious, was surprised into a smile.

"Are you all right, Lesley?"

Lesley reached out to touch his arm, her expression winsome, but Phyn moved away and stood with his back to her, appraising the decks.

Lesley sighed. "I'm fine, Phyn. How's the crew?"

"Wanting action," he said.

"I hope they get it," Lesley said.

Phyn lifted a small brass telescope from his breast pocket and put it to his right eye.

"I don't think they'll have long to wait," he said. "There. On the horizon."

Lesley came over and took the proffered telescope from Phyn.

"I reckon that's our ship," she said.

Lying between the sea and the early-evening sky, Lesley could see something resembling a dark, oblong box. It was too distant, and too dim, to make out exactly, but it appeared to be a moderate-sized container ship.

"That's going to be worth fighting for," she said. "All those containers with all that salvage. Who knows what it's carrying?"

"I'll do a final round of the crew," Phyn said. He turned and left the bridge.

Lesley remained standing at the window looking out over the forecastle. Her ship was making good time; she watched the waves peeling away either side of the prow as *Rogue Angela* thundered through a constant fine mist of spray on her way to intercept the becalmed vessel.

As they drew alongside the container ship, the first Uproar Contraption rose out of the sea portside and loosed an array of steel grapnels from a housing welded onto the side of its portholed helm. Gallons of seawater poured from its flumes and gutters, and its propellers whined in cold sea air as the grapnels drew up on their chains and heaved the machine from the depths.

Another clambered up the stern, jagged fins scoring deep channels in *Rogue Angela*'s hull. Behind the misted glass of its porthole, its operator could be seen, a shrieking thing of glass and heat, frantic with violence.

A third: surely this had been forged from some great ship's bell. It lifted from the sea on a fluttering skirt of soiled fabric and hammered the corvette like a wrecking ball.

And beyond, in the distant sky, came others in flight.

The crew of the *Rogue Angela* set about the boarders with their own weapons, repulsing the finned and clattering thing at the stern with a barrage of crossbow bolts, flue irons, and harpoons. Grode swung his mace into the body of the contraption, smashing the porthole and shattering the face of the monster within. Groaning, drawing its struts in upon itself like some dire and mortified iron crab, it toppled backward and was ground to waste by *Rogue Angela*'s propellers.

Lesley ran to the deck-mounted harpoon launcher and swung it toward the contraption grapneled to the portside railings. She aimed low and fired. The harpoon soared across the deck and buried itself deep inside the workings of the thing. Fire and dense, greasy smoke poured from a hatch that opened at the top of its casing. Something small and jagged hauled itself from the hatch and, in an instant, had snared the harpoon line and was shuttling toward Lesley at incredible speed.

Lesley made to step back but the bell thudded against the ship again and she stumbled forward, lost her balance, and fell toward the thing hurtling along the harpoon rope.

It lifted an arm like a fulgurite club edged with needles and punched it toward the side of Lesley's head.

She closed her eyes, but Phyn was there; he charged her aside and brought his own weapon, a trench raiding club, hard down onto the brittle arm.

It fragmented, and the creature screeched as it fell to the deck. Its eyes were hollow orbits blazing with rage. Along its rounded, burnished back curved spines rose, each an inch long and hollow, filled with a bluish poison. It leaped and attempted to drag the barbs down Phyn's face and throat. Phyn stepped aside and clubbed it away. It fell against the harpoon mounting and shattered. Embers and beads of molten glass rolled across the deck. Phyn stamped them out.

He helped Lesley to her feet. "Are you all right?" he asked.

Lesley straightened her tunic, examined the heel of her boot where it felt loose, leaned against Phyn as she did so.

"You keep asking me that, Phyn," she said. "Deep down, I think you really care."

Phyn frowned. There was a splinter of glass embedded in the back of his hand. Lesley reached out to remove it, but Phyn moved away, and headed back into battle.

Before Lesley could say anything, the corvette was rocked by an impact from below. She grasped the handrail surrounding the harpoon mounting and saw great plumes of spray and jets of gas explode on either side of her ship. Something large was moving beneath them, scraping its frame against the underside as it attempted to hole the corvette. The ship shuddered as some mechanism ground into her keel.

"Depth charges!" Lesley yelled, and ran to the starboard side of her ship. She peered down into the chopping water. Dimly, lit by its own core of fire, she could see the outline of a tubular submersible, its legs clasped to the sides of her ship, and a plate of drills revolving slowly as it attempted to grind out a breach.

Lesley met Fyco at the depth charge rack. It held four small dropping mines, each with canted fins, and hydrostatic pistols set for detonation at twelve meters. Lesley knew that an explosion at that depth wouldn't be enough to damage the contraption sufficiently to destroy it, but if they dropped a couple, it might cause enough pressure to dislodge the thing.

Lesley signalled to Fyco to push two of the charges off the rack and send them down. Fyco nodded, wild-eyed. All the time, the *Rogue Angela* shuddered and groaned as the vessel beneath them continued to drill. Together they shoved the charges over the side of the ship.

Lesley turned to the crew. "Charges away!" she shouted.

Everyone on deck knelt and covered their heads.

The corvette rocked as the contraption bell chimed against its helm.

The drilling stopped. There was the hollow sound of something detaching from the hull.

A moment of calm.

And then the sea erupted around the *Rogue Angela*.

"Fyco!" Lesley shouted, "Drop the rest of the charges!" She stood up and staggered across to the depth charge rack. She looked over the side of the boat and saw, as she had hoped, the vessel dropping away through fathoms, dislodged by the primary shockwave.

"Now!" she screamed. Both she and Fyco shoved the charges overboard and Lesley watched as they sank through the water, gaining on the contraption as it used its cumbersome paddles to row itself deeper.

"Charges away!" Lesley shouted again, and everyone hit the deck.

There was another moment of stillness, which was broken by the atonal clang of the contraption bell at the precise moment the charges detonated.

The *Rogue Angela* rolled to starboard, turning anticlockwise in the roiling, bubbling water. Her helm swung toward the side of the container ship. It trapped the contraption bell between their hulls and crushed it like a wooden crate. It dropped back to the water, trailing strips of its ruptured and distended skirt. Around them, on deck and into the surrounding waters, pieces of the devastated submersible rained down.

The crew cheered but Lesley shouted orders to attend to their posts; the airborne contraptions were now in range and were dropping through the sky to attack.

There were three, all of them built from scavenged metals and timbers, wrought to maraud the Quays. One had wings; two came on with great screws turning in engine blocks mounted onto their exterior. The noise was fearful: screams from pilots and engines united, clockworks ratcheting, blades scything, chains and bands and pulleys thrashing.

Lesley wound the harpoon back to its launcher, wheeled it around, and used it to take out the leading contraption. The harpoon smashed through its underside, destroying its pilot and splitting its fuel reserve. It exploded in a fireball and dropped into the sea. Lesley left the harpoon launcher and ran to the stern.

The other screw-driven contraption was hovering above the deck. One of her crew, a man named Webb who owned a stall on the market selling hardware during downtime, had been caught up in what looked like a quivering assortment of narrow, corroded band saws, which had been lowered through slots in the base of the contraption. They turned laboriously, as if cranked by hand, but Webb was entangled and suddenly there was a sheet of blood washing across the deck as he slipped, and his neck was sliced through. His eyes widened and he let out a shout. Lesley ran toward him, but he was dead as he dropped to the deck.

"Get down!" Grode shouted from behind the melee. Everybody scattered as a hail of bullets from the deck-mounted chain gun tore into the contraption, virtually disintegrating it. It wheeled away shedding perforated panels and splintered spars. It, too, was lost to the sea.

Lesley stood over her fallen crewmate. She balled her fists and shouted an obscenity at the sky. She trod through the pinkish water swilling across the deck and walked around the steps leading up to the bridge. She went to the front of the forecastle and stood staring up at the sky.

"Where are you, you *bitch*?" she screamed.

The warped and buckled frame of the old cloudbike rose above the railings surrounding the stern. Its rider howled. No thing of glass, this *bitch*. No *vitreophim*. But something worse. Nurse Melt. Cold flesh and static blood. A *Toyceiver*; bad killer-woman, black-hole soul-vandal: *Lesley's* Toyceiver. *Bitch*.

Lesley saw her and charged.

Nurse Melt shrieked and pulled back on the contraption's cow horn handlebars. It lifted higher and remained floating ten feet above Lesley's head. Lesley stood beneath it, staring up into the mad, idiot eyes of the pilot. Nurse Melt's rust-coloured hair blew around her sagging, bovine face. Her mouth hung open, a flap of torn cheek lolled, dragging her pale lower lip away from the bloodless gums. Black pegs of teeth were visible like nail heads sunk into her jaw. She chattered, madder than ever, and Lesley laughed.

"You sad, mad, *futile* whore," she said. Melt cocked her head.

Lesley had bested her once before, as a child. It had been *easy*.

"I'm not a child anymore," she said. "Get out of here."

Melt's brow furrowed, a band of flesh drooping over her vermin's eyes.

Lesley picked up a discarded crossbow and pulled back the bolt. She aimed it at the middle of Nurse Melt's forehead.

"GET OUT OF HERE!" she screamed, and pulled the trigger.

The bolt flew at Nurse Melt's face but she had already begun to turn the bike away. Instead of penetrating her skull, the bolt tore across her brow leaving a deep gash, and tangled in her flying, matted hair. Melt choked as her head was snapped back with the momentum of the bolt. She was lifted out of her seat as the bolt ripped a large chunk of hair from her scalp. She screamed, one hand clawing at the raw, seeping patch of skin. She used her other hand to turn the contraption and, still howling, let the air currents lift her higher and away from the ship.

Lesley stood with her hands on her hips, her posture defiant. Phyn came over and stood by her side. Together they watched as Nurse Melt flew higher and further away.

No cheers this time, not with a crewmate dead and in such a brutal way. But palpable relief. Lesley turned and looked up at Phyn.

Phyn turned and shouted an order to the gathering crew. Four of the men made ready to board the container ship. They would start the engines and the corvette *Rogue Angela* would escort her back to the Quay-Endula docks.

Lesley watched the men as they went about their orders.

She felt very tired all of a sudden, and tearful. She frowned and wiped moistness from her eyes with a finger. She glanced up at Phyn but he either hadn't noticed, or was pretending not to. He cleared his throat.

"That was too easy," he said, and walked away to oversee the plotting of their course home.

Lesley stood for a moment longer, breathing deeply, thinking. Then she went to join Phyn.

*   *   *

Colin poured me another pint. He'd had a few himself.

Passing me my glass, he said, "You know, I've been meaning to brew my own ale for a while. Save me a *fortune*. I'll call it Crusader. Last time I brewed beer from a kit it tasted like stummacassid."

Colin was misty eyed.

"Great story," he said. "Machine guns and crossbows. What a cocktail. I'm going for a lie down. Let yourself out and I'll see you later." He turned and stumbled off.

As he reached the door, he stopped and turned back. A couple of fly-blind strips lay across his thinning scalp like a varicoloured combover.

"Remind me to tell you something later," he said. He pointed at Bix. Bix looked up at Colin, his nose moving very slightly as he tracked the end of Colin's wavering finger. "It's about dogs," he said in clarification, "dogs with their eyes shut." And then he turned and tottered off to his caravan.

I picked up my pint, smiled at Bix, and raised my eyebrows.

I felt a bit weary, too, after my storytelling, so I drained my glass and decided to go back to my caravan and have a nap on my sofa. This was something else I'd been able to do since I'd moved up to Reservoir End, and a couple of afternoon pints and a kip was a luxury I enjoyed.

So, looking forward to dozing off with the anticipation of dreams full of mystery and adventure, I cupped my hand around the opening at the top of the pumpkin lantern, blew out the guttering flame, and then Bix and I left the social club and walked home beneath a clear blue October sky.

I was standing at the side of a wide dusty road. The road wound off to my left and climbed the side of a mountain. Behind me and opposite were small houses. People stood outside, some on the roadside, others on doorsteps or at the gates of their tiny gardens. Everyone was looking toward the point in the road where it curved around the side of the mountain.

I knew something was coming. I felt something soft nuzzle the back of my hand. Bix was standing there. He was looking up at me and there was an expression of great concern in his eyes.

He spoke. "There is such danger," he said.

I looked up and saw that the people were waving at me. There was urgency in their gestures, as if they were trying to warn me of something. I felt slow, sluggish. I looked down at Bix again. I smiled.

Bix was looking away, his muzzle rippled in a silent snarl.

"All these people are dead," he said. "We are in Hell, and now the Autoscopes are coming."

I came awake on my sofa with a shout.

Bix was there in an instant, muzzle inches from my nose, eyes peering into mine.

I was gasping, my heart hammering in my chest.

I put my head in my hands. I was shaking. I could hear rain lashing against my caravan. Where had this storm come from?

Suddenly, there was a burst of lightning. I cried out and hugged Bix.

Shivering, I stumbled to the French window and peered out into the night. As I crossed the room, there was another prolonged, stuttering discharge of lightning from overhead and an immediate barrage of thunder, which shook the caravan like a matchbox. I could hear the veranda rattling and threatening to tear loose in the force of the wind. I pulled my blanket more tightly around my shoulders and looked out. Rain pelted against the glass and tore in great diaphanous sheets across the caravan park. All was obscured until another burst of lightning illuminated the cloud base. I froze.

Something was stretched out above the caravan site, something briefly lit, like the vast steel skeleton of a wrenched and twisted super tanker, and in the sudden silence between thunderclaps, I could hear it moan as it churned through the dark rain of the night, a desolate, vast sound.

I jumped back as a pair of feverish eyes appeared at the window and a desperate, pale face loomed up.

It was Colin.

I slid open the door and he came stumbling in, drenched and battered by the wind and rain. A humid curtain of rain followed him into the lounge and the sound of it burst in, the hiss and clatter across the tarmac road and trembling boards of the caravans outside. I shut the door and turned to him. Bix was standing by his side, peering up into his haggard face. Colin looked down at Bix, then back at me. He blinked and shook rain from his straggling grey hair. Then he said, "You have to go back to sleep!"

I went over to the sofa and slumped down.

There was more lightning, followed by a blast of thunder; the sound overhead, that unearthly moan, seemed louder now, more urgent.

"I *am* asleep," I said. "I *must* be." I felt raw. I thought I must be experiencing the surreal after-effects of the nightmare.

Colin sat down in an armchair facing me. He leant forward, his elbows on his bony knees. Rainwater dripped from his hair onto the rug between his feet.

"No," he said. "You're not. You *have* to go back to sleep."

I drew my legs up onto the sofa and pulled the blanket up over them. I felt confused and frightened. My mouth was dry. Bix padded over to Colin and sat beside him.

"What's that thing outside?" I asked.

Colin looked up at the ceiling. In the lightning that flashed at that moment, his face looked more fatigued than ever.

"A *what*?" I barked. Colin's voice had been drowned out by a roll of thunder and the continual alien-engine sound above our heads.

"A *Gantry*," he repeated. "An *Ingress* Gantry." His voice trailed off, as though what he was saying sounded ridiculous to his own ears.

I stared at him. Colin patted Bix's flank.

"I was going to tell you something earlier," he said." All part of my plan to prepare you for this. But it's come too soon. I don't know what to do." Colin looked disconsolate. "I'm really scared."

I sat up and said, "Dogs with their eyes shut?"

Colin nodded. "It all seems so futile now. I've been too slow. Too bloody *pissed*."

I said, "Has this got anything to do with Bix and the dogs' home?"

"Yes," he said. "Fate. Miracles. God. That sort of thing."

I took a breath. Somewhere inside, I was beginning to feel a thrill. It was as though those dreams of Lesley were a part of every cell in my body, minute and glimmering beads of enchantment winding like code throughout my entire being.

"Then it'll be all right," I said.

Colin's shoulders slumped but he managed a weary smile.

"All right," he said. "Let's start with your real name."

Colin once asked me if I believed in miracles. I said that I probably did. If quantum theory is correct, and if matter and energy are interchangeable, then why not create an eye in an empty socket or eradicate disease by removing the substance of the germ?

Eddie D. was there at the time, smoking Marlboros and drinking a large brandy. He looked up at me. "Sudden changes," he said, and then returned to staring into his liquor.

I agreed that it would have to be instantaneous.

"I know all about that," he said.

My real name is John Stainwright.

I was given my adoptive parents' surname and knew no different.

Colin realised that I was ready to hear the truth and have other mysteries revealed to me when I dreamed about myself as a child last night. He just didn't expect things to happen so fast.

"I knew it was you the moment I saw you," Colin said.

I remembered back to that first time at the dogs' home, walking in and seeing Colin standing there behind the counter.

"You looked at me funny," I said.

"I wasn't expecting you," Colin said. He shrugged. "But then I spoke to your folks and they confirmed it. God, what a moment! I was there, just waiting, and then—bang—there *you* were. Fate."

"Ok," I said. I reached over and switched on a table lamp by the arm of the sofa. Soft light made supportable these strange disclosures, somehow. Colin looked less ragged; the light blew some of his lines away like dust from a furrow, and his eyes seemed less fervid. It kept the lightning outside, too. Now it seemed to inflame the window glass alone rather than pene-trate the entire room and throw us into constant relief. Rain dashed against the caravan and thunder rolled. The Ingress Gantry groaned. "I'm not going to ask any questions. Just talk."

Then we both jumped and cowered at the sound of a tremendous, metallic *rending* from overhead, the sound of a construction site full of cranes collapsing, of battleships lifted from the sea and wrung like cloths.

"I'll have to be quick," Colin said. "The Autoscopes are coming."

When Colin said that, I fell silent. If he knew about that, then I was willing to believe what he was about to tell me. Believe it, even though I would not be able to take it all in until much later. Colin spoke fast and he told me this:

I was always meant to find Bix. Only nobody knew exactly when. Or what kind of dog Bix would be when I found him. If I found him at all. This was chance, and fate, all rolled up. Colin said it nearly drove him and my folks mad.

I'd know him when I saw him, apparently, Colin told me. They thought maybe I'd found him once: a little puppy with a sore eye, but that wasn't to be. Colin had eventually rehomed *that* one to a nice family who had a warm house with a big garden. I was very pleased to hear this, as you might imagine.

But gradually, it became evident that I wasn't going to stumble upon the right dog as a child, and my parents agreed with Colin that they might as well stop taking me to the dogs' home. It was a risk, but Colin and my folks had faith, it seems, and well, here you go.

Bix is my Instrument. Like Lesley in the Quay, I have my own unique device. It's what sets me apart, what makes me able to witness Lesley's life as it unfolds.

When dogs sleep, they dream. And the way dogs sleep and the way they dream is very similar to the way humans sleep and dream. It's all about the eyes, and how they see things. We have a very similar design of eye. When I found Bix, the connection was made and from that day on, when Bix dreamed, I shared those dreams with him and I could go to the Quays.

Colin told me that Quays were secure places created by Firmament Surgeons to protect them and others from harm in the waking world. Firmament Surgeons were the Engineers of Creation; they kept it running against the onslaught of entropy, trying to shore it up until the re-creation of everything.

But there was opposition. The Autoscopes were fallen Firmament Surgeons, gone the way of a third of the angels and all men thereafter. They wrought havoc on the fabric of creation and tore down men's minds. Their fuel was despair, the ultimate entropy of the mind, the state we were warned not to indulge and that which brings suicide and the death of hope.

Now they were infiltrating the Quays and destroying them.

A handful of Firmament Surgeons stood between a new Creation and Annihilation. And the war was being lost.

"Lesley's in terrible danger," Colin said.

I nodded. I felt it, too.

"What do we do?" I asked.

Colin looked up at me. He spread his hands. "You go back to sleep," he said. "And Bix will take you in. You're ready now as you'll ever be."

I frowned, thinking about that lovely girl I had been dreaming about for months. Was she real?

"Ok," I said, I drew my legs up onto the sofa and pulled the blanket up to my chin. The windows flickered with lightning like screens trying to pull images out of the ether. "Let's give it a go."

Bix came over. He wagged his tail and huffed.

"Come on then," I said, and Bix clambered up and curled beside me. I put my right arm around him and rested my cheek against the warm fur on his neck. I could feel his pulse, fast and strong.

I closed my eyes.

"Am *I...*?" I started to say.

Colin tucked the blanket around me. "A Firmament Surgeon? Of course, you are," he said. "And I'm your Paladin. Now go to sleep."

We were walking through a meadow, Bix and I. Behind us, and below, a city was laid spread before a glittering silver sea.

The meadow rose, a gentle climb for us. I was a child, and Bix was a pup. Long grasses moved softly against us and the air was hazy from pollen and the downy seeds that drifted from the heads of the dandelions we brushed past.

We came upon a narrow lane bordered on one side by a low picket fence and on the other by a dark verge of tangled blackberry briars. I stopped and pulled a blackberry from its stalk. It sat in my palm, large and plump, its scarlet juice trickling along my Fate line as if inscribing it with ink. It looked like a compound eye plucked from the face of some monstrous blowfly; I could see my face reflected in every tiny globe that composed it.

I dropped it and wiped my hand on the lush grass growing along the edge of the verge.

I stood up. Bix barked, and hurtled off down the lane.

I followed, wondering what had set him off like that.

As I walked, I became aware that the lane was widening and further lanes were branching off. At intervals along these lanes, small shacks were constructed, some no bigger than sheds and each on their own plot of land with a well-tended garden. Their slat-board sides were painted in fresh, cheerful colours, and some had flags and bunting strung from lines or hanging from short poles mounted on their roofs.

I followed the sound of Bix's barking until I came to a gate surrounded by hollyhocks and wild roses. There was a little wooden post-box in the hawthorn hedge that formed the boundary to the plot. There was a name painted on the side of the post-box, but I couldn't read it. I opened the gate and walked up a short path until I reached a cabin surrounded by sapling pear trees. There was a veranda at the rear with a corrugated plastic roof supported by a blackthorn trellis. Bix was scratching at the simple wooden back door. He saw me and whined.

"What is it?" I asked. I lifted aside a thick swag of honeysuckle and tried the handle. The door opened. Bix and I put our heads in and I said, "Hello?"

I was surprised when a man's voice replied, "Hello." I was even more surprised when I recognised the voice.

*   *   *

Lesley walked down *Rogue Angela*'s gangplank and stepped onto the wharf.

The container ship was moored behind her, its long, low hull roped tight to the wharf-side pilings.

Quay-Endula dock workers were already aboard. They were trying to find a way to open the containers.

"They're all welded shut," Grode told Lesley as she drew alongside the vessel.

"*Welded*?" Lesley said. Grode nodded. He used an old Hessian sack to wipe sweat and engine oil from his huge forearms. She walked over to the gangplank leading up to the deck of the ship.

"Where's Phyn?" she asked.

"He must be on board somewhere, Captain."

Lesley went up the gangplank and walked up to one of the containers. It was approximately twenty feet long and twelve high. She lifted her right arm and banged on the side of it with her fist. Lesley frowned. It sounded empty, but then she'd not know for sure until it was opened. At the front of the container, two members of her crew were trying to hammer a crowbar into the thick rope of welded steel that sealed the doors. The metal was shiny and protuberant, and the men weren't able to put a dent in it.

Lesley strode on past the men and went up an aisle made between two stacks of containers. She noticed the same robust workmanship sealing every crate she passed. She continued toward the stern and found herself in a small square chamber made by the movement outward of two poorly secured containers.

Ahead of her, a third container had slid toward starboard and she could see that this had not been welded shut. Lesley approached it, gauging the drop, then unfastened the bolts either side of the door and let it crash to the deck.

Brushing her hands together, Lesley squinted into the darkness at the back of the container. It, too, appeared empty. She went inside and moved toward the rear.

Lesley looked over her shoulder, but there was no one about. She could hear the muted bangs and crashes of people moving around the ship, the sound of the crowd gathering on the wharf to witness the bringing home of the vessel. And she could hear something else.

At first, she thought it might be the sound of a saw as it tried to cut through one of those cords of welded steel. A metallic, angry sound. Or the heavy static of someone nearby perhaps trying to locate a channel on the ship's radio. But then, something landed on the back of her hand and she realised what it was that was making the noise. Another hit her cheek and bounced off, darting back into the darkness of the container.

She looked up and was about to speak but someone was coming out of the obscurity, someone she recognised.

"Phyn?" she enquired of the darkness.

We entered the cabin.

It was divided into a small sleeping area and, at the rear, an even smaller kitchen and dining room. There was a wooden cot bed and some small cabinets with blue Formica doors and red plastic handles. A brown curtain hung across the doorway, which led into the kitchen. We went through and pushed the curtain aside. There was a Calor gas hob, a compact ceramic sink, some cupboards and a small wooden table covered in an oil cloth.

Sitting at the table was a man.

"Hello, doc," I said.

"Hello, John," said Doctor Mocking.

I sat down in a chair opposite the doctor. It was good to see him. He looked tired, though. There was a sadness in his eyes that I don't remember being there before. He had always been so cheerful in his bright, sunlit office looking out over his tidy little apple orchard.

"I'm sorry you died," I said. Bix put his nose on Doctor Mocking's leg and the doctor scratched the side of his muzzle.

"Hiya, Bix," he said. "You're looking very young."

Bix whined and thumped his tail on the lino.

Doctor Mocking looked up at me and his expression became serious.

"Lesley is in danger," he said. "You know that, don't you?"

I nodded.

"Something from your past is here; it's been stalking her for a long time. Lulling her, duping her. It wants both of you together so that it can destroy you and this Quay you sustain. Because both of you are inextricably bound, this Quay is so powerful. And so important to us."

I said nothing. Outside, I could hear the sounds of birds and of branches moving against the side of the cabin in a gentle breeze. Sunlight dappled the sink and small drainer through a window made of a single pane of glass set into the timber wall. In the distance, I could hear the unperturbed purr of a petrol mower as someone used it to trim their plot of land.

"What is it?" I asked. "That thing from my past?"

"When you were very young, an Autoscope came for you. It was very old and very powerful. It killed every child in your village, but it was looking especially for you. You had a nightmare which made you hide from it, and when it had moved on—in terrible fury—you were taken from your parents and given to a couple who adopted you in the conscious world. All were good souls, and believers. You were kept safe, but they always knew you'd have to return home one day to face that thing. To keep your identity a secret, no one else knew who or what you were. You know what you are by now, don't you, John?"

"Yes," I said. "Are there many like me?"

Doctor Mocking spread his hands, palms downward on the tabletop. "There are only ten of us left. It's a small number to keep such rapacity at bay."

The sound of the mower was closer now, its engine rough, like it was running blunt, hacking blades.

"A Paladin was chosen for you, but he didn't know where you were or how to find you. He had faith that you'd come to him. He also knew he must find you an Instrument to enable you to return to the Quays, but again he was left mostly in the dark for your own protection."

"Must have driven him crazy. Poor Colin."

Doctor Mocking smiled. "Colin has plenty of faith, John. He did very well by you."

Now he had to raise his voice. The mower sounded like it was coming up the lane.

He leaned forward and said, "Rescue my Lesley for me."

"Is she like us?" I asked.

"Yes, but she's forgotten," Doctor Mocking said. And then he gripped my hand and pulled me toward him. I had to lean forward, and my belly bumped the top of the little wooden table. He put his face next to mine and I felt his breath on my ear. He whispered something, one word, and then released my hand. He looked at me and nodded.

I stood up. Bix came around and stood by my side. His ears were pricked and his hackles raised. He didn't like the sound of that mower.

There was a loud bang, and a splintering sound. Bix turned and ran back through the cabin and out of the front door. I heard him barking. I turned and followed him into the garden.

There was an Uproar Contraption in the lane. Half of it was up on the verge and had destroyed the gate and hawthorn hedge. Its tracks whirled and tried to gain purchase on the soft earth of the verge. It had blades, but none like I had seen before.

I shouted for Bix.

He was low to the ground and snarling at the machine. Something ratcheted from its underside, some kind of iron spar studded with tines, and lashed out at him. He yelped and leaped back, narrowly avoiding being impaled. With a great heave, the contraption rose up and came thudding down onto the lawn. It surged forward and came at us.

I dodged to the left and pelted down the garden. I leaped the fence and landed in the lane. I turned and watched it rotate on its tracks. It churned the lawn up in waves of overlapping turf.

"Bix, *run!*" I shouted.

Bix ran.

He flew over the hedge and together we sprinted back along the lane and out across the meadow pursued by that hellish contraption.

It thundered across the meadow behind us like a baroque harvesting machine. Its tracks threw up clods of dark red earth and bales of twirling meadow grass. Black smoke bloated in enormous clouds from its engine, and the air was filled with the hot, fierce stink of oil and coal dust. Fire blazed, belts flayed, and in its centre, strapped and pinioned amongst thumping pistons, its driver rang wild and unruly terror from its carillon mouth of glass.

Phyn Dakker emerged from the shadows at the back of the container.

Lesley recognised him by his uniform: the black knee-length boots polished to a high shine, the grey tunic, the belt with his trench raiding club hanging from an iron hoop sewn into the fabric.

"Phyn?" Lesley asked again. She was aware her heart was beating very fast. "How did you –"

Lesley stumbled backward.

Phyn Dakker came at her from out of the dark, his face obscured by a teeming mask of blowflies.

When I first dreamed of Lesley, she was a little girl, no more than seven or eight. She had been drifting across a snowscape in a hot-air balloon with a magical tiger as her companion. As the dreams came over the following months, so Lesley aged. She went from being a child to a young woman in less than a year.

I suppose I was a bit in love with her. She was very pretty and the emotional bond I felt with her was considerable. But whatever I'd thought was happening in these dreams, whether they were brought about by some lucky latent gift that had been facilitated by peaceful fulfilment at last, or something more preternatural, I didn't dwell on my feelings. Besides, in her world, Lesley had Phyn, and she was in love with him. I imagined Lesley creating this Quay around her, weaving its romantic threads from tender girlish ideals. The battles she fought with Phyn at her side, I believed, must have been the passionate fantasies of a maturing young woman.

I was wrong.

The Flyblown Man seized Lesley as she stumbled. It held her by the lapels of her tunic and slammed her against the side of the container. She cried out as the back of her head connected with the steel wall. She tried to reach her dagger, which was sheathed on her belt, but she was being held six inches off the ground and the sleeves of her tunic were bunched tight beneath her armpits. Her fingers scrabbled an inch from the ivory handle. Flies swarmed around her head. She closed her eyes and felt them land on her face and crawl in her ears, on her lips, in her nostrils. She shook her head. She kicked out, but the Flyblown Man pressed against her and pinned her against the wall. Lesley drummed her heels against the metal in the hope that it might raise an alarm, but she knew also that it was an insignificant noise against the backdrop of racket she could already hear.

She opened her mouth to say something, to try to engage this thing, but flies were in and banging against her teeth the moment her lips parted, so abundant was the pestilence. She coughed, choked, and spat in the Flyblown Man's face.

"*Lesley,*" it said. It no longer spoke with Phyn's warm baritone. Its voice hummed and crackled like something in its larynx was causing interference.

Lesley stopped struggling and hung limp. She tried opening her eyes a little, just a slit. She felt the flies scuttling through her hair and over her brow. She was pressed so close to the Flyblown Man that their noses were almost touching. She had to breathe through her nose as to open her mouth would invite unbearable infestation. The stench was terrible. Through those slitted eyes, Lesley could see why the flies swarmed there.

Its eyes. It had no eyes in its sockets. Its sockets were filled with shit. Dark balls of shit.

Lesley screamed, and the flies came in.

We ran, keeping ahead of the contraption by cutting through the ploughed fields that bordered the edge of a deep wood. The turned earth impeded it, rocking it on its tracks and pitching it from side to side, whereas we leaped from chunk to chunk using the hard rugged earth like stepping stones fording a wide brown river.

We crossed the tree line and fled through the wood. My breath was ragged, but here in this place I was young again, and felt capable of running forever.

Bix ran ahead but was never out of sight. I felt the presence of other living things as I skipped over roots and ducked beneath branches. As the wood became darker and the air as cool as spring water, I saw huge yellow eyes appraising me from the deeper parts of the woods.

Behind us, the contraption found the edge of the wood. It would find it impossible to follow us, certainly at any velocity, unless it employed concealed surprises. I sucked breath deeper into my lungs and put my head down as I heard the sound of what might have been huge saws start up and begin carving through the trees that barred its way.

We ran for half a mile, following a narrow path, until at last we saw a line of trees ahead, their canopies illuminated by the sun setting over the ocean.

We burst from the wood and found ourselves on a hill overlooking Quay-Endula.

It was beautiful, this city by the sea. For a moment, I forgot the thing that was pursuing us and stood bent slightly with my hands on my knees, breathing deeply, and looked out across the landscape. Quay-Endula was teeming with streets and alleyways, a labyrinth of detail. I could see how it grew like a dry reef of colour and intricacy inland, reaching out into the sea with an array of delicate, dazzling piers. There were towers and pavilions, plazas, marketplaces, parks, and great, billowing gazebos. Fountains glittered, the size of pylons, and there almost directly beneath us, the Quay-Endula docks extended their jetties and pilings into the sea.

Ahead of us was what appeared to be a shack perched on the edge of the hill. We went over and discovered that it was the landing stage for a steep funicular railway.

An old and ornate-looking coach sat by the side of a narrow wooden platform. Bix was sniffing at the doors, his tail wagging. He looked up at me and woofed.

Suddenly, there was a thunderous splintering sound. I turned in time to see the Uproar Contraption burst from the wood. Whole trees atomized beneath the grinding routers and whirling saw blades extending from its flanks. As I watched, they folded up on articulated arms and slid back inside the frame of the contraption. It emerged fully from the wood and rushed toward us.

I went beneath the low, pitched roof of the tram shed and yanked open the door to the coach. Bix and I leaped onboard, and I ran to the front of the carriage in search of some sort of operating device.

I was in luck. Built into a ledge beneath the curving split-screen window overlooking the funicular's steep, descending tracks was a brass lever. It looked easy to control. The lever was in position above a small ceramic plate designated *Brake* in large blue letters. I looked down at Bix and shrugged. Then I threw the lever.

Shuddering and clanking, the funicular began its descent into Quay-Endula.

A little girl in a red duffle coat walked along a quiet street. All the shops were shut because everyone was at the docks watching the big ship come in. She felt very happy and very safe. She looked up at her companion.

Bronze John strode beside Anna, a grand, radiant, sinuous tiger. Huge white paws padded over cobbles, his shoulders rising and falling either side of his splendid head.

Anna wanted ice cream and Bronze John had agreed to accompany her into town to see if they could find a parlour that was open. They had spent most of the day down at the docks, walking and playing amongst the crates and fishermen's' huts and now Anna was tired and hungry. They had watched *Rogue Angela* sail into harbour, the big flat boat carrying all the metal boxes following behind, and once Anna had seen Lesley and Phyn disembark, she had felt sure that all was well and that it was time for her and her companion to go and get a treat.

As they walked, she reached out a hand and ran it through the luxuriant fur on Bronze John's haunch. He turned his head and looked at her, his mighty jaws open in an easy tiger's smile.

And then, a man stepped out from an alleyway and plunged a rusty, ancient-looking sword deep into his side.

Slowly, we descended. I looked up through the rear window and saw that the Uproar Contraption had reached the entrance to the hut at the top of the hill. I crossed the rickety plank floor, holding onto the backs of the slender wooden bench seats until I reached the back of the coach. I watched as the contraption battered against the wall of the hut, smashing its way onto the platform. It teetered on the edge of the rails down which we trundled. I saw its intention and stumbled back to the front of the carriage.

"Get down, Bix," I said, and hugged him to me. We sat huddled on the floor in front of the foremost bench and I did my best to cover our heads.

I heard the sound of the contraption rocking itself onto the rails. The angle of descent was too steep for it, though, and it toppled, unable to gain any purchase on the narrow iron rails, rolling onto its front and sliding down in a caul of sparks and splintering wood. I hugged Bix to me and willed the funicular to reach the bottom, but it was slow and the contraption was tumbling toward us, wild and unrestrained, breaking apart as it came.

It smashed against the back of the carriage. The whole of the rear section crumpled and I felt the carriage leap forward, only the chain belt ratcheting us down the tracks preventing it from derailing and crashing to the bottom of the cliff. The roof peeled away and the windows imploded. One of the bench seats at the rear tore from its rivets and sailed over our heads, smashing through the windscreen. Glass showered down onto us. Bix whined but I held him tight.

The contraption trailed behind the carriage, a shattered cage. I looked back and saw that its driver was clinging to a metal prop that might have once been some kind of steering device but was now just a loose shank of iron. As I watched, it pulled loose and the creature fell. It was ground to splinters between the tracks and the chains that ran beneath them.

I closed my eyes and hugged Bix. We stayed like that for another five minutes as the funicular continued to clank and toil to the foot of the hill. Finally, it stopped and Bix and I stood, shook glass from our backs and disembarked into a tiny ticket office that led out onto a back street of Quay-Endula.

I was shaking. I looked around with wide eyes, stunned and struggling not to succumb to the dull imprecations of shock. Bix stood at my side, looking up at me. I knelt and ruffled the soft fur at his throat. He felt hot and wired, every muscle tense for more running, more exploration. I stood and looked about.

Ahead, a road ran into town. From our position, and from what I remembered of the topography of Quay-Endula I'd seen from the hill, this road would take us near the front. I took off, Bix at my heels, and ran toward the docks.

After a while, the road curved and seemed to want to take us away from the front and funnel us into town. I skidded to a stop, my shoes sliding over cobbles, and looked for options. A narrow alleyway ran off to our right, continuing in the direction I felt we ought to take, so I indicated to Bix that we should leave the road and headed into the alley.

We ran past low wooden doors built into the stonewalls, and miniature windows the size of beer mats, their thick, unrefined glass set deep into grimy, cobwebbed sills. Every so often the alley opened into a small square, something hidden like a quaint and guarded arcade within the dense walls of the city. We ran on, and came to a road at the end of which we could see the sea. And lying on the cobbled pavement at our feet, a dying tiger.

Bix howled.

I stood by the side of the tiger and closed my eyes at the sound. My heart was pounding. I knew this tiger. I knew him from my first dream of Lesley in her miraculous balloon. He had been a gift from her father, and Lesley, in turn, had entrusted the care of her sister Anna to him. Now he lay dying in a pool of blood that flowed between the cobbles in dark and mortal threads.

I knelt beside him and put my hand on the great burnished sash of his throat.

"Bronze John," I said, "Who did this?"

I felt a resonation ripple up through the tiger's trunk. I felt the words rather than heard them, a low purring insistence. One of his front paws padded at my thigh. His eyes were half closed and his jaws hung open. I felt the heat of his breath raging against me.

The man's name is Ray Cade. He has been used by the Autoscopes before. Lesley was one of five children rescued from the Autoscopes and brought through to the Quays for safety. But before the Gantry could close, something terrible happened. Cade did not escape. He hid. And in his fury, he threw himself into the gantry as it was closing. He destroyed it. The children were scattered to their Quays without protection. They need to be found. And now Cade has taken Anna. I have failed. I am dying. You have to take me to Lesley.

So now, I had to carry a tiger. As I despaired, Bix padded forward and put his nose on Bronze John's cheek. Bix licked the soft flesh beneath the tiger's eye. Bronze John closed his eyes and sighed.

There was an inrushing sound and I was thrown forward as a wild and violent wind blew past me. I went to my knees, my eyes closed against the tropical heat of it. When I opened my eyes, Bronze John was gone.

But not gone entirely.

Lying on the cobbles between my knees was a small plastic toy. A worn and contented looking die-cast tiger, his tail curling like a crook, his grin fierce, tiny and full of good cheer. I picked him up and held him in my palm. I looked at Bix. Bix huffed. I stood up, Bronze John held tightly in my fist, and we took off again down the road toward the docks.

So, this thing, this Flyblown Man, had fulfilled its purpose. As handsome Phyn it had seduced the girl, crept into her heart and mind, and helped sustain this pathetic, romantic world of hers until its time was right. So now, it had them both: the girl and the boy. And a bonus: the sister, stolen away by the monster Cade. Once they were destroyed, its Toyceivers and their vitreophim acolytes could fall on this Quay and wipe it out. There would be no more hope in the heads of human dreamers. Just deep wounds deepening and an ache for death.

It looked through its veil of flies at the girl hanging limp in its fists. The flies that swarmed gave it sight. A thousand compound images of the girl resolved in its mind. It felt her terror and despair, and it delighted in it.

And it could hear someone coming: feet running on the steel deck, echoing off the sides of the containers. Human feet and animal feet.

The girl had fainted. The Flyblown Man relaxed its grip and let her slide to the floor. It turned and looked down the length of the container. Twilight and the shadows massing in the atrium beyond the container's opening dimmed its flyblown sight, but it had a sense of something rushing toward it. The activity of the flies increased. They whirled around their host, occasionally bursting into unusual geometries before gathering again at its face.

The ancient Autoscope lifted the club from its belt and swung it at the top of the girl's blonde, bowed head.

And was thrown backward by the force of a great, blistering wind, its mind filling with a thousand facets of orange fire.

I could think of nothing else to do.

I ran through the passage between the containers, Bix sprinting ahead, the toy tiger in my fist. Behind us lumbered the giant, Grode, a look of great dread on his face.

I saw the creature standing over Lesley. I saw it raise its arm, that short, heavy club held in its fist. I wouldn't make it in time. Then I heard a voice.

Let me take him.

I was twenty feet from the entrance to the container. My arm came up and I threw the toy tiger as hard as I could, using my momentum to send it spinning into the back of the container.

Bleeding and broken, the tiger lay across the legs of the monster, pinning it to the floor. Except it was no longer the monster. The Flyblown Man was gone.

Phyn Dakker tried to sit up, but found he was immobilized by the weight of the tiger. He lifted his head and looked down at the animal that lay across him. It was bleeding heavily from a savage wound in its side and it was breathing weakly. Its eyes were shut.

"Bronze John," said Phyn. "Let me up."

Bronze John opened an eye and stared at the man.

"Let me up. I have things to do."

The tiger stretched out a paw. It rested high on the man's chest, near his throat, the weight of it pinning him further.

"You are dying," said Phyn. He reached for the club, which had fallen from his hand and lay on the floor by his right hip. He picked it up.

He felt the paw move. No: not move, but *flex*.

Something dug into the flesh of his throat.

"You can't hurt me. You're finished," he said, and then there was fright in his voice. "*Nothing--*"

I have these claws.

"*No-*"

And he dug them into Phyn's throat with the last of his strength.

Bronze John lay unmoving, the body of Phyn Dakker pinned beneath him. Grode went over to Lesley and cradled her in his huge arms. Bix nuzzled her face, whining softly in his throat. Her eyelids fluttered and she opened her eyes.

She saw her tiger, and Phyn, and let Grode help her to her feet. Slowly she approached them, her hands clasped at her breast.

Grode knelt and put his hand on Bronze John's throat. He looked up at Lesley.

"There's a pulse in there," he said. His expression was grave. "I'll look after him."

Lesley appeared stunned. She was pale and her eyes were very wide in the dark at the back of that blood-stained container. She opened her mouth to speak, and then closed it again. Her lips were dry. She walked past us and stood at the entrance to the container. She looked up at the sky. It was fully dark now, and a high and brilliant moon lent everything its frosty radiance. Bix padded up to Lesley and stood by her side.

She turned and gestured to me. I went to her.

"Who are you?" she asked.

"John Stainwright," I said, and instantly the name was right. The name was mine and always had been.

Lesley nodded. "Where is Anna?" she said. "My sister."

"I don't know," I said. "Bronze John told me a man called Cade took her from him."

Lesley made fists at her side. She closed her eyes tightly.

When she opened them, they were dry and glinted with such fury.

"Phyn was the Flyblown Man all this time. And I was stupid not to realize. Lost in this *fantasy*."

She looked at me and then pointed to Bix. "Take me with you," she said.

I must have looked baffled, because she smiled at my expression.

"Anna isn't here," she said. "Cade will have taken her back. I have to find her. Take me back home."

"I don't know if I can," I said.

"Let's see," said Lesley. "Come on."

We walked down the aisle between the containers, leaving Grode tending to the tiger. We went down the gangplank and along the Quay until we reached the *Rogue Angela*.

Lesley led us up onto the deck and up the iron steps to the bridge.

The three of us stood by the pedestal supporting the Incursion Compass. Bix lay down on the floor.

"Sit with him," Lesley said.

I sat down and nestled into Bix's side.

Lesley stood at the pedestal and gazed at the Compass. "Close your eyes," she said.

Bix settled his nose on his front paws and closed his eyes.

I took a last look up at Lesley, and then closed my eyes, too.

I heard her say, "It's moving," in a soft voice, and then we were bathed in light.

Light that took us home.

I opened my eyes. I was sitting on my sofa, in my lounge. Bix was lying by my side. Lesley lay curled up beneath my blanket, her head on my lap. It was raining on us.

I looked around and blinked. My caravan no longer existed. Something had come along and demolished it. My veranda was flattened and my white and lime green striped awning was gone. I looked out across the boulevard. There it was: wrapped around a telegraph pole that stood between the two caravans opposite mine, drenched and torn to tatters. I sighed. The rain was a constant soft, muggy drizzle, no more than a fine spray in the air. I looked down and pulled the blanket away from Lesley's shoulders.

Bix lifted his head to have a look.

"Oh," I said. "Now *that's* a surprise."

I sat back on the sofa and stared out across the caravan park. All the other caravans appeared to be standing. I wondered why no one was about, maybe going through the wreckage of my caravan for survivors. Or maybe they already had. Maybe they had found nothing and gone away again shaking their heads, thanking providence that it hadn't been their caravans that had been blown apart by the storm.

I knew this wasn't storm damage. I could see alien footprints on the shattered lath and plaster board at my feet. Something had come out of that Gantry and demolished my home in an attempt to kill us. I realized now that Bix had taken us bodily through to the Quay. No dream this time. We had been fully there.

Bix got down from the sofa and picked his way across the debris. He stood on what remained of the veranda and sniffed the air. He looked back at me and barked.

"God," I said. "Colin!"

I stood up and lifted Lesley, still wrapped in the blanket, in my arms. I followed Bix's path across the floor of the caravan and stepped down onto the road.

Lesley was no weight at all. I held her close, trying to shelter her from the rain. It glittered like dew in her soft blonde curls.

The surprise had worn off already. I had been a child in the Quay and now I was my adult self again. And Lesley had been a young woman, distorted by the quantum of her unconscious.

Now Lesley was a child again, and coming awake in my arms.

They had got to Colin as well. All that remained of his caravan was a scorched casing. Inside was burnt and blackened as if a bonfire had been set in the middle of his living room. Bits of melted plastic indicated where his gas heater had exploded.

Lesley stood by my side. She was holding my hand. She had dark rings under her eyes and she looked in shock. I wondered how much she understood. How much had her father been able to tell her before she had been seduced by the Flyblown Man's blackly tender deceits?

Now she was safe, but clearly traumatized. I had never felt like I needed someone as much as I needed Colin right then. I left Lesley standing on Colin's veranda, the blanket around her shoulders, and Bix and I went through the caravan. There was no sign of Colin. I had been terrified of finding him dead in his bed, rolled up in charred blankets, but the relief I felt at not finding him was quickly overpowered by a rising panic. Where was he?

I went back out onto the veranda. I squatted down and looked into Lesley's eyes. She focused, responding with an expression of gentle enquiry. I was so relieved to see her rise intact from what I thought might be devastating shock that I felt my eyes well up with sudden, unexpected tears. She reached out and touched my cheek.

"John," she said. "Thank you for coming."

There was only one thing left to do.

We went to the Reservoir End Social Club.

Whatever had come out of that Gantry looking for us, be they Autoscopes, Toyceivers, or their vitreophim brutes, they hadn't understood the importance of the social club and had left it alone.

I traipsed up the steps and tried the handle. It was locked. I'd latched it myself earlier that day. *That* seemed like a lifetime ago.

I hammered on the door, hoping that maybe Colin had holed up inside, but there was no reply. I walked around the side of the club and peered in through the windows but all was in darkness.

Bix barked. He nudged Lesley with his nose. She smiled and reached out to fuss him, but he scampered off down the road.

"Follow him, John," said Lesley.

I shrugged and we jogged along behind him until we came to the car park at the top of the boulevard. My Minx was parked there.

Before we got to it, I could see something white held against the windscreen by one of the wipers. It was a note, wrapped in a transparent sandwich bag. I shook the bag open and read the note.

John,

I hope you get this and all is well.

They nearly got me. I blew up my gas heater. Got a few of the bastards. Burnt my hands a bit but I'm ok. Eddie D. came and got me out. Saved my life.

Listen: we've gone to Lakenheath. It's all going off there.

Come and meet us there.

Lakenheath.
Colin.

I leaned against the off-side wing of the Minx and laughed.

Lakenheath. Now I remembered. It was the word Doctor Mocking had whispered to me in that cabin on the Plotlands. Bix sat at my feet and thumped his tail on the verge. Lesley came over and I gave her the note. She read it and looked up at me, her face alight with hope.

I knelt down and pulled Lesley and Bix into my arms. We held each other for a while. I let relief and tiredness wash over me.

"Okay," I said. I took my keys out of my pocket and opened the passenger door. "Jump in, folks."

Lesley and Bix climbed into the Minx, and I walked around and unlocked my door. I got in and put the key in the ignition.

Bix whined. I leaned over and wound the window down a couple of notches.

"Okay," I said again. "Lakenheath. That's not far."

I started the Minx and we pulled away. Lesley was hugging Bix, and as we picked up speed, she laughed as his big feathery ears blew across her face like scarves, and his eyes shut with delight.

DRIVER ERROR

I was in the car. I was driving down a country road and I had to swerve out of the way of a vehicle coming around a bend toward me on my side. I kerbed the Vectra and felt the car drag left as the tyres bit into the verge and begin to pull me into the thick row of bushes lining the road.

I flashed my lights and, after a moment of disorientation, remembered where my horn was, and leant on it. I got the car under control and felt it slide through the mud. Branches raked the side of the car and clattered against the passenger-side windows and then I was back on the lane. I glared into my rearview mirror and watched the taillights of the car as it disappeared around the bend. I was raging.

I was on my way to pick my daughter up from a friend's house. Another party, another Facebook crash, and another mass fight; and me out after midnight to evacuate Carla from the wreckage.

And then, I came fully around the bend heading onto where the road opened out onto the bypass and saw why the car had been on my side of the road.

I slowed, I had no choice: there were bodies in the road.

I stopped the car and sat there for a moment looking at the dead boys. I had a mobile, but my brain wasn't doing much at that moment other than trying to process the stuff that was going into my eyes, which was awful.

The road was dark. The streetlights didn't start for another half mile or so. My headlights provided adequate illumination. They splashed across the tarmac, throwing the three bodies into relief against the potholed tarmac. They lay, all three on their backs, each with a slick of shadow cast behind them. Their bikes had somehow ended up in a tripartite mangle at the side of the road. A couple of the wheels were still revolving, winding down like the mechanism inside was some kind of wrecked and unshelled clock. It was as though they had been riding single file, close together, and had been hit and driven into each other and then passed over and mashed by the wheels of the car.

I glanced into my rearview mirror again. Nothing coming behind me. All clear ahead. Apart from the bodies in the road. I could drive on. I thought about it.

My mobile rang. I had it rigged to hands-free, plugged into an attachment on my dash. I took a breath and looked at the screen. Carla.

"Hello."

"Dad. Where are you?"

"On the way."

"It's all kicked off here again. I'm scared. Morgan's covered in blood. I think his nose is broken."

"I'd love to do something about that, Carla. I really would."

"Dad? Are you ok?"

I looked through the windscreen at the dead boys in the road. The one nearest me was casting a shadow toward the car as though in defiance of the laws of physics. Blood, pooling around his head. I thought about driving on. I really did.

I wish I had.

"I'm fine. I'll be there in a while."

"Dad?"

"Yeah."

"Hurry up."

The connection died.

I opened the door and got out. I was alone on the road. I looked both ways but there was nothing coming. This was a well-used road, linking two major towns, and it would normally be carrying a regular freight of late-night traffic. Taxis, lorries on midnight legs, drunks hoping for a cautious run home well below the speed limit. If I hadn't been standing in the headlights of my own car on a country lane at one in the morning looking down at the corpses of three young boys, I might have thought that odd. But as it was, I was experiencing a kind of trauma drift, the sort of brief psychic harmony that kicks in for a spell and allows you to process and function in the moments following a major disturbance in the force.

The boy nearest me had been about seventeen. He had probably been at the head of the file. The reason I thought that was that he seemed to be the least damaged, as though the two behind him had been driven into him and had sprung him away from the crush of bikes. He had come down on his head. No helmet. How would a layman like me describe what I could see?

I could see his brain. I hadn't been expecting to see someone's *brain* tonight, that was for damn sure. Dreadful sentiments came to me; the last thing he'd expected as he'd set out tonight for a ride with his mates was that some stranger would be looking down at his *brain* tonight; whatever his intelligence, whatever his dreams, whatever his future might have held was bulging lifeless from the top of his head; his catalogue of memories, his personality, his character was as void as the time before all time.

I was starting to panic. My breathing was coming too fast, too shallow. The psychic harmony was fading to be replaced by numbness and dread. I stepped past the boy. His face was pale, bloodless. His eyes were open and he stared at the stars that had made him with terrible, determined senselessness.

The next boy looked slightly older, maybe early twenties. He was at an angle perpendicular to the verge. He was wearing a T-shirt that bulged at his throat with everything his torso had contained. The car had driven over him and forced his guts and ribcage up into his gullet. His pelvis had been pulverised and his legs lay bandy like a spatchcocked chicken.

The third boy lay half on, half off the verge. His arms were twisted behind his back and his legs were tangled together in an unseemly knot. Everything was smashed. His expression was one of absolute surprise. *What's this?* he might have thought. A brief insight as everything within was destroyed and he was flung forward into oblivion. How quick had it been for him, for all of them? Had there been a moment, as life had been slapped from them, when they'd thought about where they were going next? Not around the next moonlit bend in the road. Not the next town. Not home. But nowhere. Forever.

I reached for my phone but remembered that it was still strapped to my dashboard. I was about to return to the car but then something stopped me.

Something I'd noticed. Not a conscious observation, but somewhere my back brain was still processing information freely and jolted a signal through the narrow adrenaline focus I was applying to the immediate situation. It was something to do with the bikes.

I looked at the tangled wreckage. They had been forced together and driven over. Frames were distorted, wheels buckled, handlebars twisted. The wheels no longer turning, all eight wheels were still. All eight wheels.

Four bikes.

Indecision gripped me like a sudden sickness. There must be a fourth body. No. Maybe not a body. Maybe the rider of that fourth bike was still alive. I should go to the car and call an ambulance. My head was thudding. The adrenaline was gone, a lousy fix. My legs began to shake. I squatted down and hung my head, breathing as deeply as I could. The night smelt of the cold earth of the fields the road cut through, and the bitter green scent of the wet trees and bushes that lined them.

There were deep drainage cuttings behind the bushes. They were pitch dark, streams of sodden shadow filled with a sediment of leaves and sludge. I looked up as something moved beyond the tangled line of hawthorns beyond the verge.

I stood up. The hairs on the backs of my arms began to rise. Why did I feel afraid? The lane was deserted and I had three dead boys for company, all staring furiously up into the night. Three separate getaways into eternity. They now know everything, I thought. Everything there is to truly know. If there's a God, they know. If there isn't, they know. It was no privilege; just a right bestowed by the passing bulk of a murderous vehicle.

I walked around the wreckage of bikes and stepped up onto the verge. My shoes sank into the soft earth. There was a half-moon high in the clear sky above the fields and it gave enough light to make the dark red earth of the ploughed fields shine like a broken Martian beach from which the sea had long receded.

And from out of the cutting crawled the fourth rider.

I could see that there was nothing I could do for him. I stumbled backward and my hip struck against the pile of bikes. The wreckage rocked in the headlights, its complicated shadow flexing beneath it like a hellish web, and worse, as the fourth rider made it to the top of the cutting and began to push through the dense, thorny stands of the hawthorn bush, a bell clipped to the handlebars of one of the bikes began to ring in horrid elfin counterpoint to the boy's wretched progress through the barbs.

The fourth rider was as dead as the rest of them.

I turned, filled with a sudden and *clear* urge to run. I don't think I'd ever experienced such an autonomic command with the same lucid imperative before. I've read about atavistic horror, often in bad novels in an attempt to tell rather than show the repulsion a situation provokes, but I'd never expected to feel the animal uplift of fear that gave me wings that night.

The last thing I saw before I turned and ran for my car was the fourth rider pressing his shoulders through the lean and twisted limbs of the hawthorn bush, grabbing fistfuls of weeds from the verge as he reached for the open road, as he reached for *me*, with a face that must have turned and taken the full impact of the collision against the grille of that vehicle, blazing with gruesome, white-hot dismay.

I ran, and took twelve steps. And stopped.

My car was gone.

Disorientation froze me. I staggered, skidded to a stop on the bend of the road. And then I became aware of headlights behind me, and turned.

And there was my car.

In my terror, I had run off in the wrong direction. I glanced left, toward the sloping verge, and could hear the laboured sound of that dead thing dragging itself up out of the cutting. Clear thought was impossible. It was simply not something I could make sense of; the primal backup program of denial was already kicking in, that old Trojan put there in the reptile brain to provide us with the ability to shun cold truth.

There was still no sign of any other vehicles. The half-moon cast its chill light over everything. Above the scratching sounds at the side of the road, I could still hear the needling, irregular *ting* of the bicycle bell, as if its curved metal surface had been heated and was slowly cooling in the night air.

As the flattened face of the boy rose above the crest of the verge, the shattered bones of his cheeks and jaw and brow, and his teeth like tiny white stones subsumed beneath rising red waters, all wet and gleaming in the headlights of my car, I ran.

I ran past the three dead boys in the road, and their snarl of bikes, and reached my car. I scrabbled for the handle and pulled open the door.

I got in, slammed the door, and drove off.

By the time I pulled up outside the party, most of the crashers had melted away. They had done their damage, had trashed and robbed, drunk, beaten and terrorised to maximum effect. The door to the house—a spacious detached pile set back at the end of a long, curving drive somewhere in the wealthier part of town—stood open, and lights blazed in every room visible from the outside. I got out of the car and stood for a moment, listening. It was quiet, which I had not been expecting. There was no loud music, no shouts, no sounds of breaking objects or even the panicky post-party clank of bottles being cleared away in anticipation of a parent's dreaded early return. I walked across the drive to the door.

I could hear something now.

Sobbing.

The entrance hall was bigger than my lounge. To the right, a stairway curved up to the first floor. Doors stood open everywhere. I went inside and crossed the marble floor. I walked into the kitchen. There was blood on the cream-coloured tiles. It had come from Carla.

My daughter was slumped against a huge American style fridge-freezer. It loomed over her, more like the baleful entrance to a meat locker in an abattoir than the intended high-end designer convenience.

I went over and knelt beside her. She was clutching her stomach, and white, very white, and unconscious.

I remember feeling quite calm. It was detachment, I realise, brought on by overwhelming concern. I had not been expecting this, of course, and now my system was telling me it wasn't really happening, that this was probably just a dream. It wasn't an objectivity that prevented me from acting, though, and I scooped her up and carried her from the kitchen toward the front door.

As I reached the threshold, I heard the quiet, insistent sobbing again, and turned my head, and looked into the lounge.

There was destruction in there. The room had been completely turned over. Furniture smashed and upended, mirrors and paintings torn from the walls. The carpet was slashed and burned. A girl was sitting on the floor. She was holding a twisted silver photo frame. She looked up at me and her expression was at once both utterly hateful and full of despair.

"*She* let them in," the girl hissed, and I knew she meant Carla. "We told her not to, but she still let them *in*."

I didn't want to ask, but my momentum was still carrying me out of the door, and Carla was breathing in my arms and her bleeding had stopped, so what I asked was, "Let who in?"

And the girl said, without looking up this time—which saved me seeing the effect it had on her expression—something that enclosed my soul in a sudden mantle of dread.

I carried Carla to the car and placed her on the back seat. I lifted her top and exposed her stomach. There were three long gashes cut into her flesh. They were nasty but not too deep. I found a box of tissues in the glove compartment and wadded them up and placed them on the wound and pulled her top back down. Then I got into the driver's seat and pulled out, wanting to get Carla to the hospital.

As I drove, my speed increased as I thought about the last thing the girl had said, the very last thing—almost missed as I carried Carla off the porch—and it was this that made me speed, because I really wanted to get away from that house and the influence of whatever Carla had allowed in.

"The black-eyed kids," she had said. "I *begged* her not to let them in."

For a few years, I was a lay preacher in our local Baptist church, before my divorce and before Carla's incremental promiscuity became a problem. After that, my faith took a dive. Well, more of a slow yet uncontrollable tumble down a long, and seemingly endless, slope. But I did reach the bottom, eventually, and found nothing there but a plain of indeterminate distance, mostly swamped by a grey mist, across which occasional brief, deceptive sails of sunlight might drift, towing a galleon of false hope on which I had no wish to embark.

I remember my own childhood, which was happy, but my memories of it are tainted now when I found out as an adult, through my mother, how desperately miserable *my* father was. He hid it well, and I had no idea just how deep his sadness was, brought on by a lifetime of failure and loss not even my promising presence could moderate. I thought he was happy, yet throughout he grieved, so what am I to make of life? More denial?

And is agnosticism just denial? I can't reasonably be an atheist because I've seen too much of God's authority to *deny* his existence, and felt his presence, but I can't make any of it stick; I can't make sense of the mind games.

It still causes me sadness, and I still hope, maybe sooner or later, God might resume contact. I still take an interest in the supernatural, and I try to ensure that my interest doesn't take a turn into the paranoid or delusional, but I watch, and maybe I *do* hope a little.

So, I still read stuff, and I keep up with things on the Internet, and things do seem to be becoming stranger; or perhaps it's just the increasing opportunity for people to expose their madness online that's led to a supersaturation, but my instinct, my *discernment,* somehow rejects that. Something is burgeoning, gaining confidence. I think something is coming.

It may be just an urban myth, or it may be more. It may be as real as people have reported it, but something is happening, and it's worldwide. Many of the people who experience it do not report it, or want to be identified. They are too afraid.

You see, they get visits at night, by black-eyed children. I don't mean they've got bruising around their eye sockets, I mean their eyes are entirely black, with no whites, irises, or pupils. They usually come in pairs and they are usually inadequately dressed for the weather.

They visit houses, approach cars, hotel rooms, even boats. And they knock, and if you answer, they ask to come in. They don't engage in conversation; in fact, they seem to have a limited range of questions and responses, which they communicate in a demanding monotone. They are insistent and evasive, and appear vulnerable. You get an intense feeling of dread, and panic. These children terrify you. They want to come in. And sometimes, they tell you they want to feed. And then you see their eyes and your mind can't cope, because their eyes are entirely black.

There is only one encounter recorded where one of these children was let in and people survived. A woman returning from a shop with her groceries got into her car, having left her young son in the back seat, and saw that a black-eyed child was sitting next to him. Her son said the boy had tapped on the window and asked to come in, so the boy had let him in hoping they could play. The woman grabbed her son and fled, leaving the car in the car park. Later, the boy became ill and fell into a coma. His condition remained untreatable until a member of the mother's church rebuked the spirit afflicting the boy and bound it in Christ's name. He remained weak and sickly for years. Later, the woman's husband was driving the car they had recovered from the car park, and he was involved in a near-fatal collision. Evidence seems to point to a spiritual, or interdimensional, element; nephilim hybrids, demons, fallen angels? These children can appear at, and disappear from, various windows and doors around a house in an instant. But they want in, and they seem to want to feed on your fear.

They often appear to people in authority: policemen, nurses, firemen, and once to a soldier in a barracks. Or maybe these people draw on the inner resources available to them that have enabled them to gain such positions, their strength or their will, to resist the cunning presence of these children. It must be assumed they have less fortunate victims. As I said, people seem loath to report these experiences. Denial is, as they say, a wonderful thing.

But Carla had let them in.

I drove fast, too fast. Carla was making noises on the back seat. I could hear her moaning. I could hear the sound of her legs moving against the fabric of the back seat. I glanced in my rearview mirror as I approached a blind bend, just for a second.

She was sitting up and looking at me.

But it wasn't Carla in the back.

Dead black eyes looked back at me.

I lost concentration; I was no longer driving a car at sixty miles an hour, I was gone for an instant. My mind blanked. I heard something, and it was the monstrous whistling dismay of the eternal void. I had preached on Hell, on separation from God, and now I could hear what the damned hear, and for a moment I saw into the eyes of something released for a time from that unendurable vault. There was pressure and temperature in those eyes; what you might experience waking forever in the heart of a collapsed star. It was both cold and immeasurably hot, ever expanding and as massive as a neutron star. All physics was behind those eyes, all the grotesque complexities of imaginary numbers.

And the car came around the bend and I snapped back and saw them, but too late.

A convoy of boys in single file, riding home on their bikes, suddenly thrown into film-set relief in the headlights. And I hit them, and drove through them, driving one into the next and feeling the wheels bounce and smear through them. The noise was awful, like driving through scaffolding.

I swerved, but I had already gone through them, past them. As my car drifted right, into the oncoming lane, another vehicle had to veer onto the verge to avoid me. Headlights dazzled me and then I was past. Moments later, in response to my recklessness, a horn blared from the darkness behind.

I pulled the car over in a lay-by a hundred yards down the road. I swung around in my seat, my heart pounding, fists clenched. Whatever had been in the back seat was gone. Nothing. Apart from me, sweating, shaking, terrified, the car was empty. What had I carried from that house?

I put my hazard lights on and in their intermittent orange flash, I got out of the car and stumbled back toward the scene of the accident. My shadow appeared, and then disappeared before me, growing shorter, losing assurance, until I was at the bend and in darkness. The moon was a mist-light behind a streak of delicate, nervous cloud.

I approached the scene. My hands felt like numb weights at the ends of my arms. I flexed them, but that just made it feel like more blood was flowing into my extremities, leaving my core cold and hollow.

I stood, wavering, skin prickling, by a pile of broken, twisted bikes. Three boys lay across the surface of the road, dead, still warm; warmer, perhaps, than I felt. Their bikes were enmeshed. Six wheels and a confusion of turning shadows. My memory flickered, stuttered like old celluloid running through a disused projector. Three bikes?

The fourth bike I had imagined; had it been just an adrenaline-enhanced perception? Had it been shadows of wheels I'd seen and miscounted?

I stepped nearer the edge of the road, toward where the verge sloped down into the field and the hawthorns that concealed them.

And saw the wreck of the car.

It had gone off the road and ploughed through the bushes. It was on its side, the chassis only just visible as the moon broke and reflected briefly off the exhaust. It was a new exhaust, fitted only last month.

I stepped forward, and then I was turning, running in the wrong direction, disorientation blinding me, as I tried to escape the thing heaving itself up that bank, using fistfuls of weeds, labouring out of the cutting of dirt and clambering shadows.

If I could just get up the bank and reach the road...

I could warn him...

Is my daughter dead? Broken in the car wreck I have crawled from...

Is she even there?

If I could get to the top, with what life I still had, I could warn him...

But I can never make it...

Footfalls behind me, slow, two pairs, now standing either side...

My hands in the weeds...

Voices, monotonous, insistent...

A cycle I can never break...

A pale face, like plastic in the moonlight, down near my ear...

The last thing I hear before he speaks is the sound of my car, driving away again, at the top of the slope...

And he speaks, and he tells me this won't take long...

But, of course, it goes on forever.

CARRION COWBOY

ktomi meets the North Dakota cowboy where the streambed is wide and dry. It is nearly dark, and Iktomi has just kindled a fire using green willow sticks. A young moon draws its way across the prairie sky like the tip of a duck feather.

Iktomi is a spider fairy. His face is pinched and very brown. He wears deerskin leggings with tiny beaded moccasins. He paints his face red and yellow and draws black rings around his eyes. His long black hair is parted in the middle and is wrapped with red bands. Iktomi dresses like a Dakota brave.

He looks up at the North Dakota cowboy who sways in the saddle. The cowboy is dead. Iktomi can smell the rich, red rot. He can see the dark skin of the cowboy's face in the shadow beneath the wide brim of his hat. It hangs like a dirty cloth mask. The North Dakota cowboy has one eye, his left eye. His right eye is gone, all but a rim of gristle.

Iktomi is a wily imp. He cannot find a friend to help him when he is in trouble. No one really loves him. He lives alone in a cone-shaped wigwam upon the plain. He hops and scuttles around the dusty feet of the North Dakota cowboy's worn-out horse like a hungry bird.

Iktomi claps his hands and the North Dakota cowboy slides from his saddle and falls to the streambed. Iktomi shouts, "Hin, hin!" and the horse bolts away. Iktomi hoots and capers, his red and yellow face with its big dark ringed eyes shining with mischief.

Iktomi begins to chant his charm words. His fire crackles and glows with a bright green flame. In the glow of that wicked fire, Iktomi casts his scuttling shadow. The North Dakota cowboy begins to rise.

I will have fun with this, thinks Iktomi. He spins a web and with these strings he makes the cowboy dance a puppet's dance around the fire.

In his filthy bloodied shirt and ragged pants, the North Dakota cowboy topples to and fro. Iktomi laughs and throws his arms about and leads the corpse around the fire. "Ha! Ha!" laughs the wayward imp and does not see the shadow that draws to the edge of his camp while he frolics and spins.

Drawn to the fire, and to the smell of red, rotting meat, proud Coyote comes. Coyote narrows his eyes. "My, my," he says to himself. "Who among us has not been tricked by that crafty fellow Iktomi before? Now we shall have some fun of our own."

Iktomi jumps upon the cowboy's back and hoots and hollers as they jolt about on the dry streambed. As they spin toward the edge of the circle of light, Coyote speaks. "Iktomi," he says, "I see you have found a friend. Will you introduce us?"

Iktomi is startled. The North Dakota cowboy stops his dance and stands at the edge of the fire. His arms hang at his sides and his head nods as Iktomi climbs onto his shoulders and peers over the crown of his hat. "Come out where we can see you," says Iktomi.

Coyote pads out of the shadows. His pelt is yellow-green and his eyes glow like minerals in the firelight.

Iktomi watches as Coyote circles the North Dakota cowboy. Coyote is grinning, his big, dark tongue hanging over his teeth.

Coyote stands on his hind legs and puts his claws on the cowboy's shoulders. He breathes on the cowboy's dropsied face, puts the tip of his thick tongue into the abandoned socket and tastes the salt-blood-gristle. Coyote feels a great hunger and wants to eat this thing. Coyote's narrow belly rumbles like a cart full of stones.

Iktomi scrambles down the cowboy's back. He jumps into the dust. He knows Coyote of old and knows his hungers and his pride.

"Vain Coyote," Iktomi chides. "My friend would like to dance. Have you the patience to indulge before you feed?"

Coyote gapes and rolls his moon-drenched eyes.

Iktomi folds his arms. The North Dakota cowboy does the same and pulls Coyote to his breast. Iktomi begins his dance. With flying hands and jumps and shuffles, Iktomi spins a web. He wraps Coyote in the cowboy's arms.

Coyote howls, a-stumble in that bitter clasp. Together they spin around the fire. Coyote smells his partner's high decay. He cannot move against these bonds Iktomi weaves.

"Dance, vain Coyote!" Iktomi shrieks beneath a night of wheeling stars.

Coyote, cunning spirit and ancient rival, trickster, sometimes wise and sometimes cruel, is helpless in these mystic ropes. He knows Iktomi has him fast; he curses his stupidity. What can he do to free himself from this dreadful carousel?

Coyote bites away the cowboy's throat. He shoves his muzzle in the rent and bores it down toward the heart. His tail whirls, a bouquet of prairie grass, and he claws the bloody shirt and flesh beneath until they flutter like red ribbons in a *Wi An's* hair.

Iktomi skips and plays his webs. The North Dakota cowboy twirls like a bobbin across the shadows of the streambed.

Coyote can do but one thing against the trick and trap of this potent imp; he climbs inside the North Dakota cowboy and wears the corpse like a fresh-skinned hide. The stink of meat and the wet-slip-slurry of putrid guts drive Coyote's fury, hunger, and pride.

Iktomi claps his hands and the webs break free. The North Dakota cowboy reels across Iktomi's camp and into darkness beyond the rim. Coyote cannot break his bonds; in fury, his spirit seeps into the bones of the North Dakota cowboy and, now trapped inside this shambling thing, Coyote's rage and hunger does not dim. It grows, consuming him.

Iktomi, fickle, bored and weary, waves his arms and sends the North Dakota cowboy home. He sighs and throws earth upon the embers of his fire. Soon this mischief will be forgotten, and Iktomi will find other tricks and traps to work.

And so it is that when the dead arise, their first hunger and their craving is for flesh, to feed the vain Coyote's raging at Iktomi's insolent arrest.

With foul, wet tread, toward his lighted town of shacks and bars, the North Dakota cowboy starts to lurch, his hunger great, and his belly growling.

NIGHT CLOSURES

They slept cuddled up beneath the blankets, using each other's body heat to keep warm. They tried making love but it was too cold. Their feet were freezing and wouldn't heat up despite being wrapped in the folds of the blankets at the bottom of the bed. She put her hands on him but they were cold, too, and he had shrunk up small and tight. She plucked at him with her slender, icy fingers but he pulled away, laughing, embarrassed.

"Blow the candle out," he said. "Let's have a cuddle.

She leaned across him, her breasts soft against his chest, and blew out the candle.

Across the hall, the boy slept. His nightlight guttered down, the stub of wick almost horizontal in a pool of liquid orange wax. The boy stirred; his dry mouth opened. The flame brightened once and then went out.

Outside, all was in darkness. Every streetlight was out; there was no light in any of the windows along the street. An occasional car drove by, and then headlights dragged slow luminous oblongs across the bedroom walls. The car's tyres murmured on the wet road and the light was snatched away as it passed.

The man and the woman slept. They were young and happy. Their breath clouded from their sleeping mouths in the cold of the room. Condensation formed on the glass behind the net curtains and ran in quicksilver threads to pool on the sills.

Sometime in the night, the boy awoke and sat up in his bed.

He was crying. His pillow was wet with tears. He blinked and wiped his face.

Across the hall, his parents were gone.

They had been gone for a long time.

*　　　*　　　*

The boy was in the kitchen. His mother was there. She had lit the gas oven to keep them warm and give them some extra light. The boy stood and looked up at the fluttering blue rings of flame on the hob. He liked the sound they made, like a constant exhalation. The wireless was on and they listened to Radio Two. He sat at the dining table and coloured some pictures by candlelight. The rest of the house beyond the closed dining room door was in darkness. His mother gave him a plate of mince and mashed potatoes for his tea, which was his favourite. The kitchen windows were like black mirrors. He watched his mother's silent reflection move across their blind surface. Outside, the back garden and alleyway at the end were unlit and mysterious as a jungle. He imagined the house was floating in space, snug and warm and safe. He tried drawing a picture of a rocket but it wasn't much good, so he went back to drawing the UFOs that his friend Jamie had shown him how to draw. They looked like little bowler hats and they fired death rays like lots of dashes - - - - - - -. He destroyed some tanks and a few submarines and a lot of buildings and then decided that enough was enough, and blew up all the UFOs with flame-like scrawls from a fat red pencil. The boy went upstairs to his bedroom and looked out of his window. He heard the watery sound of the car's tyres on cinders, and then the alley was lit by the headlights on his father's car.

The boy turned and ran downstairs. When he went into the kitchen, it was cold and empty and the oven had not been lit for years.

He sat at the dining table and put his head in his hands.

*   *   *

They had owned an old mono record player. It was a black box the size of a small suitcase with a lid that was opened by unclipping two clasps and lifting it up on hinges. It had a speaker in the front, and at the back was a dusty grille through which the valves were visible. When it was plugged in, the valves glowed and warmed and scorched the dust that had gathered on the bulbs.

They didn't have much but enjoyed what they had, and every now and then, like a small, special ceremony, his father would come home from the factory with a record he had borrowed from a workmate and they would sit around the record player in the evening after dinner and listen to it.

The boy loved the smell as it warmed up, the anticipation of hearing the new record, the delicious pleasure of sitting on the floor in the lounge with the light off and the gas fire whispering, while his father performed the ritual. One time, his father brought home *War of The Worlds* and they sat for three nights in a row being transported to that time of heat rays, tripods, and red weed, and the boy spent hours wondering over the pictures in the book that came with it.

The boy sat on the sofa and looked at the floor. He had gone through to the lounge when he thought he had heard the sound of a needle crackling in the grooves of a record, but the lounge was empty and chilly and the sound must had been an illusion made by February weather blowing leaves against the front door.

He could have turned on the lights but preferred to remember things this way. He went back into the kitchen and opened the cupboard under the sink. He squatted down and fished out some old candles that were in a box at the back. He stood and looked at them, lifting them out one at a time to inspect them. There were memories trapped in the wax of these old candles, like messages embedded through sticks of rock. The candles were heavy and sooty in his hand, ridged with thin, brittle spines of wax. There were smaller nightlights at the bottom of the box, half-used slumped-shouldered chunks that had been used to light his bedroom. He could remember the placing of virtually every candle. They had dotted the house, melted bases pressed onto saucers, providing fluttering alcoves of light like little shrines. He remembered having a pee in the candlelit bathroom, aiming into the wobbling shadow in the toilet bowl. He closed his eyes and summoned the warm tang of pink paraffin to mind, which his father had used to fuel the little heater they carried up and downstairs to heat the house during the power cuts.

That had been a hard winter.

2.

The boy had had a friend called Andrew Vincent. Andrew had an older brother, an almost mythical figure of twelve years of age who had a good haircut and slept all morning at the weekends and stayed up late to watch films with unsettling names like *Asylum* and *Psycho*. His name was Stephen. He wore flared jeans and tee shirts cut tight to his waist, with faded psychedelic illustrations on them. Stephen Vincent could draw very well and decorated the inside covers of a green ring binder with ballpoint sketches of skulls and racing bike insignia. He said they were tattoos he was going to get. They lived in a council house down Brinkley Road, and their dad stubbed his morning cigarettes out in the stiff corona of his fried egg. This disturbed the boy a little. Andy's dad had *an ulcer* and he could be heard coughing and heaving in the small dingy toilet that was off the kitchen. When he did this, everyone in the house took on expressions of great apprehension, and crept about the house, or left the house entirely, in fear of this tall, grim, unemployed, and consumptive man.

Andy had innumerable little sisters. The boy could never remember how many exactly, but it might have been about four. They stood blinking and dirty-faced in corners behind soiled armchairs, tousle-haired and dumb. The house smelled of their musty urine.

The boy was one part in awe of Stephen, and one part scared of him. Andy said that he was a *bully* and that he had a knife and that he used it to hurt small animals. Sometimes Stephen would summon the boy and give him ten pence to go up to the shop and buy him some sweets. One time, the boy came back with a

Texan bar and Stephen let him keep the change. He experienced a rush of intense feeling as he walked back down the short path to the street clutching Stephen's largesse. He felt he was a component of the world, a partaker in life.

The boy would spend all day out with Andy. Andy was a liar, a storyteller, a deceiver. But the boy found him exciting company. They played in the alleyways that ran along the backs of the houses. They raided garages for tokens to justify their trespass; they stole screwdrivers and bolts and cogs and fled laughing, never keeping their plunder, slinging them into the low, oily bushes that ran along the edges of the cindered alleys.

Sometimes Andy would take the boy further afield. They would leave the warren of alleys, cross the street, and go on up to the allotments. Andy called them *the allockments.* Another alleyway ran alongside the allotments and if they followed this, it led to Boscombe dump. It was a council tip. It was a wet, filthy expanse of ground containing a colossal mountain of rubbish. It stank like the insides of death and gulls wheeled and cried around its faces like flecks of a neurosis.

The boys could climb the concrete wall at the end of the alley and drop down into the dump. They would scoot across the uneven ground and pick through the detritus gathered at the base of the mountain. They did this because Andy had told the boy that sometimes marvellous things could be found here. Once, Andy had said, he had found a box of watches here, and rare coins and wallets full of tenners. A tenner was almost as fabulous to the boy as Andy's brother; it was something rarely seen and virtually *unspendable*, it was so huge. The thought of finding these treasures filled the boy with a hunger for sudden and complimentary riches. Of course, they never found anything when he went with Andy, but often Andy would tell the boy that he had found things of great value on other trips there, with the other boys from Brinkley Road.

Two roads further down the high street from Brinkley Road was Longfellow Road. These were *all* council houses and had been built just after the War. Some of them had become derelict and were being slowly demolished. It would be unthinkable now, but these children played amongst the ungated and unfenced ruins, inside the shells of these small buildings, ran up staircases open to the sky, leaned out from teetering sills and skipped through cold, tiled kitchens and pulled wires from the walls.

These stripped, unroofed terraces made perfect castles; breezeblock and plaster crenelated forts from which to defend against marauding gangs from other streets.

It was Andy who first showed the boy the row of abandoned houses. He called them *bombsites*, but of course they weren't. They were being demolished because they had been neglected.

They played there all day. Their boundless child minds imagined whole worlds, entire regimes, rules and laws, quick and bright as summer lightning. There were microsecond rows and a battle that drew out over days but in reality, lasted less than an hour. They carried half-bricks and filled their pockets with acorns and small, hard green apples they scavenged from the trees that overhung the alleys. There was an inexhaustible supply of rusty ironmongery buried in the cinders: nails, screws, hinges, bolts, and they filled boxes with these tetanal horrors and toted them to the tops of their towers and placed them like ordnance to be hurled from the battlements.

And then, across the rest of the day, came the occasional boy from other roads. Wiry-haired Nigel, flaking with eczema and the feral trace of the hamster cage about his body odour. Stan: scrawny, daft but disconcerting, motherless and able to gob tiny specks of foul-smelling saliva with commendable accuracy over noteworthy distances. Danny, who was known to be *hard* but was always oddly kind to the boy, this inconsistent with the regular beatings he dished out to his own younger brothers. And there were others, drifters; some ginger and unappetising, some on bikes from further out, a set of pale-eyed twins who didn't go to the boy's school but got a special bus every morning and who were always vaguely moronic, aggressive, and defiant.

Andy knew them all, and led the boy through the manners and submissions necessary to negotiate all these possible threats. The boy stood quietly by as Andy weaselled and bragged, threatened and oppressed, and while he did so, something broke away from the boy, drifted up from his guts and passed like a numbing gas through his brain. It was a primal realization that, despite his occasional perceptions of some cavernous potential at the heart of life, something there for the taking, he would never experience the easy participation in any of it. He felt blocked, somehow, and at once terribly afraid of what that meant.

And perhaps it was this insight that Andy—in some cunning and unconscious way—understood, because in time, Andy dropped the boy for other, worldlier companions. The boy missed the adventures and the possibilities, and the empty promises. What he didn't miss was the feeling he experienced when he returned home to the warm little house in the nice road, and his mother's kiss, and snacks, and his father's authentic curiosity about his day. It was guilt, he realised later, because he did things when he was out that he was sure might break his parents' hearts.

3.

Friends come and go like shadows on an overcast day when you're a child. You can spend a whole summer holiday knocking about with someone, only to find that they drift into formless acquaintance the moment you're back at school. Or you go away on holiday with your folks and spend a week of intense frolic with someone you know you'll never see again but can remember for the rest of your life.

Ghosts of the mind. Nostalgia. Imprints. These moments are as significant as trauma; they lay down deep pathways in the brain and can be triggered in aching flashbacks by the simplest things.

The boy's world was full of ominous words that year; those announced on the news and on the front pages of the paper and those whispered by his parents when they thought the boy couldn't hear. When he heard those hushed conversations, the boy felt utterly isolated, terrified that his parents were discussing a looming death.

His father worked in a factory that made metal cabinets for offices. He worked in the packing shop. The government had put everyone on a *three-day week.* This was because miners were striking for more pay and coal reserves were running out. There were *power cuts* and *blackouts.* His parents were young and had a *mortgage* and his mother did not work.

Andrew Vincent used to say things like, "*When* I go to prison." Not *if*, but *when*. This staggered the boy, who couldn't bear the thought of doing anything to upset or hurt his parents. In their love for him, and in naïve attempts to guide and contain his behaviour, they had disciplined the boy with more than his fair share of emotional blackmail. They didn't know any better, and did it out of love, but they nonetheless *had*. Especially his mother, who loved the boy so much, but who could make him feel desolate instead of cherished when she told him that there were things he might do that would cause her intolerable pain.

The boy spent a lot of that winter worrying he might have done something so awful that he would be disowned by this mother whom he adored. Or that his father, a sweet, easy man who loved nothing more than to play with his boy no matter how tired he was after working all day in the factory, would suddenly turn with pyroclastic fury against him because of something that he had inadvertently done to ruin their happiness.

It caused the boy to lie awake at night and fret. He could hear then the whispered conversations from the room across the landing, and he wondered if he had done something dreadful, and that now his parents were discussing what must be done with him.

*　　　*　　　*

On one of the days he was not working, the boy's father had been in his garage making Tilley lamps out of old glass baby food jars. He was trying to keep busy and economise at the same time. He had moved the car out of the garage and parked it around the front of the house on the street. He stood at his workbench and hammered short pieces of narrow steel tubing through the metal lids and then pushed small pieces of torn J-cloth into the pipes. He half-filled the jars with paraffin and then screwed the lids down.

The boy watched all this. There was a large black oil stain on the concrete floor of the garage. There were shelves full of paint pots and jars of nails and screws. The boy thought that there was nothing interesting in this garage to nick, should boys come nicking, and he was quite pleased. He didn't want anyone to take things from his dad.

When the boy looked back toward his father's workbench, he saw that he was alone. The oil stain beneath his feet had faded, had been absorbed into the fractured concrete until only a dusty silhouette remained. The boy looked up and saw on a shelf above the bench the three small glass lamps his father made. They were huddled together like a peculiar little sculpture, coated in dust and smudged with soot. The boy's mother had never let his father use them in the house. She had scolded him for making dangerous things. She called them *Molotov cocktails,* which sounded exotic to the boy, who had no idea about things like improvised incendiary devices, although he had been starting to develop embryonic worries around things he heard on the news, baleful words like *the provisional IRA* and *rubber bullets* and, most disquieting to the boy, *urban gorillas,* which created fantastic images in his mind and perplexed him regarding the nature of reality.

There was a character called Gus Gorilla in his *Cor!* comic. The boy didn't like him much. There was something coarse and oafish about him that made the boy think of the fat boys who lived down Brinkley Road. They were the Canavans, and they trudged slowly around their house like nudged balloons, dragging their elbows along scuffed and greasy halls, pressing up narrow stairs, their thighs bulging against the fabric of their trousers like the spines of great, overstuffed encyclopaedias, and resplendent with massive guts that filled the boy with a prim disgust. They were unusual, this fat lot, because everyone else seemed thin, wasted a little, compared to the boy, who was always so rude with scrubbed, mothered, sheltered good health.

The boy imagined these fat things with old-style satchels, and schoolboy caps like Gus in his comic askew on their swollen heads, lurking in the dark and broken shells of the part-demolished houses in Longfellow Road; he imagined dim and brutal eyes gazing out at him from the ruined shadows; he imagined the slow and deliberate movements toward him as they crept on huge, hairy hands and feet, their protuberant primate mouths like leathery capsules a-gash with grinning, comic-strip teeth.

It was night in the garage. Moonlight made a line where the doors hung broken on their hinges. Pale stripes of light reflected from the bodies of the glass lamps and their tiny metal chimneys like filaments of cold flame.

The boy felt cold. He always felt cold.

He hadn't wanted anyone to take things from his dad; he had been so terribly wrong to think that there was nothing worth taking from the garage that winter's day.

4.

The boy found himself alone that long summer holiday. He had tried knocking for Andy, but there was no reply. He felt a nagging sense of isolation. Everyone he passed was an adult; nobody saw him. He tried knocking for some of the other boys but they weren't about either. In desperation for some company to fill the endless day ahead, the boy wandered the alleyways at the backs of the houses until he got as far as Longfellow Road. There were a couple of boys who lived down there who were unpopular and were generally ostracised, but today the boy felt a need to connect that overrode anything else, and so he walked in hope up their short garden paths and knocked for them.

When nobody answered at either door, the boy experienced for the first time a sense that the world could turn on him, reject him. It frightened him. The day was now *his* responsibility to fill. He could go home and be with his mum, but a whole day was out here with him, throbbing with light and time and possibilities. He thought for a moment about his house; his bedroom, the constant concern of his mother and the gentle sounds of her moving around the house, about the slow drift through to mid-afternoon when there would be snacks and children's television.

And always, there was this nagging guilt that troubled him now. An anxiety deep in his gut, a light and unpleasant flutter in his chest that made him feel inordinately sad. He had no conscious strategies to cope with it because he was so young, no modifications to be made to his thoughts. He did what any child would do: he avoided the thing that caused it, which happened to be proximity to his loving mother.

The boy considered alternatives. He returned to his road via the alleys, scuffing his Clark's Attackers through the cinders and mud. He found an old biro in some oily grass and was pleased to find that it still wrote despite the greenstick fractures to its transparent plastic case. He stood for a moment and tried to copy from memory one of Stephen Vincent's arty drawings, but gave up when the ink blobbed and smeared across the back of his hand. He luzzed the pen back into the grass and went on. *Luzz* was a word Andy had taught the boy. *Chucking* things and *bunging* things seemed so old-fashioned, lame. You luzzed things nowadays.

Not having children of his own age to play with, the boy decided it was time to approach one of the older boys he knew lived nearby. This was always risky, because the bigger boys— only a year or two older in fact, but empirically different in many developmental ways—could turn nasty, become unstable, and end up applying pressure and demands on the boy he found impossible to resist.

A devious, undependable eleven-year-old called Darren lived opposite the boy. His parents were old. Late forties at least. Darren had two older brothers. Dale was the eldest. He could drive and owned a very modern Triumph Toledo. He had met a woman who already had children. The boy's father didn't care for this arrangement and called it *Dale's instant family*.

The other brother was called Graham, a distant, languid figure glimpsed mostly through the living room door with his feet up smoking cigarettes and reading *The Daily Mirror*. Of the three brothers, Graham had the nicest temperament, but was in his late teens and had shoulder-length hair and sideburns, so the boy was of no interest to him. He did speak to the boy, though; short, mostly monosyllabic interactions, but enough to create a strange fascination for the boy. Once, when he had gone knocking for Darren and had found him to be out somewhere else, Graham had made him a drink of lemon squash before disappearing up to his room to listen to Led Zeppelin on his record player. This had all made a huge impression on the boy.

But Darren was the last resort; his slyness made the boy feel on edge, too aware of his own wavering innocence and vulnerability to manipulation; and so, he decided, with ill-defined self-reliance, that a day like today needed elements of control and choice he had previously been too susceptible to grasp.

A second option was Wayne. He lived next-door-but-two, in a large and richly extended semidetached house across from the entrance to the alley that ran behind their gardens. His step-dad was a builder and had recently been in prison for stealing wood from a timber yard. Now he was out, he was spoiling Wayne. He had built him a tree house, which had proper walls and a trap-door. It overlooked the alley and was a vantage place the boy coveted greatly. Wayne's dad was called Chas. He was a big bear of a man with a thick black beard and small, murderous brown eyes. He called his new wife *lover* when he spoke to her, which the boy thought both daring and a bit vulgar. She was pretty in a dusky way that made the boy think of gypsies, and she often wore tight tie-dyed T-shirts and no shoes. Chas used to touch her in ways he had never seen his father touch his mother. Wayne, the product of a previous relationship, was dark also, but mostly with dirt. Wayne lived there on a permanent basis but had a younger brother called Liam who visited occasionally. The boy preferred Liam as they were closer in age, but he had long since given up knocking for him as his visits could never be predicted and he was scared of alerting Wayne to his presence. The boy was frightened of Wayne and would rather avoid him if possible.

A third boy, and a catalyst for Darren and Wayne's most fertile and imaginative discrimination, was Peter Besant. He was a concave-faced boy from the next road with flared nostrils persistently running with snot all shades of a spectrum that incorporated glassy through pear to an alarming electric green. He had curly hair and a speech impediment that prohibited his ability to give his speech any of its normal characteristics of tonality or modulation. Had the boy known anything about neurological speech disorders, he would have understood that Peter was suffering from *dysprosody* as a symptom of a brain tumour that would kill him a few days before his eleventh birthday. He could be stupid and suffered occasional absences that made him an easy target for bullying and derision, but he was unfettered by any sense of responsibility or empathy, and that made him an exciting if unpredictable companion, even though he was repulsive.

So, it was Peter the boy tried first. He strolled to the end of his road, cutting through the grounds of the Anglican church on the corner and locating Peter's house on the even side past the church hall. It was a semi-detached running to disrepair. Peter's dad was dead and he lived with his mum and his aunt. He, too, was an only child. The boy stood at the gate and, for the first time, felt some trepidation.

This was because his mum and dad had forbidden him to play with Peter. Peter was a bit unbalanced, a *naughty* boy. He had no dad and wasn't being brought up with enough discipline. He'd *gone off the rails*. Peter smoked. And nicked.

The boy remembered with some shame—and this *shame* was a newly emerging emotion, a complex mixture of embarrassment and rage that the boy experienced with blushing and vexation—being summoned home by his mother, singled out from a group of children who were standing on the corner of the alley watching with fascination the incongruous sight of a nine-year-old boy puffing on a cigarette nicked from his mum, and blowing smoke rings with a virtuoso pop of his jaw.

The boy's mother had made him suffer for sins not yet committed after this. *If I ever catch you smoking* and *If you ever steal from me.* Admonitions against all possible disgraces. But all the boy heard was *I'll stop loving you.*

The boy could have turned away. The thought of his mother and a drink and a biscuit came to him, some tenderness to entice him home, but it was brief and gone in an instant. She would always be there. Today was still bright and edged with an infinity of possibilities, like glimpsing spectacular reflections in the near-hidden periphery of a mirror. Things to discover and places to explore. And it looked like Peter was in; his new Chopper bike stood at a jaunty angle on its kickstand by the front porch. The boy *craved* a go on that bike.

He walked up the path.

5.

The boy's dad used to get his hair cut in a tiny barbershop at the end of an old arcade at the bottom of the high street. There were two barbers there, Johnny and Carlo. Johnny was a short, rat-thin Londoner with greying hair and glasses. Carlo was Italian, larger built, entirely white-haired and full of good cheer. They both wore long dark blue coats and had combs and scissors sticking out of their top pockets. Their chairs were at right angles to each other; Johnny's to the right of the door opening in from the arcade, Carlo's opposite the door. The floor was scuffed egg-shell-blue lino and the walls were covered with perforated display board on which hung postcards and advertisements for hair products. There was a shaving brush in a bowl on a shelf above the sink and a pile of newspapers on a table next to Carlo's chair. The barbershop was redolent with the oily smell of men's hair. Small drifts of it lay in choppy piles beneath the barbers' chairs.

The boy's dad had taken him there once to get his hair cut. His dad favoured Johnny's style of cut and therefore presumed his son would, too. The boy had enjoyed the process at first: the warm welcome, the good-natured teasing, the high, shiny, bright-red upholstered chair in front of the big speckled mirror, and the warm apron that was produced, shaken ceremoniously and then used to tent him into the chair so that only his tousled head stuck out. He even enjoyed the *snip-snip* of the scissors as they pruned his soft, flyaway curls.

But he hadn't liked the clippers.

Without warning, some cold, throbbing machine had been pressed up against the back of his head, the force of it reverberating against his neck bones and ringing in his ear like some gnawing, febrile beast. It scraped up his nape like a handful of shuddering dinner forks and the boy had shrieked and thrown himself off the chair. His father was staring at him like he had lost his mind—which, for a second, he probably had—and Johnny was standing, still hunched over the back of the chair, with the clippers held aloft, eyeing the boy with a perplexed look of reproach, while Carlo pointed to an evil-looking rubber chimpanzee sitting slumped on a small corner shelf above and to the left of his chair, and proclaimed in a loud, *Latino* bellow: "*Hey, bambino! Lookadda monkey, he don' cry!*" All of which made the boy cry harder, now in genuine terror.

His father was disappointed and not a little embarrassed. When he took the boy home, hair half-cut, he suggested his mother take him to the salon with her next time she went. The boy was relieved. He preferred the softer smells and glossier magazines.

His mother's hairdresser was called Sheena and she was Greek. She had a son in the boy's year at school called Panikos. Panny had all the latest things. They lived in a flat above the salon on the high street. Sometimes, after school, the boy's mother would have her hair done and the boy could play with Panny in the back of the shop and in the rooms upstairs. It gave the boy a perturbed, giddy feeling, being in a living room that was *upstairs*. The rooms were really just a small apartment above the shop, but a wide stairway led up from the rear of the salon, where the dark hoods of hairdryers stood bowing over plastic chairs like helmeted aliens from out of *Dr. Who*, and it gave the whole place an open-plan aspect which seemed very modern to the boy.

The boy was becoming very impressed with modernity, and the trends exploding around him. He felt stout, unfashionable in his sensible Clark's shoes and his hand-me-down checkered cotton shirts. His hair felt fine and fluffy. He knew he would never have one of those cute and silky hairstyles that the button-nosed American children had on the programs he loved like *The Banana Splits* and *The Monkees*, or the more tearaway British pageboy chic of the *Children's Film Foundation*, and this knowledge filled him with a low-grade feeling of despair.

Panny was fun to be around, but he had the detachedness and confidence of a boy being brought up by young, trendy parents who trusted him with a large degree of self-sufficiency. Sheena was small and pretty and had a beehive haircut with a silver butterfly clip in the front. She wore mini-skirts and enjoyed yoga and a variety of crafts like origami, macrame, and hook rugs. Her husband, whose name the boy did not know, was in the army. He came home at weekends and the three of them went out on picnics in a battered old orange split-screen camper van.

The boy's thoughts lingered on such things, and he lost hope that he might ever live a groovy life. This, too, caused him to lie awake at night and fret, but it was a deeper and more defined worry, as vain as the fear of death and just as unfathomable.

6.

Something had happened that previous winter to badly scare the boy.

He had gone out one morning to find Andy, hoping to play out all day. His mother had taken a job working one night a week as a nursing assistant in the psychogeriatric hospital at the top of the high street. She came home at half past seven in the morning and went to bed. The boy loved getting up and going downstairs on his own because his mum always left a thermos flask full of milky coffee, some biscuits, and a list of television programmes he liked with their times and channels written beside them. There were only three channels and the TV was black and white, but the boy thought sitting on the sofa watching *Champion the Wonder Horse* while sipping creamy, steaming coffee from the flask's little plastic mug was about the best thing ever.

After he'd finished the last drips from the flask and eaten his *Club* biscuit (the purple ones were his favourite—he liked the raisins), the boy let himself out of the front door and stood staring at the world in wonder.

It was freezing cold and his breath billowed like smoke; there was a rind of hoar frost everywhere, everything was white. It was beautiful. The boy felt an odd thrill; it was as if he'd stepped out and caught the world aslumber; in a second it would realise and dash its colours on like paint. But nothing happened. The boy stood for a while transfixed. Then he walked slowly up the path to the gate. There were puddles on the pavement but they were now just platters of ice.

And there was a dense mist. The boy looked around. He couldn't see much of the opposite side of the road, just the outline of the bottom ten feet or so of a telegraph pole at the edge of the pavement and the indistinct humps of his neighbours' cars parked at the side of the road. The frosted road disappeared into the nebular whiteness in both directions.

The boy pulled his parka's hood up and blew into his cupped hands. He had mittens in his pockets but wanted to feel the cold working before he put them on. He waggled his fingers, blew fuming breath over them, saw how white they looked. He placed the sole of his shoe against the pane of ice that lay on the pavement. He pressed down and both heard and felt the *crack* as it fractured beneath the pressure. He lifted his foot. The puddle looked like a broken mirror. He bent down and lifted one of the shards of ice from the pavement. It slid away from him and dropped to the kerb where it shattered.

The opening to the alley that led through to the next street was just two houses along, but it was not visible from where he stood just outside his front gate. It emerged from the mist as the boy approached. He felt very alone, but in a serene, cocooned way that wasn't unpleasant. He imagined he was adrift somewhere in the depths of some great pale gas giant (the boy had become fascinated with planets since seeing a gate-fold picture of the solar system in an encyclopaedia at school), and he was an explorer on an outcrop of unexpected land. He stood for a moment at the entrance to the alley, pulled an imaginary ray gun from his coat pocket, and then marched on into the mist.

*   *   *

The boy and Andy had played all day as hoped. They had run alongside the allotments, the thin cold air chapping their faces, drying their lips. They had stomped through hundreds of bleached and brittle puddles and slapped rime like dust from railings with sticks. They had crept along the foot of the pale concrete wall that bordered the dump, trying to scare each other with ghost stories. The leaves of the trees dripped and dripped, and the dump was a silent, vaporous region that neither of them dared venture down into that day. The boy was not really much good at telling spooky stories, but there was something about Andy's talebearing that rang with a touch of the fearful and strange, and felt more like rumours of bad things rather than spontaneous, ticklish fibs.

Andy told of unnerving, proximal horrors like, "Two kids came down *this* alley and a face was painted on the wall of the dump in *blood* and the words appeared: *the devil!* They were both found hung from *that* tree over *there*."

The boy felt a little like crying with fear, and managed to encourage Andy, who was still frothing with terrifying fabrications, his eyes wild and his corpse-white fingers clawed, back through the misty lane and onto the perimeter of the pallid and isolated allotments.

The boy felt better now that he could make out the blurry outlines of fences and garage doors. They walked on through the flat stillness of the dampening fog until they reached the road. Andy decided that it would be fun to head down the high street to Longfellow Road and spend the day barricading themselves into one of the derelict houses.

So that's what they did.

*   *   *

The boy didn't notice how dark it had become. They had played for hours amongst the fog-bound ruins and their play had been lit by diffuse and gloomy sunlight. They had found a couple of old cardboard boxes and made gas masks out of them, patrolling the rubble like soldiers under mustard gas attack. They chased each other through the debris in a mist that tinted orange as the streetlights came on; it enhanced the sense of menace as if the vapour was becoming polluted, more toxic. They choked and collapsed against the cold tiled walls of an old, abandoned kitchen and fell on their backs, kicking their legs, coughing and spluttering, laughing like loons.

A person passing on his way home from work might stop for a moment, hearing the sounds floating out of the fog, and pull his coat collar more tightly up around his throat and hurry on.

And one did hear, and he did shift more stoically beneath his heavy coat. But he did not go on. Not at first.

* * *

When the boy realised it had become dark, he panicked.

He called for Andy, but there was no reply. He stumbled over a pile of bricks that had once been the wall beneath a bath-room window. Broken lead pipes stuck out from the walls like the damp rifle barrels of the ghostly regiment they had spent all day fighting. The boy was suddenly alone and could feel the dread presences conjured by his imagination magnify a hun-dredfold as the fog closed in on him. He couldn't breathe. His voice, hoarse with fear, called Andy's name once more, but it got no reply. Andy had gone home.

The boy's eyes were wide in the foggy orange twilight as he picked his way across the building site to the edge of the road. His breathing remained fast and shallow. As he stood at the kerb-side a car crawled past, its headlights no more than cataracts in the fog. The boy had a decision to make. He could run up the hill to the high street, turn left, and go home past the shops, or he could cross the road and cut through the alleys, which was by far the quickest option. His familiarity with the kinks and ruts of the alleys made the decision easy. It was his world and he knew it like the back of his hand. He needed to get home because his parents would be furious if he missed his tea. He had no idea what the time was but there were people about—they passed behind him like shadows, and their footsteps sounded muffled and wet—and so the boy assumed they must be coming home from work. And this galvanised him further because if they were coming home from work, then his dad would be coming home from work and he couldn't begin to imagine what would happen if he wasn't home before his dad.

He hurried across the road and ran toward where he knew the entrance to the alleyway was. The fog drifted like a screen awaiting projection, and as the boy started to walk up the car-wide alley, his shoes sinking into the mud and cinders, things emerged from the margins then sank back as he passed, like images flickering and dying: the broad, eldritch back end of an old Ford Zodiac parked half inside its cluttered garage, dustbins like squat little sentries crouching outside back gates, a rusting mangle with fissured rollers half open; things he was used to seeing became unusual in the fog, and the boy felt teased by his fickle periphery.

His mind started to make unwanted connections, combining sounds and glimpses of things, to enlarge little fears into cold, creeping dismay. It was dark in the throat of the alley and as he rounded the corner at the top to make his way down the long stretch that split the back-to-back gardens, the boy realised he would be feeling his way almost blind the whole way. Gulping, the boy turned back, but something was standing in the centre of the alleyway behind him.

It said nothing, just stood there, tall and still.

Then it moved. One step toward the boy, its right foot gritting through the cinders.

*　　　*　　　*

The boy, who was already a-twitch with nerves about many things, a spectator in a world that was billowing with terrors, disappointments and possible—*probable*—losses of insurmountable magnitude, had somehow made it out of the alleyway and onto the pavement. He had flown the length of the alley, trusting his internal knowledge of its contours, knowing the man—it was a man, he *knew* it was a man, it *had* to be a man—was following behind. Andy's earlier amusing diversions sprang to the front of his mind; the boy saw what must have been paint slapped against the sagging doors of an asbestos-sided garage become words and devilish, bloody faces; he ran past these, the nerves in his belly crawling, and felt rather than saw that there was someone standing in the swirling gap between the doors, staring at him.

And then he was out. He took a moment to orient himself, and then took off up the road toward the comforting lights on the high street. He wasn't quite old enough to have learned to reflect on his experiences and laugh at them, but in his own way, the boy knew that he had only been scaring himself, and that his imagination had created the threats unleashed along that silent back alley. But he didn't look back. He didn't want to see the figure he knew would be standing at the neck of the alley, beneath the lamppost in a dank caul of alien light, with rods that looked like levers clenched in its fists.

7.

Peter Besant was in.

He looked a little bemused for a moment to see the boy standing at his front door, but when he was asked whether he wanted to come out, he nodded and went back inside to put on his sandals and a paisley woollen tank top.

Peter knocked up the kickstand on the Chopper with his heel and began wheeling it down the path. The boy felt a thrill—both of anticipation and of guilt—that was as close to anything sexual he had ever experienced. It was so subtle a duet that it didn't register with the boy as anything more than a tingle in his belly and a momentary light-headedness; it consisted of maybe getting a chance to ride on that lovely, curious bike with its high backed padded seat, exaggerated cow-horn handlebars, gear stick and red-lined tyres, combined with the knowledge that it was forbidden to him to do so—his mother had told him that the Chopper (and its moderately less groovy cousin, the *Tomahawk*) was a dangerous bike, that it had a design fault that made braking hazardous. Children could be sent flying over the handlebars if they squeezed too hard on the front brake before exerting sufficient pressure on the rear.

The boy trotted alongside Peter. In profile, both Peter's forehead and chin protruded beyond the clogged stub of his nose, giving him the likeness of a crescent man-in-the-moon the boy had seen on the front of a story book.

They walked through the churchyard and turned down the boy's road. Peter stopped by the glass works at the top and fished around in the front pockets of his jeans. He pulled out a battered pack of ten Benson and Hedges. Frowning, he lifted the flap on the top of the bronze-coloured pack and peered into it. He shook the pack and tipped it toward the boy.

"Fag," he said, and owing to the peculiar lack of emphasis or tone in Peter's voice, the boy could only assume that he was being offered a cigarette to smoke for himself, as opposed to being bluntly informed about the contents of the pack and nothing more.

The boy refused, hoping this wouldn't alienate himself from Peter, not when he was this close to a go on a real Chopper bike, but Peter only shrugged and put one of the Bensons in his mouth. He took a box of Swan Vestas out of his pocket and struck one of the flaky, pink-headed matches against the side of the box with an assured flick of his wrist and lit up. He stood there puffing.

Again, the boy was thrilled and horrified. Didn't Peter care about being seen? And then, on the heels of this thought, one that was far worse: what if he was seen with Peter and his mother found out? They couldn't stand there in full view; his complicity was assured. His parents would see him as a smoking, nicking, Chopper bike-riding young offender. He would be put in borstal.

Taking the lead, and with great anxiety, the boy began to walk away, hoping Peter would follow. Peter was fairly compliant—the boy remembered once watching him tip a bin full of rubbish out over the bonnet of a neighbour's silver Hillman Imp under orders from Darren and Wayne—and so he followed, pushing his bike and puffing on his cigarette. Every so often his right eyelid drooped slightly, leaving a dilated hemisphere of pupil squinting at the world from beneath a curtain of sticky lashes still crumbed with yellow nuggets of sleep.

*   *   *

The boy led Peter to the allotments. Peter stood staring across the rectangular plots at a point in the far distance. An elderly man wearing blood-red Wellington boots, an old trilby hat, and carrying a watering can in each hand toiled bandy-legged to and from an old steel tank full of stagnant rainwater. A pepper-spray of midges swarmed above the surface of the water whenever he dipped the cans into it. He stopped when he saw the boys and stared at them, his eyes in shadow beneath the brim of his shabby hat. The watering cans swung like heavy pendulums sloshing murky arcs of water from their brimming spouts.

The boy, who was used to following others, felt at a loss. His companion continued to stare across the allotments. The old man must have thought Peter was staring at him, because he put the cans down on a verge that ran between two of the narrow patches of turned earth and began mouthing something. He flapped huge, swollen grey hands at them. The boy took a step back in sudden alarm, but even as he did so, he saw that the old man was afflicted with nothing worse than outsized, saturated gardening gloves.

The boy looked at Peter. Peter was no longer staring out across the allotments. He was looking at the boy with an expression that combined low curiosity with a fair amount of perplexity; it was a facial idiom too subtle for the boy to properly read—and if he had, perhaps he would have just turned and taken Peter home and had done with the day—but he interpreted it as a look of boredom and so decided that it was time to do something more daring.

The boy began to jog along the path at the side of the allotments bordered by rusty, nettle-bound iron railings. He looked back over his shoulder and saw that Peter was following, leaning on the handlebars of his bike as he trundled it over mud and cinders. The boy ducked beneath a grimy canopy of privet and led the way up the lane that ended with the wall to the dump.

Peter stood beside the boy, his bike propped up against a tree trunk. He was looking down into the dump, at the great and teeming mountain of rubbish that filled its rank and vitiated expanse. Lorry tyre tracks had churned through the pale, mud-spattered filth that surrounded it and had made wide whorls like giant thumbprints. Peter looked expectant.

Feeling suddenly elated, the boy began to spout the nonsense he had been fed by his friend Andy about the dump and its reserves of seductive riches. The pace of his life had taken a jolt; he was in charge here. Peter regarded him with solemnity. He nodded and grinned, showing a row of crooked teeth.

*   *   *

They dropped down into the dump. Peter's socks became instantly befouled as the sopping muck underfoot welled through the gaps in his sandals. Nevertheless, he followed the boy, as, keeping low, they ran across to the huge pile of refuse. Gulls lifted, squealing like rusty bolts pulled from their sockets, and hung, bobbing on the warm, stinking draughts above the mound.

They skidded to a stop at the base of the mountain. The stink was enormous, deathly and sour. Together they rummaged for boxes containing treasures. Peter picked up an old radio, the oval of plastic pores covering the speaker clotted with some kind of fat. He peered into the back of it, then shrugged and threw it aside. They edged around the mountain together, the boy keeping an eye out for the boiler-suited attendants who worked at the dump, but they were alone. Whoever was employed to keep watch over this foetid pile was absent, probably drinking tea in a shed by the entrance gate encircled by the traditional decrepit pile of salvaged junk they might be able to flog on for a few bob.

They trod through bin bags full of sodden clothing, examined discarded televisions and the shell of an old, cylindrical spin dryer. The boy dragged the frame of a pram down from where it sat marooned on a ledge of swollen suitcases and set it aside. He thought the wheels would do for a go-kart he had been thinking about building with his dad.

They found nothing of value, but the boy was delighted that Peter was having such a good time. He was really getting into raking through the rubbish and had already filled his pockets with old lighters, a couple of smoky valves, and a rotten (and empty) leather wallet.

They had gone halfway around the mound when the boy stopped. Peter came and stood next to him. They both looked at the large, white *English Electric* refrigerator that sat on a low pile of flattened cardboard boxes at the edge of the mound like a huge tooth snaggling from a pale, diseased gum. It had a large chrome handle halfway up the right-hand side of its door that looked to the boy a bit like one of the door handles on his dad's Ford Cortina.

They approached the fridge. The boy reached up and pulled the handle. There was a click and then a sucking sound as the rubber seal around the door parted company from the body of the fridge and the door swung open.

Peter stepped around the boy and went up to the open fridge. The shelves had been removed and so had the small freezer compartment built into the top. It was about the size of an upended bath inside. It was quite clean, as if the owners had been ashamed to dump a dirty appliance and had scrubbed it before disposing of it.

Before the boy could say anything, Peter stepped up into the fridge. His sandals made filthy prints on the smooth plastic. He turned and looked down at the boy. One of his eyes was half closed. He grinned, and there were thick deposits of spittle in the corners of his mouth, which made the boy think of the nests of spider's eggs he had seen clustered along the edges of the window frame in his dad's garage.

The boy felt a sudden revulsion grip him. It came over him without bidding and it was brief, but it was also intense. He suddenly despised this fatherless creature that stood looking down at him, and he felt powerful, and that power was cruel. He was not a bad boy, and he was usually kind and gentle in his own cautious way, but now he was overcome with the base thrill of casual, breath-taking malice.

He slammed the door shut.

The boy stood back, eyes wide, panting. There was no sound from within the fridge, no hammering or shouting. His hyper-arousal vanished. Shame thundered into the void left behind. He leaped forward and yanked the door open.

Peter stood in exactly the same position, his arms hanging limp at his sides. His eye remained half-lidded but he wasn't smiling. His expression was flat, erased of emotion. The boy reached up, took Peter's hand and helped him down.

Peter remained blank, his glazed left eye staring at a point above the boy's head.

The boy was horrified. He had done something truly unkind, truly hurtful, for the first time in his life. He hadn't been led into it. He had *chosen* it. In a deep, unknowable part of his mind, his unconscious marked the moment of his fall from grace. He felt panic rise, and a terrible broken sadness.

"I'm sorry, Peter," the boy said. "I'm so sorry." He wanted to make everything all right. "Look," he said, "Peter, look. I'll do it. I'll do it, too. Then we're even. It can't be that bad, Peter." And even as he stepped up into the fridge and pulled the door closed behind him, he was still thinking that maybe he could get to ride Peter's bike on the way home. If Peter forgave him.

"It's not *that* bad, Peter," the boy said, as the door sucked shut and the latch on the handle locked him in.

But it was. It was appalling beyond belief.

*   *   *

Peter continued to stare into the distance for a while and then came back to the world. He blinked and wiped his mouth with the back of his hand. He was thirsty. He frowned, his wide, heavy brow creasing like the instep of a well-worn shoe. He realised that he had stuff in his pockets that was important. Treasures. He tried to remember where he had left his bike.

Carefully lifting the things from his pockets and examining them with great and involved interest, Peter wandered home.

8.

Without shadow, the boy walked up the moonlit garden path.

There were no footballs hidden beneath the shrubs and his slide had been dismantled a long time ago.

He drifted through the empty kitchen, past the door leading onto the chilly lounge, through the hall and out onto the pavement at the front of the house. He was cold, this boy.

And as the coldness settled in, he found himself at the dump. The dump was different now. There were ranks of large rectangular skips where the old pile of rubbish had been. People recycled nowadays.

But the fridge was still there. It waited for him, on its dais of rotted cardboard, like an archetype.

The boy walked up to the door and opened it, and once more he stepped inside forever.

As the door began to close against time and the night, the boy reached down into the shadows welling at his feet and picked up a battered box of Swan Vesta matches.

He held the matches in his left hand. In his right hand he held tight to something else. It was the stub of his tiny orange nightlight.

VILLANOVA

By the time they arrived at the campsite it was dusk. They had been driving all day on foreign roads and they were cramped and irritable. Ken had misjudged the distance from Calais to La Tranche-sur-Mer; what he'd estimated to be a four- or five-hour drive through picturesque French countryside incorporating a couple of comfort breaks along the way had turned into a ten-hour slog along undistinguished motorways in heavy traffic.

To compound the experience, an inexplicable satellite navigation error had led them off the toll road and on a detour through a town at rush hour with only about a hundred and fifty miles remaining on their journey. The name of the town mocked Ken: *Angers*. He knew the pronunciation would soften the word, but nothing could be done to soften his mood as he cursed and sweltered through jammed and unfamiliar boulevards. He had to make a U-turn but had no idea of the legality of such a manoeuvre. The satnav remained mute on the subject. Finally, he summoned his resolve and swung the car around at some traffic lights; no indignant horns blared, and so he assumed he'd got away with it.

Finally, back on the motorway, Ken had put his foot down and, despite protestations from Katie and Holly, had finished the journey in one go. He refused to stop again and lose any more time. They would have to hold it in.

Holly was almost in tears as Ken swung the car into the campsite. He stopped at a barrier and waited. To the right was a single-storey building designated *Reception*. Next to that was a clubhouse. Ken could see the rapid fluttering of lights on a fruit machine. And behind that was a low concrete wall that appeared to encompass the pool. Just visible above the wall, Ken could see the bright amber display of an L.E.D indicating the temperature of the water, the date, and the time.

"Look at the bloody time," said Ken. "Where is everyone?"

There appeared to be no one about. The barrier remained down. Ken opened his door and stepped out. The ground was dusty and Ken could feel the heat rising up from it through the thin fabric soles of his holiday espadrilles.

More doors opened, and then slammed. He turned to see Katie and Holly hobbling away across the road toward a toilet block. Ken opened his mouth to say something, and then closed it again. He watched them, his face expressionless, and then resumed looking about the campsite.

Further to the right, a short flight of wide wooden steps led up to a glass-fronted chalet. There were notice boards outside and a desk visible inside piled up with glossy flyers. Ken wandered over. One of the notice boards was pinned with timetables for various local amenities: fresh bread was delivered at 0800 every morning. There was a market in town every Tuesday and Saturday (well, they'd missed *that* for today, Ken thought with a fair bit of ill will), and the Super-U was open every day from 0800.

Ken went up the steps and slid open the glass door, which gave entrance to the chalet. Inside were more leaflets on wire racks and sliding cupboards full of communal toys, board games, and packs of cards.

Ken was about to have a look in the desk drawers when a voice said, "Hi! Just arrived, have you?"

Ken started and looked up. A young man was standing on the top step grinning at him. He was wearing a light blue T-shirt adorned with the *CampEuro* logo, a pair of knee-length brown linen shorts, and flip-flops. He had short, slicked-back hair, large prominent ears, and bad skin. Ken stepped around the desk and, as he did so, noticed two quite recent-looking burns on the boy's forearms.

The boy must have seen Ken's expression. He held his arms out in front of him, slender wrists turned outward to better display the wounds. "Accident with one of the barbecues," he said, still grinning. "Got a bit carried away with the liquid fire-lighter. Sorry if it alarms you, but I thought they might heal up better if I got a bit of sun to them. My boss would have me wear long sleeves but they rub, you know."

Ken pursed his lips. "Looks nasty," he said. Should he tell the boy he was a doctor? No, probably not. Ken got a strange sense from just looking at the boy that there was something a bit *needy* about him. He'd had dealings with people who liked to display their injuries. Borderline personality disorders, most of them.

"You're English," Ken observed. Then he added, "Obviously."

The boy nodded. "Yep. We're all English here. Me and the girls. I'm in charge this week, so if there's anything you want, that's cool. I'm Steven, by the way."

Ken looked out across to where his car still sat behind the barrier. "Well, Steven, you could start by letting us in."

"Oh, right. Cool." Steven said. He turned and skipped down the steps. Ken followed, and noticed another burn, about the size of a coffee-cup ring, livid on Steven's right calf. Ken made a mental note to increase his vigilance around the complimentary barbecue set.

Steven produced a thin electronic key from the pocket of his shorts and passed it across the face of a small black box attached to the housing of the barrier. The barrier lifted, shuddering through its elevation with an odd slow crackling sound, loud in the warm twilight air, and for some reason it made Ken think of hot fat popping on a griddle.

"These must be yours," Steven said.

Ken looked up to see Katie and Holly returning to the car. "Yes," he said. "They're mine. Come on, girls, jump in."

Katie scowled but Holly, brightened by her evacuations, said, "Hi, have you got *Boggle*?"

Both Ken and Steven appeared to be at a loss for a moment, and then Holly said, "The game? You know? The game *Boggle*? You've got lots of games in that hut. We saw them on the way over to the loos."

Steven laughed and glanced at Ken. "Hah, yes. Of course. I don't know. Maybe. We've definitely got Monopoly!"

Both girls screwed up their faces.

"And Scrabble. Probably."

I hope you're not running the Kids Club, thought Ken. "Let's sort things like that out in the morning," he said. "I want to get unpacked."

"Yes," said Steven. "Let's get you up to your holiday home and show you what's what. Follow me."

Ken watched Steven go around the side of the Information chalet. Seconds later he emerged, wobbling on an ancient-looking bicycle. He waved and indicated a dirt road that forked right and curved away behind the pool. Ken climbed back into the Audi and started the ignition. Holly was leaning forward, her head between the front seats. "Who's that?" she asked.

"He's one of the couriers," replied Ken.

"A what?"

"A member of staff, Holly. His name's Steven."

"Oh. He's a bit of a creeeepo," she said, and Katie spluttered a laugh from the seat behind Ken.

"Don't talk about people like that, Holly," Ken said, trying to sound stern, and then ended up just sounding lame when he added, "We're on holiday." He pulled away and followed the boy on the unsteady bike beneath a thick canopy of trees that overhung the track.

Hidden behind high partitioning bushes and positioned well back on their individual lots, looming like shanties in dim and dusky arbours, were rows of static mobile homes, each with their own wooden veranda and barbecue pit. A few lights burned in the windows but nobody seemed to be about.

Ken squinted through the windscreen. In the gathering darkness, it was getting difficult to see the boy on the bicycle ahead of them; somehow, he kept ahead of the light thrown from the Audi's headlamps and appeared as a flickering sketch in the road ahead, weaving from one verge to another. Ken wound his window down. It was getting humid. He could see midges fuming around the muted bulbs in the intermittent streetlamps set back on some of the lots.

After another hundred yards, Steven stopped on a corner and indicated a plot to his left. He climbed off the bike and leaned it against the veranda.

Ken swung the Audi off the track and killed the engine. He got out and went over to the courier. Holly and Katie clambered out of the back of the car and joined them.

"Home for the next week," Steven said. If he was smiling as he said it, the expression was lost in the shadow that fell across his face as he tipped his head to peer down at what his hand was doing in his shorts. "Ah, here you go," he said, and produced a Yale key on a large red plastic key ring with the *CampEuro* logo embossed on both sides and: Villanova 48. *Adrienne*.

Ken took the proffered key and went up the plank steps leading to the area of decking, which abutted half the length of the mobile home. The door was of a cheap-looking UPVC variety, windowless and scuffed. He tried the key in the lock beneath the white plastic handle.

"We're in," he said. He pushed the door open and ushered the girls through. There was a light switch on the wall opposite and he reached across the narrow hallway and flicked it on. A low light came on above his head, which did little but illuminate a door to his right and part of a tiny galley kitchen to his left.

"Get some lights on, Holly. Katie—kettle, please. Let's have drinks and settle in." Ken was about to go back to the car and start unpacking but as he turned, Steven was standing in the doorway blocking him. He was blackened by shadow and for a second, Ken could smell burning. He jumped and the back of his head knocked against the bulb in the low ceiling. He ducked in reflex and where he had been blocking the light, it was now cast back across the young man standing in the doorway, revealing a face expressing some concern.

"I think you've burned your hair," Steven said. "Against that bulb." Ken reached up and patted the top of his head. Difficult to tell, but maybe there *were* a few crinkled hairs up there, wizened by proximity to the bare bulb.

Ken shrugged and felt himself grin. The poor lad looked utterly bemused. "I'll live," he said. "Excuse me, Steven, I need to go out to the car."

Steven didn't step aside; instead, he went past Ken and moved farther into the heart of the mobile home, where the girls were clumping about.

A lamp came on as Ken crossed the veranda and made his way back down the steps. He opened the boot and lifted out a large plastic picnic box. As he turned to go back up the steps, another light came on illuminating the window at the far end of the mobile home, probably one of the bedrooms. *That kettle better be on*, he thought, and trudged back up to the open door.

He put the picnic box on the tiny narrow work surface next to the cooker. There was a metal coffee pot on the stove and a kettle with a whistle. He lifted the kettle; it was cold and empty.

"Katie!" Ken snapped. "I asked you to boil the kettle."

There was no reply. Then he heard a giggle. It was coming from his right, past the shower room. Ken replaced the kettle on the hob and ducked through the corridor linking the lounge and kitchen to the bedrooms. He was just reaching out for the handle when the door sprang inward and Holly and Katie came piling out.

"What are you playing at?" Ken said as they tried to squeeze past him and continue their flight into the lounge. He grabbed Holly by the shoulders and looked into her face. Holly's eyes were large and a bit wild. Her cheeks were flushed, hectic blooms on her pale face, and her long dark brown hair was plastered to her forehead and throat with perspiration. "Holly!" Ken said more sharply.

As he spoke, he looked up. Steven was standing in the bedroom. There was a lamp on somewhere in there, probably by the bedside, but its light was meagre and what struck Ken with immediate force was the heat that baked out at him from the bedroom. It was stifling. Ken could feel the hot air rushing out of the room past his face, sucked out into the night through the open front door.

"Steven was showing us a trick," Holly said.

"A trick?"

Holly wriggled free and scampered away into the lounge. Ken heard the kettle clank and the tap run in a hollow sputter as one of the girls began to fill it. He turned to Steven.

Steven was no longer in the bedroom.

Frowning, Ken went through into the small back room. There was a double bed that filled the entire width of the room and a bank of cupboards built into the wall above the headboard. There was a flimsy wardrobe and a chest of drawers against the wall near the door and a hairdryer fixed to the side panel of the wardrobe. Ken could see himself reflected in a mirror bolted to the wall above the chest of drawers. The room smelt a bit damp but then the walls were little more than sheets of plasterboard; you could make them warp just by pressing your palm against them. Ken sidled his body along the foot-wide aisle allowed between the foot of the bed and the chest of drawers and slid open the wardrobe door. It was empty but for a rack of coat hangers fixed to a bar and a couple of shelves. Ken closed the door and stood looking around. The walls were covered with old, faded wallpaper with a tired and oppressive vertical yellow stripe pattern. Ken felt suddenly claustrophobic; he felt like he was in a giftbox that had been wrapped without much love and then turned inside out and thrown over his head. The room was warm, and musty, but no longer contained that fierce heat of moments earlier. It must have dissipated through the rest of the building and out of the door.

Ken went back out into the kitchen. Katie and Holly were sitting on the padded seat that ran in a large L-shape along two walls of the lounge. There was no sign of the courier. Ken took a step back and knocked on the shower room door. No reply, so he pushed the door open. The shower room was dark. Ken groped for a switch, found a light-pull, and yanked the light on. Another dim uncovered bulb lit up the cubicle. There was a shower, a tiny dolls-house sink, and a toilet. Ken pulled the cord and turned out the light. He went out onto the veranda. There was a misty half-moon masked by the high leafy branches of the trees that grew in close around the back of the mobile home and along the side of the lot. It had become very dark very quickly.

Ken noticed movement on the rectangle of grass beside the veranda. He crossed to the waist-high balustrade and saw that it was Steven, standing staring at the barbecue pit. He had his back to Ken but Ken could see that he was shaking.

"Steven?" Ken said. It came out more sharply than he'd intended, but he was tired and starting to feel a little unanchored by this young courier's erratic behaviour.

Steven started but didn't turn around.

"*Steven*?" Ken enquired again and began to descend the steps leading down to the grass.

Steven whirled around. He held out his hands, which were black with soot. "I was just trying to get this grill off the barbecue for you. It seems to have got a bit stuck."

Ken looked down at the barbecue, which was a small three-sided brick construction with a shelf for charcoal and a metal grill that rested over it, supported by an inch-wide steel lip. The grill was buckled and appeared to be soldered in places to the steel.

"Don't worry about that now," Ken said. His irritation was returning. Their first holiday in three years and they'd managed to pick a real winner. The plan had been to keep it simple, low-key. No airport stress, no lost luggage, no anxiety. Just a drive and a week of beaches and markets and games in the evening. But now they had arrived late, everything was shut, and this *wally* was starting to get on his nerves.

Steven had returned his attention to the barbecue. "I would have done this for you earlier," he muttered.

So now it was Ken's fault? He considered some kind of retort, but then Holly appeared on the decking behind them and called down, "There's no milk, dad."

Ken bit his tongue and stamped back up the steps, leaving Steven still pondering the barbecue.

"Where's my Welcome Pack?" Ken's voice was muffled but his indignation was clear. He withdrew his head from the empty fridge and slammed the door. He stood looking around the kitchen with his hands on his hips. He rechecked all the cupboards but found only the same collection of old pots and pans, mismatched cutlery and crockery, and cloudy drinking glasses he had located on his first search. "I've bloody paid for that!" he said.

Three mugs sat on the draining board ready for hot drinks. Behind him, the kettle was whistling with a panicky shrillness, which made Ken think of a lookout at a crime scene trying to get the attention of its gang as the security guards approached.

"No bread, no milk. I ordered tea bags and coffee, butter pats, and croissants for the morning. Now we've got nothing until the supermarket opens tomorrow." Ken was fuming.

Steven was standing in the kitchen. He had to hop and scuttle out of Ken's way as Ken rifled through the cupboards.

"I can only apologise again," he said. Ken was starting to sicken of Steven's menial responses.

Ken went to the cool-box and rummaged through the wrappers and tangerine peel and empty cartons.

"Right, girls, we've got a sachet of hot chocolate and a Capri-Sun. *And...*," Ken paused for effect, slowly withdrawing his hand, "a box of *Tuc*!"

"Great," said Katie.

"Yeah. *Suck-u-lent,*" said Holly.

Ken could identify with their lack of enthusiasm. He lobbed the box of biscuits onto the sofa between the girls. Then he turned to Steven. "Is the bar still–," he started to ask, but Steven was gone again.

Ken let out an exasperated breath. *If he's fannying about with that barbecue...*

Ken went out onto the veranda but there was no sign of the courier. He went down to the car and opened the boot, looking around as he did so, an unpleasant temper tightening his chest. Then he paused and let out a small, dry, humourless laugh.

Steven's bike was gone.

Ken stepped around the side of the car and peered along the lane. There was nothing to be seen but a few screened-off pools of light from the subdued streetlamps amongst the trees. He shrugged and began unloading the last bits from the car, and elected to leave Steven, and his decrepit old bike, to withdraw into the deep charring shadows of the hot French night. He'd deal with him in the morning.

2.

Something woke Ken up. He lay in the darkness, eyes wide, heart beating hard. He'd been dreaming about walking through a music shop after a fire. Everything he picked up crumbled to a wet sorbet of coal dust in his hands. He trod through black puddles, and the air was like the end of October. There was a grand piano in the middle of the room. It was burnt through; even the white keys were chunks of charcoal. Ken stood and flexed his fingers. He raised his arms like a virtuoso and plunged his hands down onto the keyboard. The piano exploded around him in a storm of colliery dust.

Gasping, Ken struggled into a sitting position. The bed was lumpy and sunken in the middle. There had only been a pile of thin grey blankets in the cupboard above the bed and they enwrapped Ken like an enchilada. He found the button on the wall above his head that switched on the reading lamp. The striped walls seemed to pinch in toward the light and enhanced Ken's claustrophobia; he blinked, trying to dismiss the lingering residue of his dream and the teetering sense that the washed-out golden stripes were piano wires still resonating in the scorched and blistered music shop to a single sustained and pitiable note.

eeeeeeeeeeeeeeeeeeeeeeeeeeeeeeeeeeee

Ken shuffled his blankets off and slid himself to the foot of the bed. He pulled on his dressing gown and went out into the kitchen.

EEEEEEEEEEEEEEEEEEEEEEEE

Ken switched on the light and blinked and drew a breath. The kettle on the hob was shrieking. Still half asleep, Ken reached out and lifted it from the gas ring.

"*Shit!*" he roared and threw the kettle across the lounge. It was red hot. It hit the floor and bounced, emitting a hollow clang. Ken nursed his hand. A red line was scorched across his palm. He ran the cold tap and held his hand beneath the tepid water. As he did so, he looked around. The gas was off; there had been no flames beneath the kettle. It lay on its side beneath the little folding dining table. Ken wrapped his hand in a wet dish towel and went over to the kettle. He picked it up using the towel.

"Daddy?"

It was Katie. She stood in the kitchen and rubbed her eyes. Ken turned to look at her. For a second, he felt suspended in the dream again. She looked so like Elaine it was agonising. Where Holly was all darkness and obscurity, Katie was light. They were like something out of a Bradbury short story. Blonde and blue eyed, his younger daughter stood and peered into the gloom of the living area, her hair flossed up into a web of spun sugar on one side of her head from where she had been sleeping.

"Hey, sweetheart," said Ken. How odd must he look standing in his dressing gown with a dishtowel wrapped in his hand, holding a kettle in the middle of the night?

"Heard something," Katie said. She took a few bare-footed steps into the lounge. "Had a dream."

Ken went over to his daughter. He put the kettle back on the hob and scooped her up. She was already drifting back to sleep.

"Come on, love," he said.

"Mmmm."

Ken carried her back to her room, a narrow space no wider than a walk-in wardrobe situated between the toilet and his own room. It contained nothing more than a bunk bed and a side table with a lamp on it. Snuggled up in a ball beneath her ratty grey blankets, Holly snored on the top bunk.

Ken put Katie back on her bunk and covered her up.

"Night, baby," he said.

"Daddy," Katie said.

Ken paused at the door. "Yes?"

"Had a dream."

"You said."

"Nice."

"That's good."

"Mummy was playing her piano."

"Sweet dreams, Katie," Ken said, his mouth suddenly very dry.

Ken went back to bed and slept without any more dreams. By the time they were all up the next morning, dressed and washed and ready to go shopping as early as he could possibly coordinate, Ken had forgotten about the unsettling synchronicity of his and Katie's dreams. He had also put from his mind the fact that the kettle, picked up from the floor in his dishtowelled fist, had been empty and in no way boiled dry. It had been stone cold.

The Super-U was 500 yards from the campsite so they decided to walk it, Holly and Katie both carrying canvas Bags-for-Life bought from Tesco's back home. Again, there was no one about when they walked past the reception and bar.

When they arrived, the large looping car park that surrounded the supermarket was empty. They walked up to the doors and Ken was relieved when they slid open. The first thing that struck him was the smell. It was the brash and unfettered tang of strong cheeses fused with locally caught fresh fish. The girls wrinkled their noses. Ken thought it was marvellous. You wouldn't get a smell like that anywhere in Britain outside of a nursing home.

Ken had anticipated the layout to be unusual, but he wasn't expecting the first aisle to be crammed with such an eclectic array of goods: beach toys, men's shorts, games, deodorants, gardening equipment, flip-flops, magazines and fruit juice. They wandered past the shelves toward the back of the store, following the stink from the fish counter.

Holly and Katie crowded up against a display in the middle of the tiled floor at the end of the aisle. Upon it, made docile by a bed of crushed ice, was a pile of spider crabs jumbled like a cache of rusty medieval coshes. Holly poked a finger at the spiny haul and gasped when they shifted and flexed their legs in a stuporous response.

"They're *alive*!" Katie said, her eyes wide in surprise.

Ken laughed and came over. He plucked one of the crabs from the pile and held it up so that its artfully articulated underbelly was visible. Its legs curled in on itself, and its claws parried in cantankerous slow motion.

"That's cruel," Holly said, but her eyes were bright and she said it with a rapt expression on her face.

Ken placed the crab onto its bed of ice. "Not really," he said. "They're all dopy this way when you boil them alive."

"*Noooo!*"

"Oh, yes." Ken pressed the heels of his hands together and clawed his fingers and thumbs and wriggled them in the girls' faces. "Aghh, I'm cooking!" Ken cried, laughing. "I'm *cooking!*" and then stood wondering whether his pantomime had been a little misjudged. Holly paled; Katie shrieked; both girls turned and fled away up the next aisle looking a bit sick.

They lugged their bags to the doors and stopped so that the girls could look at the souvenirs and trinkets on a revolving rack by the magazine counter. It was hung with a variety of nameplates that displayed French forenames and their meanings, presumably for children's bedroom doors.

Holly and Katie pored through them looking for versions of their own names. Holly found *Holland,* its meaning unambiguous: named after the Netherlands. And Katie failed to locate anything close to her own name, although she did pour scorn on a number of *Janelles* and *Cherelles,* which she thought sounded chavvy. Ken pointed out that these names were originally French and had been appropriated by the British working classes, thus cheapening them. "Whatever," said Katie.

"Oh, look," said Holly. She held up a nameplate.

Ken looked. *Adrienne*, it said.

"That's our caravan's name," Katie said.

"I *know*," said Holly. "What does it mean?"

Ken translated the simple definition beneath the name.

"Oh," he said.

"What?"

Ken replaced the nameplate on its stand. "It's not as glamorous as it sounds," he said. "It means 'black earth.'"

Ken carried the bags back to camp. The girls trotted along ahead of him. The road was dusty and the edges of the pavements were bordered by narrow strips of dun-coloured stones. Already it was warm, but there was nobody about. The beachfront was deserted; the sails of the windsurfing boards and small boats ranked along the front fluttered and thrummed in the breeze, and somewhere a line had come untethered and rattled its clips against a mast.

Ken watched the girls as they ran shadowless in the early morning light. The bags weren't heavy but he ached from yesterday's drive and a poor night's sleep. He hoped he hadn't made a mistake bringing the girls away on his own. They were at a strange, baffling age, and although his love for them was immeasurable, often he felt as detached from them as he was from images on a screen.

He imagined Elaine's response. *Just persist*, she would have said. *Just keep going. Do normal things. Have fun.*

Ken stopped and looked out across the bay. He could see a bridge, so distant on the horizon it was no more than a misty thread, linking the mainland to an island. He sighed, and the emptiness of the beach and the whitewashed promenade was suddenly unbearable.

Ken turned and hurried after his girls.

They hadn't been back long and there was a knock at the door.

It was Steven. He was holding a small cardboard box.

"I found this," he said, offering Ken the box.

Ken reached out and took the box, and then he noticed what appeared to be fresh burns on the backs of Steven's hands. He looked down and saw more, nasty-looking pink scabs on the boy's ankles. They couldn't be new, but how had he failed to notice them last night?

"Steven," he said, and against his better instinct, "let me look at those burns."

Steven reacted with immediate and unexpected refusal. He stumbled backward and collided with the balustrade surrounding the veranda, his hands held high above his head.

Ken was stunned by the reaction.

"I'm fine, I'm fine." Steven said. Somehow, he kept a sickly salesman's grin on his face. "Really, I'm cool."

"I'm a doctor, Steven. I'm not going to hurt you."

Steven backed away. "I don't need a doctor, thanks. All's well. Just enjoy your holiday." He stood on the grass beneath the veranda. He stared up at Ken, his arms hanging by his side. There were dark smudges on the collar of his *CampEuro* shirt. His bike was leaning up against the side of the mobile home.

Ken looked down at the box he was holding. It was about the size of a shoebox. Ken lifted the flaps, which loosely covered the contents.

"Oh," he said. The girls would be pleased.

Boggle.

Ken looked back to where Steven was standing. He was gone.

"Bloody hell," said Ken.

Later, he made them all *carbonara* for lunch using the fresh ingredients they had bought from the Super-U. It was very good, very rich and filling. The girls were in their dressing gowns and lay next to him on the sofa playing *Boggle*. Ken thought about going for a beer at the bar. They'd be safe enough for half an hour. He felt the need for some adult company, even if it was just a stranger serving cold beer. He looked at his watch. It was nearly eight o'clock. The girls laughed, the dice clattered. *Where had the day gone?* Ken wondered. They'd done nothing but laze about on the site today. Normally, Ken would have considered this a waste, but right now he was glad to do nothing, glad to just relax and enjoy the time with his girls. Tomorrow they could hit the beach.

3.

Elaine had been a concert pianist. She had been due to play a Chopin recital at the *Rudolfinum* in Prague, but the night she arrived, there had been a fire at her hotel and she had died.

The girls were in the shower. Ken sat on the edge of his bed and listened to the sound of them shrieking beneath the jet of water, and the thumps and creaks as the moulded plastic walls gave beneath their weight as they bumped against them.

He looked at his suitcase. He hadn't unpacked; rather he would select items from it as he needed them. He sighed and lay back on the bed and closed his eyes.

He must have dozed, because when he became aware of his surroundings again, it was quiet. He sat up. He couldn't hear the girls.

Beneath the mobile home, amongst the leaves and litter and darkness, something moved.

Ken lifted his feet off the floor and sat cross-legged on the edge of the bed. He peered down at the strip of floor between the end of the bed and the chest of drawers.

Again, furtive movement. And then a bump, as if something had tried to stand up and hit their head on the underside of the mobile home.

Ken stood up and slipped on his shoes. He went out into the hallway.

"Hi, dad," Katie said, looking up from the sofa. Her hair was damp and tied back in a ponytail.

"Where's Holly?" he asked.

Katie shrugged and went back to her magazine. "Dunno," she said.

Ken pushed the girls' bedroom door open and looked in. The beds were empty. He knocked on the bathroom door and went in. Holly wasn't in there, either.

Ken strode into the lounge. "Has she gone out?" he demanded.

"She might have," Katie said, still vague. "She didn't say."

"Katie! It's ten o'clock at night. Where is she?"

"Look," said Katie. She was staring past Ken, toward the hall. Ken turned around and saw that the door leading out onto the veranda was open.

Ken frowned and went to the door. There was no moon tonight, just low racing clouds like smoke from a factory chimney. He could smell meat burning on a barbecue. It was still very warm.

"Holly!" Ken shouted.

Something moved to his left. Ken crossed the veranda and peered over the balustrade. In the darkness beneath the mobile home, he could just make out the curved shoulder of the gas cylinder that fed the cooker and water heater.

Ken went to the car and got a torch from the glove compartment. He crossed the grass and went around the barbecue and knelt down and played the torch beam beneath the mobile home.

Something was under there. Ken leaned further into the darkness, his shoulder brushing against the pipes that fed the gas up into the mobile home. Suddenly something rolled away from behind the gas cylinder. Ken flicked the torch beam to the right and it slid across the back of something glistening and black. It looked flaky, crinkled, like a bin liner rolled up and melted by a blast of heat. Ken jumped and banged his head on the underside of the building.

Ken withdrew and stood brushing the dirt from his knees. It had looked like a bin bag, so that was probably all it was. There were a few bags, filled with rubbish and loosely tied, still lying in a pile at the side of the barbecue.

Then Ken heard Katie cry out.

He ran around the veranda and up the steps. In the lounge, Katie was sitting with her legs drawn up on the sofa and one hand pressed to her mouth. She was in tears.

"What is it? What's the matter, Katie?"

Trembling, Katie extended her other hand and pointed at the table.

"I don't like it, daddy. Make it stop."

Confused, Ken walked over. Katie was pointing at the dish of dice sitting amongst pencils and bits of scrap paper. He frowned. "Is this a joke?"

Katie shook her head, tears running down her pale cheeks. "It keeps doing it. Every time I shake them, they say the same thing."

Ken was about to ask her to demonstrate, to prove what she was saying, but then he heard Holly call from outside.

"Daddy, look. She's coming!"

Ken looked up. From where he stood, he could see through the wide window at the back of the mobile home along the lane leading back beneath the canopy of trees. A figure was approaching.

With slow tread and a tightening in his chest he recognised, Ken walked out onto the veranda. Holly was standing there by the picnic table. She smiled up at her dad, came over, and took his hand.

Together they watched as the figure resolved itself out of the dark tunnel of trees. A streetlamp delineated her features, her black dress, and the spray of white lilies she carried in her arms.

"She's still so sad, daddy," Holly said. Ken squeezed her hand.

"So am I," he said.

"Me, too." Holly squeezed back.

Ken and Holly watched for a little longer as the woman approached their mobile home. The ache in Ken's chest became unendurable and he wept as she placed the bouquet on the ground at the foot of the steps.

"Mummy didn't die in a fire, did she, daddy?" said Holly, and Ken felt some small comfort for a moment, just a moment.

"I don't think she did, baby," he said.

Inside, Katie called, "Steven's here."

They went inside.

They were sitting together in the lounge. The curtains were drawn. Steven, their courier, was standing before them. His arms were spread wide and Ken could see the burns on his forearms. They had grown, consuming the flesh of his biceps and underarms.

On the table, their game of *Boggle* was still underway. The lettered dice were in their grid and a pen and paper lay beside them. Ken drew his eyes away from Steven and looked at the sixteen dice and at what they spelled:

BURN

URNB

RNBU

NBUR

Ken closed his eyes.

"You come here all the time," Steven said. "*All* your holidays are here."

"No," Ken said.

"You have your own *key*!"

Ken's hand went to his trouser pocket. He felt the shape against his leg.

Steven was nodding. Now his face was gone, his baked-fish eyes looked down at Ken from the black smouldering flesh of his skull.

"I wish I could have saved you," he said, grotesque now, those blind, boiled eyes unable to intimate any of the emotion carried in his voice. "But I'll always be here. I'll always keep trying to warn you."

Warn us? Ken thought, but of course there was no memory of the explosion, of the fire that followed the gas leak from the rotten valves around the pipes beneath them. Pipes that had been knocked loose by Holly, playing under the mobile home while Ken fixed the barbecue. No memory of the lighter fluid, the embers, because they hadn't happened here yet. Not yet.

Ken felt despair crawl through him. He turned to his right and his face crumpled, twisted into a grimace by what he saw sitting propped up next to him. Their heads were together and their fingers were interlocked. His girls, like scorched china dolls, their skin curling off their muscles like newspaper lifting from a bonfire.

Ken raised his hand and looked at what it held, what was melted to his fist.

Villanova 48. *Adrienne.*

Black earth.

Now he remembered.

He opened his mouth to howl, but the flames had seared his throat to ash.

ACKNOWLEDGEMENTS

I'd like to thank Tim Lebbon for the warmth of the introduction, Brandon Nolta for the wisdom of the edits, Ben Baldwin for the elegance of the cover, and Charlie Franco for the encouragement and belief.

AUTHOR INFO

Paul Meloy was born in 1966 in South London. He is the author of the novels The Night Clock and its sequel, Adornments of the Strom, and the short story collection, Islington Crocodiles. His work has been published in Black Static, Interzone and a variety of award-winning anthologies. He lives in Devon with his family.

www.ingramcontent.com/pod-product-compliance
Lightning Source LLC
Chambersburg PA
CBHW020605260626
47157CB00003B/873